GUARDIANS OF THE SKYRIDERS

Skyriders Book 2

FLORENCE PHILLIPS

To all those I left behind.

～

'Home is not where you were born; home is where all your attempts to escape cease.'

Naguib Mahfouz

PROLOGUE

T he year was 2326.

People in the Wastelands still talked of a long-lost golden age when men flew not on the backs of birds but inside metal machines, wore clothing made of oil and worshipped things they could neither see nor touch.

Most of us didn't believe such tales.

We believed in wood and water and in what we could eat.

We believed in bringing forth the right children for the work that needed to be done.

Above all else, we believed in absolute loyalty to each other.

Outsiders stared at our tall, strong bodies, elaborately braided hair and harmonious features. They marvelled at our feathery mounts and wondered how we kept from falling out of the skies to our deaths.

They called us Skyriders.

We just called ourselves the Clan.

Following the Quake that destroyed our Village and killed our families and friends, there were only eight of us left in our makeshift camp.

It was enough. We were young. We were strong. Together, whatever it took, we would survive.

∿

For news of upcoming book releases and for free short stories set in the Skyriders' world, join our mailing list on http://florencephillips.co.uk/join-the-clan-2/ or by clicking on the link at the end of this book.

Follow me on Facebook (www.facebook.com/clanoftheskyriders) or on Instagram (www.instagram.com/florencephillipsauthor).

∿

MAIN CHARACTERS

Morgunn Ulfborn
    22, Chief and Hunter, son of Ulf Svordborn, Clan's Chief, and of Brynis Attaborn, Healer

Efalaa Vonaborn
    20, Hunter, apprentice to Morgunn, daughter of Vona Taniborn, Singer, and Berjast Strumborn, Master Maker

Vidris
    17, daughter of Fan, Teacher, and Melli, Keeper

Aalma Randborn
    59, Master Healer, daughter of Rand, Healer, and Uria, Singer

Veiti Calliborn
    25, Gatherer, daughter of Iilios, Gatherer, and Calli, Cook; mate to Ollo and mother of Leif

Leodurr Pernaborn

35, Master Farmer, son of Gust, Guardian, and Perna, Farmer, father of Leif

Steon Hildenborn

29, Guardian, son of Hilden, Guardian, and of Gaia, Farmer

Leif (also, Leif the Lucky)

Baby son of Veiti Calliborn and Leodurr Pernaborn

Sili

25, Outsider, friend to Efalaa

~

For more information about the Clan, see the 'About the Clan' section at the end of this book or visit www.florencephillips.co.uk

❦ I ❦

Sili

Efalaa sauntered past me down the mountain path, her perfect braids dancing around her slender shoulders. I glanced at my grotesquely pregnant belly, and bile rose in my throat.

'How much longer?' I complained. 'My mantle is not as warm as your cloak. I'm frozen.'

The winter had started in earnest. Efalaa and I had been out in the cold for hours, foraging for plants and nuts. She wore one of the Clan's traditional travelling cloaks; made of waxed sheepskin and rabbit fur, it covered her from head to toe. I had to make do with a knitted mantle which kept my shoulders warm but not much else.

I struggled on the rocky path, my swollen feet adding to my ridiculous gait.

I had tried everything to convince Efalaa to abandon this

expedition: faking interest, displaying boredom, pretending to trip and pleading exhaustion. Nothing had worked.

'Walking is good for you, Sili,' she said, not for the first time. 'It's a beautiful day.'

'No, it's not. It's about to rain.'

'Anyway, you need to learn about edible plants if you're to make yourself useful. Everyone works in the Clan.'

'You said it takes twenty years to make a decent Gatherer. I've only been here two months,' I retorted, without much hope of changing her mind. Indeed she went on as if I hadn't spoken.

'Oh, curly dock,' she said, pointing at some ugly greenery. 'I once ate nothing else for three days.' She wrinkled her nose at the memory.

'Was that while you sulked in the Wastelands for weeks because Morgunn wanted to marry you?' I jeered to avenge myself for the hours of walking.

'That's one way to see it,' she replied, unamused.

I ignored her and her cursed plants and made no further attempt to keep up with her pace. She slowed down to match her steps to mine. As we carried on down the treacherous path to the Orchard, we were both quiet.

My thoughts found their usual furrow – back to my safe and comfortable life in New Bodie, the city beyond the Wastelands. My childhood in the ochre and green valley by the Two Rivers delta had not prepared me for what fate had in store.

My mother's death when I was fourteen had started a long list of disasters.

On my twenty-second birthday, my father was murdered, forcing me to seek refuge with my indifferent uncle. Only a few months later, I was kidnapped by a group of Raiders and given a comprehensive insight into their peculiar brand of hospitality. Then, six months pregnant, I narrowly escaped their camp with Efalaa and, after a terrifying journey through the skies, was begrudgingly given shelter by the surviving members of her clan—the once mighty Skyriders.

The Skyriders were a group of reclusive hillbillies who rode monstrous oversized birds. The Clan had a reputation for breeding like animals and killing their own babies, but few people had ever clapped eyes on them, and these rumours remained unconfirmed. Many beyond the Lowlands did not believe the Skyriders even existed.

For centuries, they had lived in complete isolation on the upper reaches of a group of two mountains, surrounded by brambles taller than trees. They claimed their territory was only accessible by air, although Efalaa had somehow made her way through the hedge on foot.

The Skyriders had suffered their share of disasters. A few weeks before my arrival, an earthquake had destroyed their village and killed all but eight of their hundred and forty-strong community.

The survivors now appeared determined to carry on with their odd way of life, no matter how outlandish the rest of the Wastelands and Valley folks found their customs. They showed no interest in anything beyond their immediate survival or spartan comfort but seemed deeply attached to each other, possibly as a result of their recent losses.

Due to this long chain of calamities, and so close to the end of my pregnancy, I lived in a ramshackle, muddy camp where grieving people fought winter for every morsel of food.

Still, my father had taught me to keep my face smooth and my bearing confident regardless of the turmoil inside, and I refused to appear a victim. As long as I could pretend to be unaffected by life's trials, I retained my dignity, and that was enough for me to carry my losses and my fears through yet another day.

However, each passing hour brought closer the moment I

feared above all others. It was my first thought of the day, and my last. The impending birth of that most unwanted child could mean life or death for me. If I survived, I could go back to New Bodie and resume the course of my life, but judging by recent events, the alternative seemed a more fitting end to my sad story.

Efalaa suddenly came out of her pensive mood and spoke to me, but once I ascertained she was still talking about plants, I returned to my own thoughts.

I had been a sex slave in a Raiders' camp for over a year when Efalaa was dragged by her perfectly braided hair into the captives' tent.

She had left the Clan shortly after the destruction of their village when their young Chief, Morgunn, invoking some long-forgotten rule, had tried to make her his wife. Neither Efalaa nor the rest of the Clan appreciated this departure from tradition. In a fit of temper, she disregarded the fact he was utterly in love with her, hit him squarely in the face and flew off on her bird.

Homeless and starving, she roamed the Wastelands for a few weeks before being captured by the Raiders who were holding me.

Her misfortune was my long-awaited luck. The revulsion in her eyes when she realised where she was told me everything I needed to know about her. Unlike the other captives, she wouldn't just whisper about leaving. She would kill and die trying. She was the perfect accomplice for a heavily pregnant woman more used to scheming than fighting.

Between us, we killed four men in cold blood and four more in self-defence before escaping on a couple of stolen horses. This ought to have ended my pregnancy, but it didn't.

The leader of the Raiders – a vain wisp of a man called Torston – soon caught up with us. What I knew of his character helped me to forget my fear of heights, and I didn't hesitate when Efalaa ordered me to ride her bird to safety.

This journey back to her village was the worst experience of my life. I still had nightmares about it. Veiti thought I was reliving my ordeal at the hands of Torston's Raiders. In fact, night after night, I pictured myself falling off Efalaa's bird.

A storm in shades of grey gathered overhead, and the wintry wind turned into a gale. A long shiver went down my spine: we would not make it back to the camp before the rain started. Yet another one of my days would be spent stomping in the mud, huddling around a weak camp fire and eating rabbit roast and leaves.

Efalaa was still chattering. 'Foraging is the perfect job for new mothers. You'll see. It's helped Veiti to get her strength back, and the fresh air does wonders for little Leif's sleep.' She smiled at my pregnant belly.

A ball of anger rose from my stomach and lodged itself into my throat. How quickly had she forgotten why I had someone growing inside me! As usual, I pushed my wrath down where it could not be seen or heard. When the paralysing fear that followed any thought of the unborn child came, my mask was already firmly in place. Efalaa never realised the torment she had caused. My father had taught me well.

As we walked on, I noticed a lone pebble amongst the rocks of the path, dark and perfect next to its jagged neighbours. Despite my bulk, I bent down and picked it up. I was about to offer it to Efalaa, who collected pretty things, when the sky darkened again.

Looking up, I saw this was not the cloud I had expected. Instead, a large shape loomed still for an instant before resuming its inexorable descent. My heart raced against my ribs. A giant bird – larger than a pair of horses – flew in front of the sun and cast its awful shadow over us.

It let out a blood-curling shriek and headed straight towards me. My vision narrowed to near blindness until there was nothing left in the world but the beast rending the air, claws first. It was now beyond my powers to hide what I felt as the monster grew and grew against the clouds. I covered my head and cowered down.

Efalaa, eyes wide, pressed her hands across her mouth. Her reaction increased my panic.

I threw myself on the ground and landed painfully on my bulging stomach. I felt the beast's heat when it crashed next to me. I screamed, and my body gave up. Ignoring the warmth spreading across my lap, I waited for the sharpness of a beak or a claw cutting through my flesh.

When none came, my brain took a few seconds to reconnect with reality. Efalaa, pale-faced, knelt next to the animal.

'Frid! Oh, Frid,' she said over and over.

The giant bird lay in a heap next to me and twittered pitifully, exhausted or half-dead. It was harnessed with one of the leather saddles and braided bridles the Clan lovingly crafted for their mounts. When Efalaa threw her arms around the bird's neck, I finally accepted the evidence of my senses. The animal posed no immediate threat.

The puddle around me was quickly absorbed into the ground, but the dirt of the path stuck to the wet streak on my tunic. My face glowed red, and I felt fresh shame at my inability to hide my emotions.

But Efalaa didn't notice my wet skirt or my flushed face while she whispered hushed questions into the bird's feathery neck. This particular bird was unknown to me. It was even larger than Morgunn's bird, stony grey with a collar of black feathers.

'Frid,' Efalaa said again, stroking the bird's face in between the plaited leather.

Angry at my demeaning display, I had no interest in

learning about the new arrival. I struggled to my feet and took a first step down the path toward the Orchard.

'Stop!' shouted Efalaa, her voice like a whip. She leapt to her feet, and – without any warning – started down the hill at full speed. 'Stay here and hold on to him,' she ordered over her shoulder.

My mouth fell open. Efalaa could sometimes be blunt, but this was the first time she had ever given me an order. Her concern for this riderless bird seemed excessive, yet the urgency in her voice stopped me from ignoring her instructions.

With a trembling hand, I approached the bird. The closer I got, the more my knees wobbled and my vision blurred. I struggled to control the panic and thought briefly of letting the creature go. After all, no one would ever know. But even an Outsider like me could tell the bird's arrival was momentous news. Efalaa was my only friend. She had rescued me from the Raiders, and I owed her my freedom – and probably my life too. When it came to it, my loyalty to her was stronger than my fear. So I controlled myself and, inch by inch, reached out until my hand grazed the leather of the bird's strap. Blood rushed in my ears as my fingers closed around the bridle, and I held fast with shaking hands.

❦ 2 ❧

S ili

Minutes passed slowly. The large bird cooed a tale of woe beyond my understanding. Its doleful sounds helped soothe my nerves, and its proximity became an inconvenience rather than an impossibility. He pecked at the ground nervously and gobbled long white worms with a relish born of insatiable hunger.

When Efalaa finally returned on her bird, who was called Mila, she wasn't alone: little Keeper Vidris and Guardian Steon were following her path in the sky. As the three dismounted, I was struck by their improbable good looks. It was one of life's ironies that, ugly as I was, I had to share my life with such men and women.

Morgunn had explained this baffling beauty stemmed from the Clan's revolting practice of controlled breeding. For generations, the Chiefs had systematically chosen the better looking parents out of those of equal skills, in the cynical belief their mating instructions would thus be easier to obey.

Despite their physical beauty – or because of it – the Skyriders were not at all vain. They cared only about cleanliness and neat hair. Strangely, their Chief Morgunn did most of the braiding. Every evening, he sat someone at his feet and spent hours twisting their hair into complicated plaits and patterns. I found it unseemly. My father would never have included hairdressing duties in the long list of his responsibilities.

Vidris and Steon were first cousins, although he was twice her age. They had the same blonde hair and sun-kissed skin. Steon was a taller, broader and more rugged version of Morgunn. His eyes could have been beautiful, had they been less dull. As for Vidris, she was a little thing not yet eighteen, with a round face and soft blue eyes. Despite her apparent meekness, she deeply disliked me and made her opinions heard.

Beside the cousins' display of goldenness, Efalaa stood out with her glossy dark hair, clear blue eyes and rosy skin. Now that she was home safe and well fed, she was the most beautiful of the Clanswomen.

I too was pale, dark-haired and blue-eyed. I hadn't seen my reflection in nearly two years, but I could easily guess how plain I must have looked next to Efalaa, especially with my ridiculously distended stomach and borrowed clothes.

When the riders landed, my first reaction was relief. Despite her young age, Vidris was in charge of the birds. She would become the Clan's bird Keeper as soon as she came of age. The burden fell off my shoulders when she took the reins out of my hand. I retreated to a more comfortable distance.

My second reaction was renewed fear, as I was now surrounded by four birds of varying colours and sizes.

Steon had arrived on Morgunn's bird, Eko. I'd never seen the hulking Guardian ride before. I wondered why Efalaa had brought him.

Since my enforced stay with the Raiders, men filled me with nearly as much dread as giant birds did. Yet, for Steon, I felt mostly scorn.

Bred for the sole purpose of fighting, he was a man of few words, scant emotions and indiscernible personality. But, as he rushed towards me, his face alive with what resembled concern, my breath caught in my throat. I was struck by how different he looked. I thought his concern was for me, and despite myself I was touched. Then he stepped past me and had eyes only for the new bird.

He didn't even noticed the wetness on my skirt.

Little Vidris hugged the animal as a long-lost friend. 'His harness cut into his neck,' she lamented. 'He's been mistreated, but his wound is nearly healed already. It must be at least five days old.'

My mind was working at full speed to puzzle out what seemed so obvious to the three of them. I was clearly missing some vital piece of information. Why was this bird here?

'Where did he come from?' Steon asked Efalaa without unclenching his jaws. I was surprised he should address her so rudely, and my eyes darted to his face. There I saw no disrespect, only pain. Efalaa must have seen it too for she did not rebuke him.

Skyriders were strict on gender equality, and none of those great lumps of men normally spoke down to the women. It was one of their more endearing qualities. Steon's roughness confirmed the situation was highly unusual and involved a significant level of danger.

Unruffled by his gruff tone, Efalaa pointed at the sky.

'From south-south-east, or perhaps due south, I'm not sure which. He was flying like a mad bird.'

Steon and Efalaa stared first at the sky, then at each other. My irritation grew. Some unspoken communication passed between them and – without so much as a glance at me – they climbed on their birds and flew off towards the storm.

Vidris showed no surprise at their actions. With many words of encouragement, she got the exhausted bird onto its feet. Misreading my bewildered look, she sought to reassure me. 'Don't worry, he's just shocked and tired,' she said, and she presented me with the reins. Instinctively, I stepped back, but Vidris thrust them into my hand, and with no further instructions, she too leapt onto her bird and was gone.

Stunned by the unfolding events, I watched as the three riders scattered through the sky, their shapes darker against the dark clouds. The way they had sprung into action with so few words spoken was frustratingly typical of Skyriders caught in a crisis. And no one had given me a second thought. That too was becoming a habit.

I resumed my waddling down the hill towards the Clan's camp, with a creature out of my nightmares at the end of a length of leather. My weak knees made my walk even more unsteady than my cursed belly. I only managed a few yards before the skies broke open. Heavy rain soon ran freely down the path and my boots started to squelch in the mud.

I hated my fate and every single person who'd ever had a part in bringing me here. At least the rain would wash the urine out of my clothing.

I arrived at the camp predictably soaked, with water dripping from my hair and sleeves.

Morgunn, who was a Hunter like Efalaa as well as being the Clan's Chief, walked out of the greenwoods with two bags full of dead rabbits.

The hood of his travelling cloak covered the upper part of

his face, and his knee-high leather boots were caked in mud. He stamped his feet a few times but managed to dislodge very little of it. This childlike manoeuvre reminded me that, although we were almost the same age, Morgunn was still a very young man. In fact, probably too young to be leading anyone.

He pushed back his hood, and raised his face towards me. His greeting smile died when he saw the bird behind me.

Like the others, he ran towards the animal and held it close to his chest.

'Frid! How is that possible? Where did you find him? Where are the others?'

He shouted his questions in such quick succession I had no time to answer any of them. I pointed in the direction of the path, and he grabbed my shoulders.

'Where's Efalaa?'

'She flew off with Steon and Vidris,' I started.

'Had they seen Frid?'

I nodded yes. For the first time he relaxed, and his green eyes softened.

'Where did they go?' I asked, but he didn't reply.

Instead, he turned to face Leodurr and Veiti, who were walking side by side down the path leading from the Farming Fields.

Leodurr, a Farmer, was older than Morgunn and Steon, perhaps in his mid-thirties. He was pale like Efalaa and had long auburn hair and kind light-brown eyes.

Veiti, the Gatherer, was another blonde beauty with glowing skin and a full smile of shiny white teeth. She carried their son Leif on her hip, safe under the cover of her cloak.

Veiti and Leodurr had been sharing a joke, but when they saw the bird, they both froze.

'Ollo!' Veiti cried, as she ran towards us, Leodurr on her heels.

Morgunn shook his head. 'Frid returned alone.'

Veiti made a guttural sound and half-collapsed into Leodurr's arms. He went even paler but held her fast. Morgunn grabbed the baby and cradled it against his chest.

'How can this be?' said Leodurr, the first to recover from the shock. 'Where's Ollo?'

That name was familiar, and it only took me a moment to remember why I knew it. Before the Quake, Ollo, like Steon, had been one of the nine Guardians of the Clan. He and Veiti had been together for several years, and because I shared her hut, I well knew she still cried for him in her sleep.

Leodurr steadied Veiti and wiped tears from her cheeks with the back of his hand. 'If Frid wasn't in the Village when the mountain came down, maybe Ollo wasn't either,' he said.

'He might be alive,' added Veiti tremulously.

My heart sank, my patience already wearing thin. I never could stand people deluding themselves. I liked to look truth in the face, and I was needled by their unrealistic notions about long-dead people being found alive.

Morgunn didn't contradict them. This angered me even more, and I made no attempt to stop myself from voicing my opinion. 'It's been months since the Quake. The dead are dead, and no amount of wishing ever brings them back,' I said despite murderous looks from all sides. 'For all you know, all the birds escaped the earthquake.'

They looked at me uncomprehendingly.

I continued. 'The birds could save themselves in one beat of their wings. Why would they not?'

Their slack jaws indicated they had never before considered this possibility. They did not like it. Leodurr looked away with a pained expression. Veiti's mouth hung open, and Morgunn held the baby closer.

He looked ready to punch me when he said, 'Our birds love us as we love them. They chose to die with us.'

I snorted and stared scornfully at the muddy water pooling around my feet.

The silence stretched until Morgunn broke it. 'You Wastelanders know nothing of loyalty,' he spat angrily.

'I'm not from the Wastelands,' I started, but he snatched the bridle out of my hand and turned his back on me.

'Frid is still alive,' he said in a gentler tone as he carefully deposited Leif into Veiti's arms. 'Ollo is a Guardian. The strongest of the strong. He's not afraid of anything.' Morgunn rested his palm on Leodurr's chest. 'All of us here survived against the odds. Maybe Ollo did too.'

I rolled my eyes.

'We must not get our hopes up,' said Leodurr cautiously.

'You're right, elskan, let's keep our heads,' continued Morgunn. 'But, Veiti, I promise we will look everywhere for him.'

'I know you will, sweetheart,' replied Veiti as she patted Morgunn's face. 'I know you will.'

'Leodurr, feed and water Frid for me,' he said. As Leodurr ran to the birds' shed, Morgunn got an armful of supplies out of the food store.

Within minutes, everything was ready. Veiti handed Morgunn a waterskin and gave him the woollen muffler from around her neck. 'It's going to be so cold flying through that rain,' she murmured.

'Don't worry, dearie, I'm used to it,' Morgunn replied, but he accepted her gift.

Morgunn straddled the bird. It seemed happier than could have been expected of the exhausted animal I had led into the camp.

'Good luck,' said Leodurr.

'Be safe,' cried Veiti.

Morgunn held his hand up in sad farewell. 'For the Clan,' he called out.

'For the Clan,' Leodurr and Veiti answered with one voice.

Then Morgunn was gone. We watched his progress through the sky until he was just a dot.

'Why do you have to be so mean, Sili?' Veiti said turning on me. 'Have you never loved anyone?'

I shrugged and walked away. I could understand why, after losing their families and friends, the thought of one of their own stranded, birdless, in the Wastelands should weigh heavily on their minds. But Morgunn was a fool to risk all their birds and half of their dwindling numbers for a man who was most probably lying dead under the rubble of their village or somewhere in the Wastelands.

For all we knew, the bird everyone fussed about had eaten his corpse.

All this sentimentality annoyed me. Sentiments didn't keep people alive.

It was still raining.

჻ 3 ჻

S ili

As the evening approached, the rain finally stopped, and the mud hardened, imprisoning a tangle of broken twigs and half-mulched leaves into a dirty crust.

My Clan-made boots were ugly but well stitched and kept the rain and cold away from my feet. The Skyriders made everything themselves, even what they could have more easily purchased or traded. Their clothes were all the same: rough woollen cloth or knit, brownish dyes and unbecoming cuts. They wore shirts or tunics over leather trousers, tied at the waist with plaited leather belts that resembled the birds' bridles—which maybe they were.

I hid the drab dress they had given me under a bell-sleeved tunic inherited from the Caravaneers. This tunic was the only pretty thing I owned. In fact, it was the only thing I owned.

My layered clothing doubled my bulk, but in the midst of winter not even I was vain enough to remove a single thread. As my distended middle grew, I had to sweet-talk little Vidris into stitching patchworks of side panels into my clothes. They looked worse, but finally I could breathe.

The Skyriders used no currency of any kind, nor did they own anything privately. Efalaa was the only one with any leaning towards private property. She was excessively attached to the little house Morgunn had built for her and clearly enjoyed having sole use of it. Everyone else shared dwellings, in the same way they shared every other resource. Everything was freely lent and borrowed, and even the gifts exchanged on their Clan's Day soon started changing hands. Leodurr had carved wooden spoons for everyone. The one with the bird in flight belonged to Efalaa, and the one with the man supporting a house was Morgunn's. Mine had an eye gouged into it, and I often wondered whether it meant I noticed things or that they were watching me. The spoons could easily be matched with their owner, but the Skyriders all ate with whatever utensil they were given. My attempts at trading for my own spoon usually fell on deaf ears.

As the night closed in, Veiti, Leodurr and I silently attended to our chores. There was always much to do in order to feed and shelter eight people and baby.

I scrubbed carrots and potatoes for a stew while Leodurr started the evening bonfire. Food was plentiful here, which made a welcome difference from the near-starvation I had endured at the Raiders' camp. Meals were exceedingly simple though and mostly did not taste of much.

Morgunn had left without preparing the rabbits, so our dinner would consist only of boiled vegetables and leaves, with a few pieces of dried fruit.

Veiti, her eyes empty, was bouncing baby Leif on her

knees while he smiled and gurgled, unaffected by the sombre mood around him.

Alma, the Clan's Healer, was the last person to return to the camp that night. She arrived breathless just as we started to pass the food around, mud up to her slender thighs and bits of twigs in her snow-white hair.

'Sorry I'm late, darlings. The ground is so sodden down by the clearing I couldn't get up the slope,' she started cheerfully. 'I had to go round the—' At that moment, she took in our downcast faces. 'What?' she asked simply.

Leodurr and Veiti looked at each other hesitantly instead of answering, so Aalma turned to me.

Hiding my irritation, I replied, 'Frid arrived just before the rain started. They've all gone to look for Ollo.'

Uncharacteristically showing her age, Aalma sat down heavily. Her face was so pale that I thought she might be sick. She stared at the fire in silence, deep in her thoughts.

'How could that be?' she wondered in a whisper.

'Maybe he didn't know we'd survived the Quake...' tried Leodurr before his voice trailed off.

No one spoke after that, and we ate little. The stew tasted bland despite the various herbs floating wilted in the stock.

Aalma attempted to lift the mood with a lighthearted song. Leodurr dutifully joined in, and the baby gurgled happily for a while before falling asleep against Veiti.

I spent the rest of the evening twisting rainwater out of my hair and drying my clothes by the fire.

The embers were almost dead by the time Morgunn returned. The bird was too tired to fly, and the rider was in a foul mood. 'I'll leave again at first light,' he promised Veiti.

I stared at him open-mouthed, wondering how long they would spend on this fool's errand. He gave me a fierce look and said, 'The only reason why you hate this is that no one ever looked for you when you were taken.'

His words slid down me like rain on a coat of armour. I didn't rise to the challenge, but he was right. My life would have been different if our community had been half as strong and loyal as theirs. I was still seething that neither my uncle nor his many sons had ever come after me when I was captured. In contrast, the whole Clan had set off in search of Efalaa, no matter how desperate the rescue mission, the minute they heard I had seen her alive.

I remembered that evening well. My arrival on the back of Efalaa's bird was a shock for my hosts. Morgunn stopped just short of accusing me of killing Efalaa and stealing her bird. He had murder in his eyes, and I struggled to keep my composure. Fortunately, he wouldn't raise a hand to a pregnant woman, and allowed me to relate the events of our escape.

Once reassured Efalaa was still alive, the Clan offered me hospitality until the child was born. Aalma took me to one of the huts to examine me. She knew what she was doing, and her touch was gentle. She helped me wash off a year's worth of grime in their communal bath tub. I remember my delighted surprise at finding the water clean and warm and the soap rough but pleasantly scented.

The evening of Frid's return was arguably worse than the day of my own arrival. Leodurr, grey-faced, fidgeted about, moving firewood from one side of the firepit to the other. Veiti, disappointed that Morgunn had returned alone, was crying into her hands. The rest of them exchanged worried looks every time she whimpered. Aalma settled by her and rubbed her back.

Veiti was taking this badly. Ollo had been her partner for many years although according to the Clan's unnatural customs, she had conceived her son with Leodurr, the man chosen by the previous Chief to carry on her line.

'I don't want to hope, but I can't stop myself,' warbled Veiti.

No one could find anything to reply to that, and we waited in silence as the night darkened.

When, one by one, we retired to bed, Aalma followed me into Veiti's hut. I lay on the fur I had been allocated, in the corner furthest from the door, and faced the wall while Veiti cried soundlessly into Aalma's lap. After an hour, I offered Aalma my bed and found somewhere else to sleep.

Vidris returned halfway through the night, drenched to the bone. We all stepped outside our huts to hear her news.

'What did you find?' said Morgunn.

'Nothing. I searched the Wastelands as long as I could towards the south, but the darkness was falling, and I saw nothing.'

'Why didn't you turn back earlier?' scolded Morgunn.

'I turned around after sunset.'

'Still you made the return journey in the dark.'

'It wasn't my first night flight,' she argued in a small voice. 'Everyone would have done the same in my place.'

Morgunn sighed. 'Go to bed now, you can continue your search in the morning.'

The Skyriders' treatment of Vidris was odd. They expected from her the courage and fortitude of an adult, but in every other way treated her like a child. For her part, she obeyed Morgunn's orders without question, like a daughter eager to please or an infatuated young girl hoping to be noticed.

Morgunn was sombre and restless as Vidris scurried away.

'Don't worry about Efalaa,' Aalma said to him. 'She must be camping somewhere in the Wastelands. She won't return for another day or two. She wouldn't give up the search so easily. Not after what we did to find her.'

Despite the manner of her leaving, the Skyriders had searched high and low for Efalaa. Miraculously, Morgunn and Steon had found her at the edge of the Clan's territory. More than half-dead of starvation and exposure, she had managed to crawl through what they called 'the Hedge' – a wall of brambles that separated them from the Lowlands.

Morgunn gave Aalma a pained look, and she put her arm around his shoulders.

'Go to bed, Morgunn Ulfborn. We need you strong,' she said gently.

He obeyed her without a word.

As I lay frozen on my pallet, I wondered if Steon would return at all. The memory of his unguarded expression at the sight of Ollo's bird was still fresh in my mind. He had launched Eko into the air like a sleeper finally awoken.

No, Steon would not come back without Ollo. Morgunn could forget about his bird and his last Guardian. Typically, no one had mentioned that possibility. I was, as per usual, the only one to have followed the facts to their proper conclusion.

I tossed and turned in my improvised bed, but sleep eluded me. My huge stomach made sleeping on the floor a new kind of torture. I missed my soft bed at home in New Bodie. I also missed simpler times when my place in the world was assured, when my happiness mattered, and when my orders were obeyed.

When I was born, my father had already been the city's Lord Mayor for many years. He was a strong man, cunning and sometimes ruthless, but under his rule New Bodie had prospered. We were the envy of the other Valley dwellers.

We had clean water at our taps, brick houses and plenty of food in our larders. We wore tastefully cut clothing of silk and fine cotton, and we sent our children to school. Our walls were well defended, but nevertheless we traded with our neighbours – mostly for cloth and manufactured goods. We had no slaves, only workers organised with a strict hierarchy of foremen, supervisors, managers and directors, all reporting to my father.

Dissenters were swiftly dealt with. Everyone knew where they stood.

I too knew where I stood, and that was at the top, one small step down from my father. He trusted me and valued my opinions, and when I turned twenty-one, he started preparing me for leadership. He was pleased with my progress. Life was good.

My world collapsed on the evening of my twenty-second birthday party. While everyone lay this way or that, inebriated, a group of traitors slit my father's throat and left him to bleed on the floor of his office. I received word of his death seconds before the assassins arrived at my own door.

I only had time to leap out of the window and hide in the sewers under the street. I bet my life on them thinking me too vain to spoil my beautiful party dress. Indeed, no one looked for me among the detritus and excrement.

I waded through the muck and soiled water until I was able to force my way through a grate at the end of the tunnel, dislocating my shoulder in the process.

It was in that sorry state that I arrived at my uncle's camp outside the city. Gond was my father's younger brother. They had chosen different lifestyles and never saw eye to eye, but he and his Caravan of more than a hundred chariots had been invited to join in my birthday celebrations.

Gond and his five sons were suddenly my only family. They took me in, pushed the head of my arm bone back into its socket, poured bucket after bucket of water over me and burnt my ruined gown.

I started my new life empty-handed and just as naked as the day I was born, depending on charity for every thread on my body and every crumb of bread.

On hearing the news of my father's death, the Caravaneers made swift preparations. We were gone before dawn. At the time, I concluded their haste was a sign of their concern for me. Later events showed me it was in fact their own lives they had been keen to save.

Life in the Caravan was tedious. We stopped in every town, village or camp – no matter how small or poor – and bought and sold goods. I soon became convinced that every stop on our way would be equally squalid and depressing.

The trading of badly made pots and second-hand fabrics never captured my interest, and I dreamt of returning to New Bodie and reclaiming what was mine. This time, my place would be at the top, with no one above me. I didn't care how many lies I told, or how many lives I took if it brought me closer to my goal.

My uncle and my cousins were not interested in risking their position in life in order to restore mine, so I started working on the hearts and minds of a carefully chosen selection of their men. I traded whatever favours I could in order to secure a following. In those days, I was still sure of my charms and powers, and I never once doubted that I would eventually succeed.

Unfortunately, that plan never came to fruition. One night, as we camped near the Dry Lake, our convoy was attacked by two dozen Raiders. In the wrong place at the wrong time, I was snatched along with some crates of well-worn poplin.

I never saw the Caravaneers again.

Whilst I was being raped for the first time by my captors, I squarely directed my rage and hatred at the men who had failed to defend me rather than at those violating my body.

In time, this changed.

After my escape from the Raiders' camp, returning to New Bodie on my own would have been suicide. Assuming I survived the long journey home, I could trust no one there. The traitors would kill me before I opened my mouth.

Neither could I return to Gond's caravan. The Wastelands were an open desert where they roamed at will. I had no chance of finding them before the Raiders found me.

Having strictly nowhere else to go, I now lived in a camp composed of hastily put together wooden huts that only kept out the very worst of the winter nights. The Skyriders seemed immune to the cold and washed in their draughty bath house, whatever the weather. I spend my days shivering and my nights frozen.

At least I did not go hungry, nor was I beaten or raped. So I rammed my throat full of unsaid words and did my level best to avoid undignified displays of rage and disgust, despite the unrelenting memories of betrayal, humiliation and violence that swirled inside me.

❧ 4 ❧

S teon

Efalaa and I were entirely unprepared when we launched the birds into the air, on the afternoon of Frid's return. By heading straight into the storm with a civilian, I'd broken every rule of Guardianship. The Master would have turned my skin into breeches for this.

I hated being the Clan's last Guardian. Hundreds of years ago, the First Twelve had decided the Clan needed nine Guardians—never more, never less. And now, I was on my own.

Even in the Clan's close-knit community, the Guardians stood out as a tightly bonded band of brothers and sisters. Our Master, Erlen Durrborn, used to say that we were united like the fingers of a fist, and – behind his back – we used to joke that he couldn't count. We nine spent most of our time together and made few friends outside our group.

Our parents were carefully selected for size, strength and courage, and we were bred for combat and raised as warriors. From the age of eighteen, a Guardian was expected to lay down his or her life whenever the need arose. No complaints, no questions asked. Our dedication set us soldiers apart from the rest of the Clan. The other Clan members all took their own vocations seriously, but nothing compared with living and breathing your mission like a Guardian.

Our job was simple: we kept the Clan safe. We warned travellers to avoid the Lowlands around the Clan's territory. We protected the Chief, the Gatherers or the Healers when their jobs called them beyond the Hedge. Once every few years, we even fought off Raiders if they came too close to our lands.

It was also a Guardian's job to rescue any Clan member lost outside the Territory, but the odds had never been as poor as they were in our search for Ollo. Of course, I still hoped to find him somewhere in the Wastelands, but I had a much greater chance of getting myself or, worse, Efalaa killed.

We scoured the skies in the beating rain. My fingers became cold and stiff, and I struggled to keep hold of the reins. I thought of Efalaa flying directly behind me. She had tiny hands, and I hoped she had remembered her gloves.

The only thing we saw during that afternoon was a long line of Raiders walking north, with twelve chariots and perhaps a hundred men. They were en route to attack some unsuspecting settlement—or anyone else they might find along the way.

Efalaa reacted swiftly and gained altitude. It was the right evasive manoeuvre, and without delay I joined her above the clouds. We could not fly that high for very long: the air was too thin for our lungs and the cold even more intense, but the last thing we needed was some grubby archer shooting our birds out of the sky.

We'd been flying south-east for an hour when lightning struck close to us, followed almost immediately by the boom of thunder. I felt Eko's tremor of fear. We could ask no more of the birds' loyalty, so I signalled to Efalaa, and we landed by a group of pine trees that would give us some shelter once the storm passed.

'Not even a Guardian and a Hunter can start a fire in this weather,' she remarked. 'How are your hands?'

'Cold.'

'Let me see.'

She held my hands with the very tips of her fingers, as if frostbite was contagious.

'You're lucky, they seem alright.'

'Stop worrying,' I replied.

From her saddlebag, she pulled a pair of man-size fur mittens and handed them to me. 'Morgunn always forgets his gloves, so I keep these with me,' she smiled.

My hands immediately warmed up, and I thanked her with a nod.

She was quiet as we sat side by side and petted the birds to keep them calm.

Our travelling cloaks would protect us from the cold and rain for now, but this was the worst possible night to spend outdoors without food or supplies.

'Any chance of a catch among those trees?' I said half-hopeful, half-joking.

Efalaa shook her head. 'What could possibly draw a rabbit out of his burrow in this weather?' she chuckled.

'I don't know... Flooding?'

She laughed.

'Did you have weather like this when you were away?' I asked. She had spent the weeks of the late autumn roaming the Wastelands after a quarrel with Morgunn.

She flinched but answered in a level voice,'Yes. Once it rained for three days.'

We were quiet again, both lost in our own thoughts.

I was the first to break the silence. 'I can't abandon Ollo just because of bad weather,' I said, answering the many objections in my mind.

'I'm not proposing we do.'

'I think you should go home, Efalaa.'

'I'm not leaving him out there on his own, and I'm not leaving you to look for him alone. We'll cover twice as much ground if we split up.'

'It's too dangerous. Morgunn would not want you continuing this mission.'

'You don't know that,' she argued. 'He has given no orders to you or me about it,' she added with a sly smile. I frowned, and she continued. 'Every Clan life is precious. Morgunn would not want us to give up so easily on Ollo, his skills, and his bloodline.'

'This is not a job for you, Efalaa. I don't know why I took you with me.'

'I'm a Hunter after all. I go out for prey in all sort of weathers.'

'But not on your own.'

'I can take care of myself, Steon Hildenborn. I'm not a Singer any more.'

I sighed. She had a point.

As we had nothing to eat, we passed the time by collecting rainwater in our cupped hands and sipping it slowly.

'I wish I had picked up those curly dock leaves I was showing Sili earlier,' said Efalaa. 'I'd even eat them raw.'

We exchanged a smile. I had never spent much time with Efalaa before and found her surprisingly good company. She was not as troubled and complicated as she had once seemed.

'You must be used to spending evenings out in the rain.'

She nodded. 'Yes, this is nothing new.' She smiled again, 'Except you don't talk quite as much as Morgunn.'

'You two are lucky to still have each other. I've lost everyone,' I said.

She nodded quietly. After a pause, she added, 'You've been calling me Isveg all day.'

Hearing that name in Efalaa's mouth was a stab to my heart. 'Have I?' I said quickly to disguise my unease. 'I'm sorry. Just habit.'

'I take it as a compliment,' she said softly. 'She was strong. And kind.'

'And funny,' I added through the lump in my throat.

'Was she?'

'You had to get to know her.'

'I was so caught up in my own problems I never took the time. I wish I'd taken the time to get to know everyone better.'

'Me too,' I confessed. That thought made me so sad I didn't trust myself to say any more.

After a while, Efalaa asked, 'Do you think we'll find Ollo?'

I swallowed my grief before answering. 'No. But then again, I didn't think Morgunn and I would find you either, and yet we did.'

Her hood hid most of her face, but I saw her pretty smile. This encouraged me to continue. 'I've never been more surprised in my life than when you burst out of the greenwoods. Skin and bones. Covered in blood. You looked like you'd walked through death and come out the other side.'

'I had,' she said softly. 'And the blood wasn't mine.'

I chuckled. 'I'm a Guardian, I've served for eleven years, and I've never killed anyone. You're tougher than you look.'

She was suddenly serious. 'I killed because I was afraid.

You Guardians are afraid of nothing. You're so brave you don't need to kill people.'

'You sound like a ten-year-old,' I teased.

Everyone knew Efalaa's childhood had ended abruptly when her mother died young. I was touched to find such a sweet nugget of innocence in this woman who had grown up too soon. It reminded me how deeply the Clan trusted their Guardians.

The little ones were taught Guardians could drive away fear. 'If you're ever scared, find a Guardian,' the Elders would tell the children. And the Teachers would bring us the fearful toddlers or anxious youngsters they had failed to reassure. We held little hands and patted little heads, and if all else failed, we took them into Guardians Lodge and made room for them at the foot of our beds.

Arni was particularly popular with children. They sat on his lap at assemblies, and he would let them plait his hair endlessly. Poor Giselda, his lover who was also a Guardian, always ended up with the job of detangling the mess. Because Giselda was twenty years younger than Arni, eyebrows were raised when they became regular bedfellows. It all seemed so shallow now.

It broke my heart to think how much the Clan trusted us with their own lives and the lives of their children, because we had saved no one. Not a single life.

Of course, I knew beyond doubt that if anything could have been done when the mountain fell, the Guardians would have done it. I knew they had united to save the children's lives at the expense of all others, including their own.

We'd all heard tales about soldiers of old saving women and children first. That was not our way. In a crisis, women were perfectly capable of saving themselves, but children... Children had to be protected at all cost. Every precious young life lost on the day of the Quake had been fiercely defended.

Yet, what could Guardians do when boulders the size of a house crashed onto their roof? Stone upon stone fell on the Hall where everyone feasted, from Uron the oldest Helper to Geeda the youngest child. The dust alone must have been enough to kill those who escaped the crush.

The only thing the Guardians could do was to die alongside their charges. Shoulder to shoulder, arms full of children, in an unwinnable war.

Efalaa interrupted my dark thoughts. She shook me gently. 'Don't go to sleep yet. We need to gather twigs and pine needles before the end of the light. They make an uncomfortable bed, but they will keep us off the wet ground.'

I followed her in silence.

Our task completed, we waited for sleep, curled up inside our travelling cloaks. Isveg would have nestled close to me, but Efalaa kept her distance. She let no one but Morgunn into her personal space.

'I miss my bird,' I said.

'What was his name?'

'Jaavis.'

'I'm lucky I still have Mila.'

'Jaavis carried me everywhere so faithfully I never knew I wasn't the one wearing wings.'

She sighed. 'We took so much for granted before the Quake. We probably still do.'

Her words echoed in the silence.

Before the fateful day of the Harvest Feast, the only thing missing from my life was a child. I didn't care who the Chief chose to be the mother. I just wanted my own child to continue my bloodline and hopefully choose to bear my name, like I had my father's.

The earthquake had not only left me the last Guardian, I

was also the last male of my bloodline. Veiti and Vidris were my first cousins, and as such unsuitable partners. Aalma was too old to have children, and Efalaa refused to take part in our honoured tradition of purposeful breeding. When she left the Clan, she'd made it clear she'd rather die in the Wastelands than accept mating instructions. Now that Morgunn had claimed her for himself, the chances of me having a baby with her were thin.

These were uncomfortable thoughts when she was lying an arm's length away from me, so I cleared my mind as Erlen had taught us and went to sleep for a few hours.

༈ 5 ༈

Steon

Dawn had already broken when I woke with a start, my body stiff from the cold and the uncomfortable position. I often dreamt about my fellow Guardians, and that night was no exception.

In my dream, the nine of us were training together in Guardians Lodge. Delnir was there, making us all laugh with one of his impressions. Saaria worked with the skipping rope, counting under her breath while her braids beat a rhythm against her back. Rakel, only nineteen, was our most recent recruit, and she liked to show off what her young body could do. She hung upside down, doing inverted sit-ups with effort-less grace.

I was telling Isveg, a fellow Guardian and only one year my senior, that I'd dreamt they were all dead. She laughed and teased me. Isveg had such warm eyes. She found everything funny. I felt overwhelming relief and connection, as if all the pieces of my life were falling back into place after a nightmare. In my dream, I was happy.

Then the cold dawn brought back my grief.

Crushed by disappointment but glad of the company, I patted Efalaa awake.

The pools of rainwater around us had frozen over, and my face stung with cold. I broke the icy crust with my fist and washed my face and torso. I checked my braids; they were all still tight and neat.

Efalaa kept looking away from my naked chest. It took me a while to understand her concern.

'Do you want some privacy while you wash?' I finally asked her.

'Yes, please,' she answered in a small voice. 'Afterwards, I could start a fire if you want to shave, it's only drizzling now.'

'Don't worry, I'll just run the blade down my face quickly.' I walked to the centre of the group of trees and continued my morning ritual.

When I came back, Efalaa and the two birds were ready to go. 'We'd better split up,' she said. 'I'll search the south-western plains. We sometimes hunt there. I'll be able to tell if anything is different.'

I was reluctant to let her out of my sight, but she was right. 'Don't spend another night out here on your own. The Raiders are on the move.'

She nodded, but I guessed she would ignore my advice.

'Why are you doing this?' I asked.

'Same reason as you.'

'He's a Guardian. He's my brother.'

'Now we're all brothers and sisters,' she said, looking at me through her lashes.

My heart swelled, and I gripped her in a hug she didn't return. When she spoke, her voice came out strangled.

'Take care of yourself, soldier.'

'Take care of yourself, sweetheart. For the Clan.'

She repeated the Clan's words after me.

There was nothing more to say. We flew off in different directions to resume our hopeless search.

I flew east as the day dragged on, bleak and cold. There was nothing to see on the Wastelands below, only clumps of yellowing grass. Nowhere for a person to hide or shelter.

I landed three times to explore two thickets and a small wood but found no trace of Ollo.

The light was dwindling fast; it must have been around dinnertime. My growling stomach reminded me that I'd missed four meals in a row when, at the edge of my field of vision, I saw a dark lump on the ground.

It was too isolated to be a dead tree. Maybe a dead animal. I turned Eko in that direction and held my breath. This was the first possible sighting of Ollo since Efalaa and I had left the Territory.

The shape was not moving. I landed, my heart thudding, and discovered what was unmistakably clothing. The top layer was dark wool and covered the form entirely.

I should have noticed the smell, but in my excitement, I didn't.

I lifted the cloak in one swift move only to uncover a decomposing mass with bits of fabric and hair sticking out of it. The stench was powerful. This corpse must have been freezing at night and thawing in the sun for many days, perhaps weeks.

I turned around to vomit, but nothing came up from my empty stomach. I forced myself to inspect my gory discovery. The fabric seemed a different colour from the dyes we used in the Clan, but that proved nothing. Efalaa had come back dressed in Raiders' clothes. I needed to know beyond doubt that this was not Ollo.

The head was so damaged I couldn't tell whether it belonged to man or a woman, but the hair was the right sort of blonde. It was long enough to be Ollo's, although it was not braided.

The only way I could be sure was by comparing the corpse's height with mine. Ollo was taller than me, and that made him much taller than most Wastelanders, Raiders or Valley dwellers. If the body had longer limbs than mine, then it had to be Ollo.

I used a stick to peel away some of the rotting flesh from the thigh bone and measured it with a length of leather from Eko's bridle. Again, my stomach tried to empty itself. My fingers were shaking as I compared the length to my own thigh.

The bone seemed smaller than mine.

I repeated the experiment and came again to the same conclusion.

I breathed a sigh of relief, and the pungent smell invaded my nostrils. There was nothing around the body to indicate where this person came from or what caused their death. There were no visible blood stains on the decomposing clothes, so it must have been exposure, starvation or illness.

There may have been weapons or a waterskin caught between the frozen ground and the body, but I decided that my need was not that great.

I sat by the corpse, relieved and sad in the dying light, but soon I shook myself. There was still something I had to do.

Eko and I circled the area at low altitude until I found some debris of wood and stones at the edge of a murky pond. I loaded them into my saddle bags and flew back to the dead body. Just as I began to cover the traveller's remains, the rain started again.

It took me an hour to complete my grim task. Once it was done, I found the ground to be so wet that I had no choice but to sit astride Eko's back and lay my head against his neck. This was uncomfortable for both of us, yet it was better than sleeping in a bog.

I used my training and discipline to will myself to sleep.

S teon

Thanks to Eko's body heat, I was able to sleep through the hours before dawn that are always the coldest.

I woke with the first rays of sunshine peeking timidly above the horizon. It was still raining, so I took my clothes off and let the cold rain wash the grime and sadness from my skin. I was not able to wash my undergarments – the puddle water around me was too muddy – but I tightened my braids and shaved the stubble on my face. My skin stung, and my eyes were sore.

I had no food for my breakfast, but I let Eko pick at the thawing ground for worms. There was no point in both of us starving.

The sun shone cold just above the horizon when we resumed our ride.

From the vantage point that Eko afforded me, high in the

sky, I could see for dozens of miles in any direction, and a lone man on foot would have stood out like a beacon.

Poor Veiti. Was she still hoping her mate would return? She had been given the cruelest of hopes.

By midday, the hardships of the journey started taking their toll. I hadn't eaten in three days, and the cold seeped through my damp cloak, but I kept flying east, my eyes trained on the ground and my thoughts on the past.

So many stories I could no longer share with those who'd been there. So many memories were lost under the rock. Maybe that was how Sili felt. She was the only Outsider in living memory who had not spent her time with the Clan tied to a tree. She was smart and not as naive as some other civilians.

Sili knew the worst that men could do, and she'd proved she had what it took to survive. After a year of rapes and beatings and while six months pregnant, she'd escaped a Raiders' camp and came out still fighting.

Of course, this was the kind of woman who could stab you in the back without blinking, but I wouldn't have minded fighting next to her in a tight spot. Unlike Morgunn or Efalaa who were the best fighters left after me, she wasn't burdened by doubts or scruples. Both the Hunters had it in them to waste the fateful minute weighing moral considerations. Such naivety could cost them their lives and me mine. Sili, on the other hand, would plant the knife before I'd even thought of it.

Despite her fighting spirit, she was green. She didn't understand the twists and turns of combat. She thought the road to victory is as straight as the horizon, when every soldier knows it is jagged like a scar.

What annoyed me most about her – apart from her messy hair – was her blatant inveigling. It was clear her plan was to use us as long as suited her, with no respect for the extra effort it took to shelter and feed her. Whenever I saw her, I was seized by the desire to subdue her and to bend her to my will. No other woman had ever made me feel this way.

My past relationships had been simple, based on equality, mutual liking and satisfying sex. Clanswomen were beautiful. They were not coy or manipulative. Brought up to be the equal of men in every respect, they allowed themselves the same appetites. If they wanted sex, they chose an available partner and asked nicely. I had been asked often, and I'd also done my share of asking. When turned down, I moved on to a different partner without a moment's frustration or regret. Sex was good, it was fun, and I liked to keep it simple.

I could imagine that sex with Sili would be intense, but that was out of the question. With her infuriating Outsider ways, she couldn't understand that we were all equal. She thought that exiles with inflated ideas of themselves ranked higher than the Clan's last Guardian. She would try to take the upper hand and harness me like a bird. Sex with her would not be simple. Thinking of Sili made me miss Isveg even more.

As the day progressed, I flew east over the barren lands, and my thoughts kept wandering between the aggravating Outsider and my fallen brethren.

My deepest shame and regret was that I hadn't died with the other Guardians. The truth was that on the day of the Quake, for the first time ever, I had forgotten my weapons.

I can't explain how it happened. As we often did, Isveg and I were having before-dinner sex in the deserted Orchard.

Broadcasting your lovemaking was considered extremely rude amongst the Clan. With all of us living in such proximity, it was only fair that those who were enjoying each other shouldn't taunt or tempt the others. Loud noises would only bring around potential participants, so if you wanted to keep things private, you just had to be discreet and allow the rest to go about their day or have a good night sleep.

The dinner calls came earlier than Isveg and I anticipated, and we hurried back to the Great Lodge still fastening our clothes. Halfway there, I realised I'd left my dagger and my knife behind as well as the axe I had used as an excuse to loiter around the apple trees.

A Guardian without his weapons was a laughing stock. I knew Delnir would never let me live it down, and even at my age I disliked getting on the wrong side of Erlen. So I ran back to the Orchard, leaving Isveg to go home without me.

Now I was alive, and she was dead. My incompetence had saved my life.

I didn't know how I'd ended up in that ditch, still without my weapons. I could hardly believe no one, not even Morgunn, had ever questioned why I wasn't in the Hall when the mountain fell. I was grateful no one had looked too far into it, but guilt and shame were eating away at me.

❧ 7 ☙

S teon

I had never flown that far east. The muds of the narrow valley to the east of our mountain range turned into a dry craggy landscape. The cracks in the ground reminded me of the broken Lowlands after the Quake, only these were much deeper.

It was time for me to turn back. I could survive another night in the open and another day without food, but I needed to be back in the Orchard during the course of the following day or the Clan would have no Guardian left.

I was curious about the broken ground below us though, and I let Eko fly in circles for a while. Then, just as we were about to turn around, I saw something moving along one of the ridges.

It was a tall figure in a cloak, and my heart jumped. The broad shape moved slowly with dignity and poise. I descended straight towards it at Eko's full diving speed. My braids flew behind me, and the cold air made my eyes well up.

I was approaching fast when, through my tears, I saw the figure turn around and run from me. My heart was no longer beating joyfully. Ollo was the only person in the Wastelands who would not have run from a giant bird.

The traveller stumbled forward in panic. I would have normally stopped the chase, but I needed to know if he had seen Ollo, so I pressed on.

Soon we reached the edge of a deep canyon, and the shape stopped and turned to fight. I landed at a good distance and walked slowly forward, arms spread wide. The man stood his ground defiantly, his cloak pulled tight around his bulky body. I wondered what manner of weapon he was hiding.

'I come in peace,' I called out.

The man didn't answer, and the anxiety on his face grew as the distance between us shortened. Again, I wondered whether he was armed. I noticed his hollow cheeks and the bony fingers clinging to the cloth.

'I'm looking for my friend,' I said. 'I won't harm you.'

The man relaxed, but his eyes still searched my face.

'A man travelling alone,' I continued. 'I thought you were him.'

I stopped, leaving ten paces between us.

'He might be hurt. Have you seen him?'

'No,' the man replied, and he stepped back, dangerously close to the edge.

'Have you been travelling long? Where are you coming from?' I asked.

A look of suspicion returned to the man's face, and his grey eyes darted left and right.

'I'm alone,' I said.

The man's cloak rippled, and instinctively I reached for my dagger. The traveller took another step back.

'Stop,' I said. 'You're too close.'

The man's bulk somehow shifted from his side to his back, seeming to retreat further from me.

'What are you hiding?' I asked, my voice now hard. I pulled my dagger halfway out of its sheath.

The man's face lost all colour. 'I haven't seen your friend,' he hurried to reply. 'I haven't seen anyone.'

I took my hand off my weapon and started walking backwards towards Eko.

'Safe journey,' I said to the man. I hated that he was so scared of me.

'Have you any food?' he interrupted, his sallow face suddenly eager.

I was about to reply that I didn't when a pair of tiny eyes full of anticipation peeked out of the cloak. A child no older than six appeared from beneath the fabric. The man tried to push him back, but the boy planted his feet and hugged the man's leg.

'We haven't eaten in days,' said the man.

'Neither have I,' I replied. 'I have nothing to give you.'

My heart ached at their disappointment. The man lowered his eyes and bit his bottom lip hard. The child kept staring at me anxiously.

I stood frozen as their despair cut into me.

'Have you seen a settlement nearby?' the man asked eventually.

I shook my head. I could not trust myself to speak.

'Do you have a weapon? Traps perhaps?' I asked after my voice returned.

'Nothing,' said the man.

'I can give you my dagger...' I started.

'There's nothing to hunt. No trace of anything alive.'

The boy started crying silently, his eyes still fixed on me.

I gave the man my dagger, handle first. He took it with a nod of thanks.

For a moment, no one spoke. I could not utter the words in my head, neither could I leave them unsaid.

'I can take your son with me,' I said eventually.

The enormity of what I was offering hit me like a blow to the temple. The man held my eyes, and I felt I was stepping into his mind and into his pain. My own grief seemed small and unimportant compared to his. What terrible choice was I giving him?

The man stood at the edge of the precipice, and I became scared that he would jump. He looked down at the child.

'No,' said the child meeting his gaze steadily, 'No, Father. I won't go.'

The man put his finger across the little blue lips, but the boy clung to him, his fists gripping the cloak with white knuckles. The man was still undecided.

'God will provide,' the child said finally. 'Have faith, Father.'

The man shut his eyes with a look of exhaustion. He laid a hand on the boy's head and turned his gaze on me.

'Thank you, stranger,' he said. 'My son and I will continue our journey together.' His face was drained of energy, and I thought he might collapse, but he only smiled. 'I hope you find your friend.'

I saw in the man's eyes his decision was made. There was no more I could do.

With a deep ache behind my ribs, I nodded my goodbyes, and one foot after another I walked back to Eko. He clucked as I reached for the reins. The familiar noise comforted me.

Efalaa was right, we still took so much for granted: I had a home to return to where fellowship and a hot meal awaited me. After what I had just seen, I had no right to wallow in self-pity and shame.

For better or for worse, I was the Clan's last Guardian, and my mission was still clear. I would keep my people safe and protect their lives with mine. Above all else, I would protect the Clan's children. No matter who their fathers or mothers were, I would love each and every one of them, and they would all be mine.

There were still a couple of hours of daylight, and a new storm was brewing. Eko and I headed home. The time for grief was over. I was ready to carry out my mission and think no more of what could have been.

I lacked the courage to look back at the man and his son, but I saw from the corner of my eye the boy waving me goodbye.

8

S ili

I was washing undergarments that didn't even belong to me when Efalaa came back, dirty and exhausted.

I shook the tepid water off my hands and joined the little crowd forming around her. She'd been gone two days, and everyone hoped she would have news.

She pulled out of Morgunn's tight embrace to hug me, and her simple display of friendship warmed my heart. I wiped a muddy smudge from her face with my still wet hands.

'So, what news?' asked Morgunn, speaking for all of us.

'Nothing. No traces of him or anyone else,' Efalaa replied.

Veiti whimpered, and Vidris hugged her sadly.

'Where did you go?' questioned Morgunn while leading Efalaa to a seat by the fire.

'Steon and I split up on the first morning. I went west

towards the sea, and he carried on due east towards the canyons.'

'And you saw nothing at all in the Lowlands?'

'Nothing human.'

Aalma stroked Efalaa's hair and helped her out of her wet cloak.

'Are you hungry, sweetling?' asked Morgunn, and with one look at Vidris he sent her to the foodstore. She returned with soft white cheese wrapped in a piece of flatbread.

'We did see something on the first day,' remembered Efalaa in between mouthfuls. 'A troop of Raiders riding north with several chariots.'

'They must be long gone by now,' said Morgunn. 'Leodurr, prepare the bathhouse for Efalaa.' He turned again to his wife. 'I'll help you wash your hair, my love.'

Veiti blew on a mug of sage and mint tea to cool it down before placing it in Efalaa's hands.

'Thank you for looking for my man,' she said in a broken voice.

The kindness they all showed Efalaa left a bitter taste in my mouth.

Steon returned that same evening and, unlike Efalaa, he looked as tidy and clean as he always did – not a strap nor a hair out of place. It was hard to believe he'd spent two nights sleeping rough with nothing to eat and little to drink. I wondered briefly whether he'd only pretended to look for Ollo.

He resumed his duties after a quick dinner and never spoke a word to anyone about his time away. His face had returned to his usual expressionless stoicism. Perhaps I had imagined the moment of pure emotion that had threatened to change my opinion of him.

While we talked around the fire, the storm started again, and the thunder woke Leif, who had been sleeping in his mother's arms. Soon, his cries of fear were louder than the storm. Veiti did not even try to comfort him, she passed him to Steon as if it were the most natural thing in the world. No one but me seemed surprised.

Steon held the baby tight against his chest.

'Shush, little man. Have no fear, a Guardian's here,' he whispered in a sing-song voice, at odds with his bulky appearance.

This didn't work and Leif kept sobbing, but Veiti did not ask for her son back. Steon took the baby with him when he went to bed in the sleeping hut he shared with Leodurr, and he only brought him back to Veiti halfway through the night for his feed.

Although I had a bed in Veiti's hut, and I ate their food, I would never be part of this tight-knit group. They had known each other all their lives and were bound by blood and tragedy. Together, they had painstakingly clawed their way back from the brink of extinction. Together, they had survived. Now they had finally brought Efalaa home, and they were complete.

As the only Outsider, I was dispensable. I would never feel safe here. And frankly I didn't want to live in the mud and wash other people's laundry one day longer than necessary.

However, before I could return to my life, there was still one thing I had to do. After all the miscarriages I had suffered in New Bodie, I could scarcely believe this most unwanted baby, this child of a dozen fathers, was the only one I would carry to term.

In my younger days, when I was still living a free and comfortable life under my father's protection, I'd enjoyed many lovers, certain as I had become that I would never conceive a viable child.

Still, this pregnancy had served me well at first. The

Raiders soon lost interest in me, and I was able to prepare my escape in peace. I walked around their camp unnoticed, my distended stomach a cloak of invisibility. They even stopped tying me to their cursed posts, confident that in my state I wouldn't try to escape.

They had underestimated me.

I refused to think about what had happened at the Raiders' camp. They had already taken too much of my time. What I needed now was food, shelter and a trained Healer until I was strong enough to return to New Bodie, in the soft green valley where everything grows.

I didn't know what I would find there. Undoubtedly, someone sitting in my father's office, living in his house and eating his food. Of course, I was my father's heir, but it would be hard to get rid of the impostor and regain what was mine.

My plan was to leave the child behind. I didn't want it, and in any case it would be safer here with the Skyriders. I calculated that I could leave four or five weeks after the birth. Veiti still complained about having to ride a bird the day after Leif the Lucky was born. I had no desire to follow her example. I couldn't worry about the child. Veiti would feed it with Leif, I had not a single doubt about that.

I had turned the matter over in my mind for many nights, and despite my chilling fears about bird riding, I had come to the conclusion that the only way out of the Clan's Territory was by bird. It would impossible to walk away fast enough to avoid the Skyriders tracking me down and demanding I take the baby with me. Just as I knew they would look after the child once I was gone, I knew they would not allow me to leave the child behind.

I needed to learn to ride and befriend Efalaa's bird so that when the time came, it would obey me and take me straight home to New Bodie. This was a terrifying prospect, but there was no other choice. I decided to attack my fear head on and chip away at it, one day at a time.

I could hardly get the words through my chattering teeth when I approached Vidris one frosty morning. She was ladling water out of the stream in a leaky wooden bucket before tending to the birds.

'Dearie,' I called, using one of terms of endearment Clanspeople favoured.

She turned and smiled. 'Hello Sili, did you sleep well?'

I frowned. 'I can't get comfortable with my bulge.'

She laughed. 'Don't call your sweet baby a bulge. The poor treasure will feel unwelcome.'

My mask slipped and I sniggered. She looked at me questioningly.

I changed the subject. 'I wanted to talk to you about the birds. Have you got time?'

Her look of growing suspicion was instantly replaced by excitement.

'Of course,' she replied eagerly.

'You know how frightening I still find the birds, don't you, sweetheart?'

She nodded and smiled. 'I'll never forget your face when you had to hold poor Frid's bridle...' Her smile died as she remembered the rest of the events of that day.

'Do you think that, if I got to know the birds a bit better, maybe even helped with feeding or grooming them, I might in time become less fearful?'

She looked at me with surprise, and a hint of suspicion returned in her eyes. I saw she was about to refuse so I hastened to add, 'It can't be good for the baby, can it, for me to be so frightened.'

That argument found its mark. The Skyriders were fond of children, and Vidris was no exception. She would do for my unborn Raider baby what she would not do for me.

'You're right,' she said, 'and that would help the birds too. They feel your fear, and it makes them nervous. Can you start right now?'

The lump in my throat prevented me from speaking, so I simply nodded.

She relished the opportunity to show off the birds' skills and practically skipped to the birds' shed, while I wobbled behind her. She laughed when I approached her bird Oxi with a trembling hand.

'She is very gentle,' I praised, caressing its silk soft feathers with the tips of my fingers. Vidris's cheeks pinked in delight. 'Is she totally blind?' I asked.

'She can't see my hand in front of her eyes, poor darling. We've never had a blind bird before. I had to devise a new training routine for her. We've been working on her recall for many months. She's such a good girl.'

'And she is beautiful.' I never thought those words would ever pass my lips in reference to one of these overgrown eagles, but Vidris enjoyed my unimaginative compliments.

No matter how docile this bird was, her blindness required steering skills I could not hope to learn in time for my escape.

'What about Efalaa's bird? She is gentle too, isn't she?'

'Well, you know that,' she said. 'You've ridden her.'

'Is it alright if I feed her?'

Vidris paused, but then said, 'Of course. Just keep your fingers like so. Her beak is sharp.'

My hand trembled so much Vidris had to steady it with her own. Her brow furrowed.

'You don't have to feed her if you're that scared,' she said pulling my hand away.

I couldn't let her restrict my access to the animals and jeopardise my escape, so I decided to lie with the truth. 'Look,

Vidris, I've never told anyone because it is so embarrassing, but something happened when Frid returned.' Immediately, I had her full attention. 'I was so terrified. I thought he was attacking us and that both Efalaa and I were going to die—'

'Of course not!' she interrupted, shocked.

'Only I didn't know that at the time.' I lowered my voice further. 'Can you keep a secret?' She nodded yes several times like a much younger girl. No louder than a whisper, I said, 'I was so scared I wet myself.'

She looked up at me, eyes wide.

'I can't let that happen again. It's too embarrassing.' I covered my cheeks with my hands to hide my non-existent blush.

'I won't tell anyone,' she said fervently, and she stopped my hand from shaking as I fed the birds their breakfast. 'Don't overfeed Frid,' she warned, 'he stress-eats. He must have had such a hard time alone in the Wastelands.'

'I can well imagine.' I managed to keep the annoyance out of my voice, and Vidris smiled at me, blissfully unaware of my true meaning.

From that day on, I made sure I was always the one to deliver grains and treats to Efalaa's bird. While Vidris and the rest of the Clan continued to underestimate me, my fears receded and my confidence with the birds grew.

I also discovered where the waterskins were kept and found the fire-starting flints and dry food supplies. I made a note of the times when the travelling cloaks would be mine for the taking. My preparations were almost finished. I only had to survive the labour and birth.

To that effect, I dutifully practised the birthing exercises Aalma insisted on.

'You should have started those months ago,' she scolded, with uncharacteristic thoughtlessness.

I gave her a sideways look. 'Birthing exercises were not part of our lifestyle in the Raiders' camp.'

She lowered her eyes and never referred to my life before the Clan again.

My fear of the impending birth made all my other fears seem small. I'd seen women die in childbirth, exhausted by hours of pain and blood loss. I'd rather have fallen off a bird.

❧ 9 ❧

S^{teon}

The morning was sunny for a change. Veiti and Aalma, bare to the waist, squealed like children while splashing each other with icy water.

Veiti, who valued cleanliness above all things, was the only one brave enough to remove the rest of her clothes, break the crust of ice and sit in the frigid stream. She didn't stay long. She leapt out of the water and ran around to warm herself, her backside and legs bright red from the cold.

We all laughed while she good-humouredly squeezed water out of her braids. Vidris went to fetch her some dry underwear.

'You've lost a lot of weight,' said Morgunn to the still naked Veiti. 'Your stomach is nearly flat. Are you eating enough?'

Veiti rolled her eyes with a patient smile.

'She's fine,' Aalma called back from inside her hut. 'Leif the Lucky is drinking her slim!'

Morgunn turned to me. 'You can see how busy I am keeping these ladies in line,' he said with a wink. 'A Chief's work is never done!' Then he stood up and called everyone to him. 'I want everyone in the fields today. Leodurr tells me we can plant some vegetables ready for early spring. We will take advantage of the bright weather and do it all in one day.'

'For the Clan,' Veiti called, and six voices answered.

It was a joyous noise, but never again would we hear cheers like those before the Quake, when a hundred people together shouted our Clan words and when children's voices turned them into the sweetest music.

We worked all day in the vegetable patch Leodurr had brought back from barrenness, with much determination and rotten nettle leaves. The ground had thawed, and we planted five long rows of beets, two of carrots and turnips.

Sili was the only one to stay in the Orchard. If she'd even tried to bend down, she would have toppled over. Her pregnant belly made her look frail—not strong like Veiti had been. In any case, Aalma thought she needed the rest.

That evening though, Sili was not at assembly. She hadn't answered the dinner calls. We waited for her to start eating, and Veiti went to the latrines to find her. She wasn't there. Involuntarily, my body tensed in alert. Where was she? Was she hurt? Had she left? Had she been taken?

Again, I felt the absence of my fellow Guardians. I would have to deal with whatever this was on my own.

Aalma also looked concerned. 'She might have gone into labour and be stranded somewhere like you were,' she said to Veiti who nodded anxiously.

'We need to find her without a moment to spare. Night is falling fast.' I declared.

I sighed inwardly: we were forever trying to find the lost

sheep, the one that got away. Couldn't we all just stay in one place? Missing people made me anxious.

Morgunn stood up and took charge. As the son and great-grandson of Chiefs, he had an instinctive understanding of what his role entailed. I could not be seen to be making decisions. I could only follow his orders. I was grateful when he spoke up.

'Let's eat and drink quickly so that we can spend the rest of the night looking for her if we have to.'

Obediently, we swallowed our food in a hurry.

'Where was she last seen?' Morgunn asked.

'I saw her leave in the direction of the greenwoods towards the end of the afternoon. She said she would gather kindling,' I replied. Now that I took the time to think about it, this was an unlikely explanation. If she couldn't bend down for vegetables, she couldn't pick sticks off the ground either. My anxiety grew.

'I saw her after that, when I flew back from the hunt,' added Efalaa, in between two mouthfuls. 'She was walking down the west flank, half a mile from the Camp.'

Morgunn stood. 'Steon, take Frid west towards the Bridge. Vidris, take Oxi and fly over the greenwoods. They're thin enough at the moment, you'll be able to see her from the air. Efalaa, you will fly east. Leodurr, walk through the south woods. They are too thick, and we will need someone on the ground. I will fly over that area so that I can take her back to the Camp on Eko if Leodurr finds her.'

One by one, as our names were called, we jumped to our feet.

'What about us?' asked Veiti, pointing at herself and Aalma.

'Chances are she's gone into labour,' replied Morgunn. 'You two have to wait here and prepare to deliver a baby. We'll fly her back to you or come and fetch you on a bird.'

Aalma and Veiti looked a little disappointed, but both nodded their understanding.

'For the Clan,' said Morgunn in conclusion. I was interested to hear him say those words in a matter concerning an Outsider. Vidris raised an eyebrow.

'For the Clan,' we all replied.

When Morgunn gripped my forearm in silent goodbye, my eyes moistened. This was the Guardians' farewell. It had been months since anyone had held my arm like that, and I missed it even more than I'd realised. I also measured how much I'd missed my job during all these months of farming, building and gathering.

With a renewed sense of purpose, I took off on Frid to carry out my mission. Night had fallen, the moon hid behind the clouds, and I could see very little. I flew down the mountain flank towards the river, and I was reminded of the search party for Efalaa.

That day, I was only humouring my Chief, but now I felt I was doing my job as a Guardian again. I couldn't help but stand a little taller.

I called Sili's name for maybe an hour over the southwest slope of the mountain. I was flying low over a thicket within sight of the River and the Bridge, when a voice called back from underneath the tree canopy.

'Who goes there?' It was Sili.

'It's me, Steon!' I shouted back, circling over the thick leafy cover. There was nowhere to land, so I headed toward a moonlit clearing.

'Follow my voice,' I called to Sili, but she didn't reply. 'Sili!' I called again as I reached the ground. Nothing but silence. I worried that I'd lost her again.

I walked in the direction of the thicket, calling her name with more insistence. She must have heard me. I couldn't understand why she wasn't answering. Had she been trying to leave the Clan? That thought gave me an unexplainable rush of anger.

'Sili!' I barked.

After a silence, she replied from behind a nearby tree. 'I'm here.' Either she'd mastered the Guardian skill of walking noiselessly through woodlands or she'd been within arm's reach for the last few minutes.

'Why weren't you answering?' I said angrily. 'I've been bursting my lungs shouting for you.'

I grabbed her not too gently by the arm. It was bony, and it felt wrong. I wasn't used to women feeling so breakable, but I wasn't going to let her out of my sight again. Even in the dim moonlight, I saw her recoil and attempt to cover her face with her free arm. Immediately, my anger melted away, replaced by a dull feeling of guilt.

She was annoying, but this was a young woman who had been horribly mistreated and abused by a bunch of cruel men, and I didn't want to remind her of them in any way. I released her arm and stroked her hair as gently as I would have done a child's.

'Oh,' was all she said, as she looked at me from under her lashes. I could not be sure of what I saw in the moon glow, but she gave me a curious look, as if she was seeing me for the first time.

She straightened up and stood stiffly, seeming embarrassed. She wasn't the kind of person who gladly admitted to her own weakness. I was the same, and I could understand that better than most.

'Are you alright?' I asked, no louder than a whisper.

'I got lost,' she murmured.

'You got lost or you were trying to sneak away?' I said softly.

'Sneak away?' She raised her voice. 'Eight months pregnant? What kind of a fool do you take me for? More brawn than brain, as usual.'

And just like that, the good will I had felt towards her a minute earlier vanished. I kicked the frozen ground in frustration. She could look down her nose at me all she liked, she was not as clever as she thought, and I certainly wasn't as dumb as she believed. But I didn't want to let her know she could get under my skin with her offensive remarks.

'I'll take you back to the Orchard,' I said smoothly.

She didn't reply and only followed me back to the clearing where Frid waited.

'Have you seen these lights?' she asked as I reached out for the reins.

I paused. 'What lights?'

She simply pointed in the direction of the Wastelands below us, and straight away I saw what she meant.

There was a chain of torches winding around the base of the mountain, at the very edge of the Clan's Territory. I was annoyed an untrained Outsider had had to point them out to me. My mind had been too full of her mean words, and I'd forgotten my Guardian's duty to stay alert and watch for dangers at all times.

'Caravan or Raiders?' I spoke aloud the question in my mind, forgetting I wasn't talking to another Guardian.

'Raiders,' she replied evenly. 'Caravaneers don't walk in single file.'

'That's a problem,' I said, stating the obvious.

'Glad it's finally reached your brain.'

I bit back an angry retort.

'Come on,' I said as calmly as I could manage. 'I need to take you back to the camp, I'll return to investigate later.'

'Don't waste your time. We need to check this now, I have no intention of being recaptured by the Raiders.'

I couldn't believe her words. 'Do you think you're in danger here?'

'What? You're going to defend me all on your own against a whole army of Raiders?' she mocked nastily.

I heard the fear behind her words plainly enough, and I didn't take the bait. Instead of putting her back in her place, I choose to reassure her.

'No one—no one—has ever breached the Clan's defences. The Guardians have always kept invaders away.'

'In case you haven't noticed, you're now on your own.'

She'd gone straight for one of my tender spots. How could she know the absence of my fellow Guardians made me feel less safe? I told myself it was a lucky shot, and again I didn't reply to her barb.

'Let's get you back to the Orchard before you go into labour in the woods.'

'No, I want to see what we're up against,' she said firmly, and she started walking down hill towards the line of torches.

Without thinking, I grabbed her arm again, and again she recoiled. I wondered if, having noticed my reaction the first time, she was now doing this on purpose. To make me feel guilty. Knowingly or not, she'd found my other soft spot.

I knew how I appeared. Before the Quake, I'd been one of the tallest and broadest of the Clansmen, bred for strength and bulk. I'd developed early and from a young age towered over the other children. I didn't like being so much larger than the others. I preferred to feel on an equal footing with people. And what I really didn't like was feeling people were scared of me. A Guardian drove away fear, he did not inspire it.

I let go of her arm and gave up fighting with her. She was unpleasant, but at this time, she wasn't the threat. I brought my mind back to my mission.

'There's a Watch Tower nearby. From there, we can see

the defences and the Wastelands beyond,' I said as gently as I could.

She followed me without a word. One of the few things I liked about her was that she didn't waste words when words weren't needed.

We walked in silence for a while, and I didn't realise she'd fallen behind until I heard her call me softly.

'Steon?' This was the first time she'd ever spoken my name. She didn't pronounce it quite right. She made it sound longer, like two separate sounds, 'Ste-on'.

'I'm here,' I called back, and retraced my steps through the woods until I saw her shape in the dark. I held my hand out to her, and she grabbed my forearm instead. Just like it had with Morgunn, that simple gesture put a lump in my throat.

I led her back onto the path, and we held on to each other as we made our way to the Watch Tower.

It was a tall wooden structure made of mossy grey oak. Previous generations of the Clan had raised it twice to keep it above the canopy of the growing trees. It was very simple, with four huge posts supporting two platforms. The lower one was enclosed to keep spare watchers out of the wind. The upper platform was open on all four sides and had a roof made of shingles. Watchers accessed the platforms via a central ladder.

We kept some supplies on the lower level: dried fruit, some nuts and fresh water in a barrel. Normally, those on guarding duties brought their own food to stave off boredom and keep themselves warm through the chill of the night.

In recent years, the comfort of the Watch Tower had been improved thanks to Berjast, Efalaa's father, our last Master Maker. He had devised a large clay chimenea that could be lit without any risk of burning down the tower. Berjast had received many slaps on the back from grateful

Guardians when he presented his invention one night at assembly.

I tried to help Sili up the ladder, but she pushed my hands away. Hers were cold.

Once on the upper platform, I ignored her protest, grabbed her by her armpits and sat her in one of the two raised chairs. My fingers went around her arms in an unbroken circle. Even this pregnant, she was light as a feather. She must have been seriously malnourished during her time in captivity.

I let my eyes adjust to the moonlight and saw the Raiders were still there. We watched as their fiery line unfurled into a curve around the mouth of the river.

This was the weakest point in the Clan's defences, and I was annoyed they should have so easily found it.

'Forty-four torches and probably twice as many men' said Sili before I'd even finished counting.

'Eleven to one,' I added.

She followed my train of thoughts. 'You're counting Veiti and me?' She sounded surprised.

'Of course. Are you telling me you wouldn't take a few men down before you fell?'

'Not in a fight, I couldn't.' She pursed her lips.

'Nonsense,' I said flatly.

Her brow furrowed into a deep frown.

'I've had a whole year to learn I couldn't take down a man before falling—let alone eleven.'

I was on unsteady ground but chose to push on. 'You were outnumbered, and you weren't fighting for your life.'

'They were raping me every night, it was motivation enough, believe me.'

I tried to sound casual, but I'd been knocked by the bluntness of her last statement. 'Maybe I believe in you more than you believe in yourself.'

Without warning, like a branch snapping back into place, she slapped me hard across the face.

'You're dumbest man I've ever met, I mustn't listen to a word you say.' She fixed a furious gaze on me and continued louder. 'And exactly how many men have you killed in battle? All of you 'guardians', hiding behind your blackberry bushes! I'm not staying a minute longer in your presence. I'd rather wander the woods alone until morning light.'

She hurled herself down from the chair and struggled down the ladder.

'Suit yourself,' I said pettily to her retreating back. Although my task here was done, I stayed in the Watch Tower for a few minutes longer. I didn't want to give her the impression that I was following behind her.

10

S ili

I could not let this brute upset me as he had done.

'Maybe I believe in you more than you believe in yourself.' His words still rang in my ears.

I had believed in myself. In fact, I'd had great confidence in my own abilities, but when my trials started, self-belief made not a bit of difference.

I would never forgive myself for what the Raiders had done to me. My revenge felt small compared to my suffering. Yes, I'd poisoned four men, but that wasn't enough. Even bleeding dry that pig Tungor did not feel a suitable revenge. I could still feel the spray of his blood on my face as I slashed his femoral artery, but I remembered even more vividly the blood flowing out of me after the first gang-rape.

Kasha had spent an hour washing the blood out of the

tunic my uncle had given me. I thought of her kindness and her round Wastelander face, that no hardship could hollow, every time I looked at the hem of my tunic, where faded brown stains were still visible more than a year later.

Nothing ever could repair the insult and injury of my year in captivity. To have been brought so low, me, a Lord Mayor's daughter. They'd taken my pride and my dignity and left me with a child I didn't want growing inside me.

And now I was at the mercy of a bunch of uncivilised, self-involved, xenophobic bird riders, depending on them for my food and shelter and for my very protection.

As I walked through the woods, lost in my own bitter thoughts, I wandered off the path again. I stopped and looked around; I could no longer see my way through. I would have to wait for daylight to return to the camp. It would be a long cold night, and the woods might soon be crawling with Raiders.

I decided to carry on, in case the path miraculously reappeared. All I managed to do was trip over a root in the dark and fall flat on my huge belly. A dull pain went through my body, and my breath was knocked out of me. I let out an undignified wail. When I struggled to my knees, holding my swollen stomach, fear took its familiar hold of me. I imagined Raiders everywhere, hiding behind every tree. I swallowed the pain and was trying to catch my breath when a hand grabbed my elbow.

I shrank away in panic, and nearly wet myself again, but a voice said, 'It's me, Steon,' and the fear drained out of me. Easily, he pulled me to my feet.

The pain in my womb went from a dull ache to a sharp throb, and I doubled over. Steon's hand settled on my lower back, but he didn't speak and neither did I. He put his other hand on my stomach and felt for the baby. Whatever information his inspection yielded, he did not share. I imagined the worst: the birth was imminent.

In silence, he started walking ahead of me and, reaching back, he took both my hands in his. I thought of shaking off his hold but finally accepted I needed his help. He led me out of the woods then back onto the path that wound up all the way to their camp.

We were halfway back when another sharp pain contracted my womb. I yelped. Steon turned around but didn't speak.

We walked on, my breath more and more shallow. Steon looked at the sky with insistence. Then he whistled one of their shrill bird calls. Another contraction came and I stumbled. Never expecting to carry the baby to term, I hadn't kept track of weeks and months since I'd discovered my pregnancy, but I did know that it was far too early for me to give birth. At least a month early, maybe more. Fear choked me as I followed in the huge man's silent footsteps.

The next contraction came faster, and I doubled up in pain again.

'Frid!' Steon shouted at the sky. 'He's gorging himself somewhere.'

He put my arm around his shoulder, and half-carrying me, half-supporting me, he walked on.

We still didn't exchange a single word. The situation was clear to both of us, as well as the required course of action. Talking about it would make no difference.

I'd never been so afraid. For the first time, the danger was both lethal and unescapable – a combination that, despite my many trials, I had never encountered before. I was also terrified of the pain of birthing a rape-baby alone in the woods, with a taciturn soldier for my only midwife. The most likely outcome was that I wouldn't survive. My life had not turned out as I expected and had yielded unimaginable hardships, but I very much did not want to die.

My breathing became erratic, and Steon reacted straight away. He sat me against a thick tree and felt my stomach again. Another contraction came, and I gritted my teeth.

He stood up calmly and called Frid again. Then, he whistled louder. Still, nothing happened. He gave me his hand, and I squeezed it with all my strength. He didn't even flinch.

Finally, a bird-like whistle tore the silence. Steon responded and, within seconds, Morgunn landed next to us.

'Frid's not answering my calls,' Steon explained to Morgunn. 'She's in labour.'

The Chief needed no further explanation and, in complete silence, they started strapping me to Eko.

'No,' I shouted. I tried to resist, but both men worked together to restrain me.

'This is the swiftest way to take you back to the camp,' argued Morgunn.

'No!' I said louder.

'Don't be scared,' said Steon in a low voice. 'Morgunn will go with you.'

'The sooner you are in Aalma's care the better,' declared Morgunn.

Another contraction came, and I no longer had enough breath to object. Morgunn climbed on behind me and put his arm around my chest. I hated the way these two men handled me – without polite request or even warning – but, despite their firm grip, they did not hurt me.

When we took off, I saw Steon running up the hill steadily, his pace even, regardless of the steep incline.

As Eko soared through the star-strewn night sky, I cursed riders and birds. I also cursed myself and my stupid fears.

The men had followed the only reasonable course of

action. The journey back took only minutes, and soon we landed by the Orchard's fire pit. There'd only been time for one contraction, but when it came, I almost fell off our mount. Morgunn nearly strangled me to keep me in the saddle.

11

Sili

Aalma met us as I tumbled off Eko into Morgunn's waiting arms. Without delay, she led me to Veiti's hut. The women had had the foresight to prepare it as a birthing room, which terrified me even further. They were calm, and spoke in soothing tones. Dry sage was burning in the four corners of the shack, filling the air with acrid smoke.

'It is a bit early, but your baby can survive out of the womb,' Aalma assured me.

'Breathe like this,' demonstrated Veiti.

Far from reassuring me, their behaviour contributed to the panic rising in my throat. It made my situation feel too real and unescapable. Whatever I did, whatever I said, I was going to give birth to a baby. A baby I didn't want. A baby who might kill me. Anger and fear built up in my heart like a whirlpool.

The next contraction was the strongest so far, and the pain broke through my sanity. I started pushing at Aalma and Veiti who were trying to hold me down. Even I couldn't understand my muttered words of anger.

A couple of contractions later, I was screeching and scratching any flesh within reach.

'She's completely lost control,' I heard Veiti say through the red fog in my mind. The only lucid part of me was powerless to stop the unfolding events. I was a helpless witness to the eruption of my own rage.

'I'll have to prepare a calming potion for her.' Aalma replied. 'She'll hurt herself and the baby if she carries on that way.'

'Just go,' Veiti said breathlessly, 'Send Morgunn to help me with her.'

Aalma left, but a minute later she put her head through the door. 'Morgunn's gone to get Leodurr, but Steon has just arrived.'

'Send him in,' pleaded Veiti.

'No!' I shouted at the top of my voice, and I pushed Veiti off me. She bounced against the wall of the shack with a thud.

Another contraction came, and I was lost in my pain again. When I came through, Steon was stepping into the small room. He occupied most of the space inside.

'Hey, dearie,' he said to Veiti, 'How are you holding up?' He was asking her how she was! What was I to them? Less than one of their ugly birds.

'I'm a human!' I shrieked, and when they both looked at me blankly, I added, 'I'm important!' in a paltry attempt at an explanation.

They ignored me and returned to their own conversation, leaving me seething and frustrated by their incomprehension.

'I've no flesh left on my arms,' Veiti whined. 'She's clawing me like a feral beast.'

'Let me hold her then,' he offered.

'No,' I wailed. 'Go away! I don't want you here!'

I sounded insane.

He settled behind me and ignored my efforts to push him away as well as my incoherent shouting. He held my wrists flat across my chest and settled his strong legs on either side of me. He smelt of woodland and sweat.

His touch distracted me long enough for me to catch the thread of my errant thoughts. Surprisingly, my fears ebbed away. For the first time since arriving back at the camp, I dared to hope that I might survive the night.

Aalma came back a moment later, and the three of them forced a sweet liquid down my throat. I choked and spluttered, but they took no pity on me.

The potion acted fast, and against my will I relaxed. My head propped up against Steon's shoulder, I was able to ride the waves of pain coming thicker and faster.

At some point, Efalaa appeared next to my face. 'I'm here,' she said, 'I'm here.'

I couldn't even take her hand as Steon still had both my wrists caught in an iron grip. I held her gaze instead, and it comforted me. Efalaa had been my saviour, maybe she could save me again.

'Efalaa,' I breathed in between unladylike grunts.

'I'm here,' she said again, and she kissed my clammy forehead.

'If only she would get herself under control, we could be making progress,' I heard Aalma say in a cross voice. 'Come on, Sili, work with me. Not against me.'

Efalaa and Veiti were shushing me soothingly, but that didn't help. It only fuelled my anger, and soon – potion or no potion – my own screams rang again in my ears. I'd lost all composure, but the small lucid part of my brain still cursed my vulgar display.

This seemed to go on for hours. My anger was compounded by overwhelming sadness at the wretchedness of my life. What a painful and bloody end, what a waste of time. I think I was crying.

Efalaa and Veiti recommenced their shushing and soothing. It made everything worse.

'Quiet you two! Stop shushing me!' I shouted angrily. 'I'd like to see you in my place!'

'I gave birth through an earthquake,' said Veiti with a pinched face.

'She doesn't know what she's saying,' replied Efalaa to placate her.

'Go away!' I shouted, and I managed to land a kick in Aalma's stomach. She huffed in surprise and Veiti rushed to her side.

'She's gone mad,' lamented Efalaa.

Behind me, I felt Steon sit up straighter.

'Enough of the soft approach, darlings,' he said to the women. 'It's not working with her.' He added gently, 'You two go and have a rest, you've done all you can.'

Efalaa and Veiti disappeared from view.

Aalma looked up from beneath my raised knees. Her face was stern, her patience obviously thoroughly tried. 'You need to calm down, Sili. You're harming yourself and your baby.'

I took in her words, but I didn't know what to do with them. All I could think of was all the other times I had been restrained by a man behind me with my insides in agony. The fury and horror of those nights meshed with the fear and pain I was feeling. I screamed and twisted with all my strength.

Steon spoke into my ear very quietly, and I had to strain to hear him over the rasping sounds of my breathing.

'I'm more disappointed in you every second you spend

screaming like a coward. Be quiet, focus and do what needs to be done.'

His voice was controlled and emotionless. I had just been given an order that I wasn't expected to disobey. It was like a bucket of cold water thrown in my face. I calmed down, and I found I could think again. My body and my brain fell back into line.

I was back in the Skyriders' camp with Aalma who was always kind and Steon who had helped me in the woods. Another contraction brought another bout of full-throated yelling. The pain was excruciating, but I could finally see an end in sight.

Encouraged by Aalma, I took a series of deep breaths. Steon held me even tighter, like a baby in swaddling clothes. Once the pain receded, I started shivering uncontrollably. Even Steon's strength could not absorb the shaking. Both our bodies shuddered and trembled.

Aalma said, 'You're nearly there. You're going to have to push in a moment. Save your strength.'

I did my best to gather my wits and control myself. The pain relented a little.

'Good, well done,' said Steon calmly.

'Don't talk to me!' I shouted at him. 'Don't you dare talk to me!'

'I think she's ready to push,' chuckled Steon to Aalma who smiled back.

Their complicity infuriated me, and when Aalma said 'Push!' I had the good sense to pour all my frustration into my effort. This was surprisingly easy, and when Aalma told me to push again, I was ready.

Seconds later, a wet lump shot out of me with an audible squelch, and I felt unbelievable relief. I shut my eyes and let the world fade away. Even Steon's hold disappeared from my awareness. I recuperated for a few moments, safe within myself. Alive.

What I noticed first was that Aalma did not speak. Then I realised the baby hadn't cried. I looked up to Steon's face, but he was looking anxiously at Aalma.

'All this for a dead child,' I said aloud, and I couldn't decide whether I was relieved or angry.

Steon looked down at me with dismay, and I turned away. From the corner of my eye, I could see Aalma holding a newborn upside down and slapping its back repeatedly. Then she rubbed its chest vigorously. I'd just decided that I was relieved and that this was for the best when I heard a thin wail.

Aalma let out a cry of joy, and my heart sank.

Steon patted my arm gently. 'You have a daughter,' he said.

The words dragged me out of the peaceful place in my mind back into the chaos of reality. It was such a shock that I burst into sobs.

'Shhh,' started Steon, comfortingly.

'Do you want to hold her?' asked Aalma.

'No,' I hiccuped.

'I'll take her,' said Steon.

He received the baby into the crook of one arm and cradled it against his chest. With the other arm he still held me while I blubbered.

'Push again,' said Aalma, and I did. I wanted rid of everything that could remind me I had just had a child.

'She's torn badly,' Aalma said, presumably to Steon.

'Enough for stitches?' he asked as if he actually cared. I was surprised he understood the ins and outs of childbirth. Then again, the Skyriders took gender equality very seriously. If men had physically been able to bear children, the Clansmen would have been having them on a par with the women.

'Try putting the child to her breast,' said Aalma. Steon obeyed and opened my dress delicately. I tried pushing him away, but I felt too weak. He took my breast gently and held the baby close to my nipple. I felt a gushing inside as the milk came up. The baby latched on, and I averted my eyes.

'Get Veiti,' Steon said to Aalma, and this too sounded like an order which Aalma immediately obeyed.

Moments later, Veiti entered and saw me in tears with my face turned away from the child. She didn't beat about the bush.

'She's your daughter before she's anyone else's,' she said firmly. 'You owe her care.'

'I don't owe anyone anything!' I shouted back at her.

'Bring Efalaa here,' said Steon, still giving orders.

Veiti left followed by Aalma.

'Who do you think you are, ordering women about like that?' I shouted at him. 'You're just a guard dog!'

'A guard what?' he asked, surprised, as if he'd never heard the word.

'A dog, you moron.'

He rolled his eyes and didn't reply.

Efalaa entered. She took one look at the baby at my breast and flinched. Intrigued, I followed her gaze. The baby was very red and much smaller than any newborn I'd ever seen, but she was perfectly formed down to her minuscule finger-nails. She held my nipple in her tiny puckered mouth and kept her eyes closed.

Efalaa touched the back of the baby's neck. 'She's very cold,' she said to Steon. Immediately, he wrapped the corner of a blanket around the child and rested his thick forearm on top of the sleeping form.

'Let's leave them together,' Efalaa said to Steon. They exchanged a long look, and he reluctantly stood up, while Efalaa fashioned a pillow for me from a pile of furs. She shrugged off her sheepskin jacket and wrapped the baby in her pink shirt. This tugged at my heartstrings. Efalaa had given the baby the clothes from her own back as if the child was already one of them.

After they left, I was tempted to push the child further away from me. From their half-words, I'd grasped she needed my body heat to survive. If I didn't provide it she would surely die, and no one would ever know.

Then I remembered I did not need to kill the child. I could just leave it behind in the care of the Skyriders. They needed children to repopulate the Clan. They would struggle to keep their bloodlines from inbreeding with only three women and three men. A little girl entirely unrelated to them would be an asset worth the food it would take to raise her.

All I had to do was to get the baby even just once in Veiti's arms, and the handover would be complete.

Conflicting emotions swirled in my chest. I hated emotions, they interfered with my thinking. Clear thinking was what would save me and make my messy life tidy again.

❧ 12 ❧

S teon

Efalaa kept glancing at Veiti's hut.

'She won't harm her child, sweetie. No need to worry,' I said to her.

'I'm not so sure,' she replied sadly. 'How can she ever look at that little face without thinking of her ordeal?'

'With time, I'm sure she will.'

'What do you think will happen now?' Efalaa asked.

'Are you asking me? Why not Morgunn?'

Efalaa had been very friendly towards me since I'd contributed to her rescue, but I was surprised by her candour. I'd always thought she was too complicated a character for the simple friendships I favoured. Maybe her time away had changed her.

'I want your opinion, soldier,' she smiled. 'That's why I'm asking you.'

I smiled back. 'I think Morgunn doesn't have it in him to turn a woman and her newborn out of the Clan. Raider's baby or not.'

'He's strict on Clan's rules though,' she said with a frown.

'What do you think should happen?'

'I wish Sili could feel safe here. She's difficult and cross because she has no one to rely on. We should make her feel welcome and allow her to stay with us however long she likes.'

This surprised me greatly. 'You mean let her join the Clan? What about purposeful breeding? Should we let Sili breed for the Clan? What about her daughter when the time comes? Should we let them learn a vocation?' The more I thought about it, the more bizarre her suggestion was.

Efalaa listened to my objections with patience, but she held on to her strange views.

'I owe Sili my life. I think she is worthy of joining the Clan. She would make a good Teacher, maybe even a Healer— once her heart thaws a little.'

I laughed at that last comment. I was glad that Efalaa was not entirely fooled by Sili's manipulations.

'She can be rather cold, can't she?'

Efalaa smiled a little sadly. 'I've always wondered what it took to make her how she is.'

'You're well placed to imagine it,' I replied.

She looked up at me sharply with an expression I did not understand.

'You know, both of you lost your mothers when you were young, and both your fathers recently died...' I explained tentatively.

Her cheeks turned pink, and she lowered her gaze. When she recovered, she continued smoothly. 'I'm not even as bad as she is,' she joked.

'You've had the Clan on your side whether you liked it or not. You were never really on your own.'

She looked up at me again, and for an instant, I thought she might let me into a secret, but she changed her mind. She swallowed whatever words had been on her lips.

'I know that now,' she said instead. 'If she too knew that she's no longer on her own, we might see another side to Sili.'

'It will take a while to break through her defences.'

'Probably, but I think it would be worth it.'

'Is that what you are you going to tell Morgunn?'

'Morgunn is very distrustful of her. Very wary.'

'In the end, Morgunn will always do what you want him to do. There's no question about that.'

She smiled bashfully. 'That's why I have to be very careful what I tell him and what I ask of him. Not even for Sili's sake would I get him to make a decision that didn't sit well with him.'

I patted her cheek affectionately. 'Let's go and check that she hasn't throttled her baby yet,' I chuckled turning toward Veiti's hut.

'Steon!' said Efalaa, shocked.

We found our newest mother fast asleep next to her daughter and left them to their rest.

Efalaa and I joined the others around the dying embers of the fire. Vidris was yawning. It had been a long night. I sat by her side, and she put her head on my lap.

Efalaa walked straight into Morgunn's outstretched arms.

'What's wrong, sweetling?' he asked, dropping a kiss on her hair.

'I worry about what's going to happen to Sili and her baby,' she replied against his chest.

'They can stay here until they're both strong enough to go home,' he said reassuringly.

Efalaa's frown deepened. 'Sili has nowhere safe to go. She left her hometown when her father was killed by his own men, and her uncle's caravan abandoned her to the Raiders. They're not suitable places to raise a child.'

I had to admit Efalaa was right about that.

Morgunn did not feel the same. 'The Clan can take no responsibility for the problems of an Outsider. We have enough of our own. Once she's fully recovered, Sili can decide what to do. She's clever and resourceful. She can build a future for herself anywhere she likes.'

Efalaa was still in his arms and looked up at him with soft eyes.

'You don't understand,' she said. 'It's a cruel world out there.'

I expected him to surrender, but Ulf's son had more backbone than I thought.

'Recent events have taught us that the Clan's territory isn't as safe as we thought,' he retorted bitterly. 'We can only just feed ourselves.'

Efalaa stepped out of Morgunn's embrace and turned towards the rest of us. 'We're feeding her now, and it's the middle of winter. And she'll soon be able to work. I've been teaching her about foraging and—'

'Have you now?' interrupted Veiti, affronted.

Efalaa ignored her and continued bravely. 'I think Sili and her daughter should stay here and be allowed to join the Clan.'

Now that she'd said the words, they were between us like a thorny bush.

Morgunn sat down on his Chief's seat, and his face turned more serious than I had ever seen it.

'We don't allow Outsiders into the Clan,' he said firmly.

'Make an exception,' countered Efalaa.

'Are you telling your Chief what to do, Hunter?' Morgunn's voice betrayed his anger, but his face showed nothing.

Efalaa didn't wither or waver. 'I'm asking you to do the right thing. To keep these two lives safe.'

Morgunn straightened his back. 'They are not mine to protect, Efalaa. I protect the Clan. My power doesn't extend beyond that.'

The rest of us said nothing. We were all reluctant to step in.

Morgunn held Efalaa's eyes with no trace of weakness. 'I owe it to the long lines of our families to continue as they started. I owe it to my father and to his grandmother and to all the Chiefs before them to follow the rules that have kept the Clan safe and strong for centuries.'

Efalaa lowered her gaze and sighed. Morgunn would be hard to convince. Although he hadn't said so, I guessed that Clan's traditions would have felt lighter on his shoulders if he had trusted Sili.

She thought herself clever, but could sometimes be woefully oblivious to other people's feelings. She'd got on the wrong side of Morgunn more than once without realising it. Disparaging comments about our customs and semi-naive, semi-scornful questions about our history had done little to warm Morgunn's heart to our guest.

Before admitting defeat, Efalaa struck a low blow. 'I know what it's like to wander alone, friendless and hungry through the Wastelands,' she said quietly, and Morgunn's eyes welled up. 'Sili has been through enough. We can't send her back out there.'

Morgunn swallowed but said nothing. The silence became oppressive.

Veiti stood and asked Morgunn for permission to speak. I thought she would stand with him against Efalaa, but when he nodded, she said, 'Sili's daughter was born in the Clan. Like Leif. She should get the Clan's protection. Like him.'

This left Morgunn open-mouthed.

Vidris, always quick to side with Morgunn, jumped to her feet and said, 'Chief, may I please speak?'

Morgunn nodded again, but more reluctantly this time.

'Veiti, I am surprised you cannot tell the difference between Leif, who is part of an unbroken chain of Clanspeople, and this Raider's baby. The child may have been born in your house, but she wasn't born in the Clan.'

Veiti's face turned red. 'What I see are two babies, helpless, fragile, with big eyes and little noses, who need love and a safe place to grow. I can't accept this sweet little girl should be denied the luck granted to my child.'

'Luck?' interrupted Vidris. 'Leif was born in the ruins of the village that should have been his home with only the seven of us for kin. How is that lucky? Are you saying that when comes the time to wean him, you will not worry about where his food will come from?'

'Why do you call him Leif the Lucky then?' Veiti said. 'Why do you say it if you don't mean it?'

'Leif's lucky to be alive!' Vidris replied. 'But he's not lucky to be alive here and now.'

There was an eerie silence, and I was grateful Sili wasn't here to witness this discussion.

'Please Morgunn, may I speak again?' said Efalaa. He nodded yes, but shut his eyes and squared his shoulders.

'Let's not hide behind rules that were not made for this situation. Let's be honest with ourselves and each other. Unless we welcome her in the Clan, a woman like Sili will never ask us for our protection, no matter how badly she needs it. Her sense of dignity will not allow it. Unless we extend the hand of friendship soon, she will leave. What chances does Sili have to reach safety with her daughter, alone and on foot? How long before they're recaptured by the Raiders? I've seen what life is like in those camps for women and girls. They're tied to stakes in the ground.'

Veiti covered her eyes and Aalma winced. My stomach dropped into my boots. Morgunn remained expressionless. I was glad my position as a Guardian prevented me from speaking out. I didn't know what I thought or felt.

Morgunn gestured for all the speakers to sit down, then he asked, 'Aalma, what do you have to say?'.

'We do not need to make a decision today. It will be many weeks before mother and child are strong enough to leave us,' she answered. 'I respect the rules Morgunn is duty-bound to uphold, but as a Healer I will never condone a course of action that would give Sili and her baby no chance of survival. Maybe a solution will present itself before it is time for them to go.'

The silence stretched again, and no one dared meet anyone else's eyes.

Morgunn looked at me and said, 'Steon, what about you?'

I was surprised he asked me this question.

'Guardians support the Chief, whatever his decision.'

'What is your opinion?' he insisted. 'Everyone else is speaking freely.'

He gestured for me to stand, and I reluctantly got to my feet. 'I know you do not trust Sili, Chief, and to be honest, neither do I. I do not know whether her loyalty to us would hold if it ever came to the test.'

'It is hard to be loyal to those who don't want you,' interrupted Efalaa, jumping out of her seat.

'It is indeed, sweetheart,' I said to her gently.

'We haven't deserved her loyalty yet,' she pointed out.

Morgunn gestured for both of us to sit down.

Leodurr raised his hand and was given permission to stand and speak. I had no idea what gentle Leodurr would find to say in such a tense and difficult situation. He spoke quietly.

'The reason why the Clan never took in any Outsiders was to avoid mouths that we couldn't feed,' he started. 'Now that there are only eight of us, my opinion as Master Farmer is that our Territory can yield enough to support Sili and her daughter for the rest of their lives. I cannot speak for all of our dead friends or for the many generations of our ancestors, but I know my mother and my father would be ashamed of me if I stood against what Efalaa proposes.'

There was a hush of surprise, and all eyes were fixed on Leodurr.

Morgunn flinched, but bravely kept his voice steady when he finally spoke.

'Has anyone got anything else to say?'

No one responded.

'Then I've heard your opinions, and I will now think further on the matter.'

We avoided each other's gazes and went to our beds. It was the middle of the night, and I for one had had enough of that day.

❧ 13 ❧

S ili

Daylight flooded the hut when Veiti came in that morning. Without a word, she picked up the baby where Efalaa had left it and settled it in between her breasts. I hid a smile at how easily my plan had succeeded.

'We need to keep her warm against our bodies at all times,' she said. 'That's the only thing to do for small premature babies.'

'Premature?'

'It means born before their time.'

'Is she too small to survive?'

'I don't know,' admitted Veiti. 'Only time will tell. All I know is that we can't afford to put her down, not even for a minute. If you need to go to the latrines, just call and I'll hold her for you.'

My plan was working. I found myself hoping I could bring

forward my escape and land in New Bodie within a fortnight. The thought of home filled me with delight until I remembered I probably would be even less welcome there than I was here.

Aalma entered. 'Do you need to relieve yourself, Sili?' she asked. I nodded, and she helped me up.

I stumbled out of the hut, and we bumped into Morgunn who took my arm and together with Aalma walked me to the latrines.

'I would love to wash,' I said.

'It's too early for you to bathe,' replied Aalma, 'But I'll bring you warm water, soap and some clean clothes. It will make you feel as good as new.' She smiled encouragingly.

That night, I ate a good meal of rabbit stew and cooked apples and drank Aalma's special 'after birth' tea. I wasn't sure what was in it; she wouldn't say. Veiti tucked me into bed and took the baby away to sleep with her and Leif in Aalma's house. Little Vidris moved in with the birds.

I couldn't have got better care anywhere in the Wastelands, not even in New Bodie. I felt that it wouldn't be long until my strength returned.

However, the next morning I woke up with the weight of a horse on my chest. I started crying and couldn't stop. Overwhelming sadness and dread filled every part of my body. Even my toes felt wrong, and my hair hurt. A small part of my brain wondered at the drama unfolding, but the rest of me was lost in heartache. My willpower was gone. I could only cry.

By midday, Aalma had been with me all morning, and she was at her wits' end.

'I assure you all is well, Sili. You've delivered a lovely baby girl. Everything will be alright,' she said. As she left the hut, I heard her puff her cheeks in frustration.

Efalaa sat with me in silence, holding my hand sadly. She

too left when Veiti brought the baby for her feed. As the baby nuzzled my breast greedily, my eyes brimmed with tears.

'It is not unusual for new mothers to feel sad and unprepared,' said Veiti kindly. 'Don't worry, darling, it doesn't last. Get a lot of rest and make sure you drink plenty of water.' Then she went off to wash my soiled linen.

I sat alone in the darkened room and watched as my tears fell on the head of the child at my breast.

Aalma visited me a few times. She brought me some tea and sweet gruel for my lunch and checked my pulse.

'You've had a difficult labour, Sili, and you're still very weak,' she declared. 'That's why you're not yourself. You will be fine in a few days.'

She didn't stay long, and I reflected that she didn't care for me as well as she had for Veiti. I was an Outsider, I was not important. The pain from the birth was still strong.

As the day drew to an end, a cold gale was blowing under the door. I shivered despite the furs. Efalaa sat close to me, and neither of us had spoken for at least an hour. The rest of the Clan were preparing dinner. I could not believe that even on such a cold day they were going to eat out in the open. They would spend several hours outside around their fire, talking and singing. Without me. Useless tears flowed from my sore eyes.

I was startled when the door slammed open and Steon entered, both hands full of earthen crockery. He held a wooden spoon between his teeth. I noticed it was mine, the one with the wide-open eye. He closed the door with his shoulder and crouched next to me.

'Go and stretch your legs, chickling,' he said to Efalaa. 'Dinner is nearly ready.'

'Thank you, elskan,' she replied. 'I'll see you there.'

I refused the plate he presented. I was not hungry, but my tetchiness was due to their annoying habit of calling each other all these ridiculous pet names. What on earth was an elskan anyway? It was driving me mad. Especially now.

Steon didn't speak. He put the plates on the floor and sat down. I braced myself for an argument that did not come. He blew carefully on the thin broth contained in the larger bowl until it stopped steaming. Then, to my surprise, he grabbed me round the neck firmly and poured the liquid down my throat. I struggled to swallow and clawed uselessly at his hands.

The bowl finished, he put a piece of flat bread next to my bed then left with the dishes in one hand and the baby in the other.

It took me long minutes to recover from my shock. I realised I had stopped crying and I did not feel as wretched as before. The way he'd treated me, like a petulant child, was both infuriating and reassuring.

I lay in my bed shivering and wondering whether he would come back, but he didn't. I hated myself for feeling a tiny twinge of disappointment. Then I fell asleep.

It was Veiti who eventually came back with the baby.

'She's hungry,' she said.

'Can't you feed her?' I asked.

'She needs your milk, not mine. I can feed her for you in a few days, but not yet.'

She helped the baby latch on to my breast and watched while it fed. There was nothing I could do but lie there like a milking cow. It wasn't worth attracting Veiti's wrath at this time, but I felt used and depleted.

After a while, the baby fell asleep at my breast, and Veiti took her away. 'Get some rest,' she said. 'I'll come back when she's hungry again.'

As silence returned in the draughty hut, I felt desperately alone. I wasn't wanted anywhere. Not here, not in New Bodie, not in Gond's Caravan. The only people who wanted me were the Raiders. I had enough sense of irony to laugh bitterly about that.

I slept badly and had many nightmares. In one of them, I had given birth to a giant pebble. In another, I was sitting in the middle of a ring of fire, sweating and shivering, and my heart was ripped out of my chest by invisible hands.

❧ 14 ☙

S^{ili}

I woke at the first light of a cold dawn, feeling all-encom-passing sadness and self-pity. Lying on my pallet, I felt my strength ebbing away; soon, I would no longer be able to leave this place. The future towards which I had worked was gone. The child had taken it away from me.

The door opened quietly, and Steon walked in.

'How are you feeling today?' he asked cheerfully. He carried a steaming bowl with two hands, and my spoon stuck out of his left arm brace.

He smelt of cold wood smoke and dried fish.

'Potatoes and smoked trout,' he announced.

'You stink,' I replied scornfully.

Unfazed, he laid the food down and turned to leave. Before reaching the door though, he stopped and sniffed the air.

'You stink too,' he said, matter-of-factly. After a pause, he added, 'You reek of bad blood.'

He didn't give me time to reply and hurried out. This was the first time he'd ever retaliated to my mean words. My cheeks burnt, and I was grateful no one was there to see that.

I wasn't alone long though. The door slammed open, and Steon and Aalma burst into the small space one after the other.

Without warning, Aalma lifted the furs off my body and knelt at my feet. I was so surprised I didn't think to argue.

'How could I have missed it?' she lamented when she saw my birthing wound. I recoiled from her touch as the pain shot through me.

'Don't worry, my girl,' she said. 'I'll make the infection go away.'

She applied an unguent that set fire to my already tortured flesh and made me drink a bitter potion.

'Do you want me to feed you?' offered Steon after she'd left.

His face showed no trace of mockery or spite, and I struggled to gather enough anger to shout at him to go away. But I succeeded. He left without another word.

Later on that morning, Morgunn entered the hut and greeted me with a smile. The others had been distant and wary, and my brain started whirring with a range of possible explanations for this change of mood—none likely. I watched him closely and hoped to read the meaning behind his words.

As he looked down at me with his open face, I saw nothing there but the unusual green of his eyes.

'Hello, Sili, time for breakfast,' he said simply.

'Steon's already brought me something,' I replied curtly.

'A bit of fresh air will be good for you,' he insisted and easily lifted me up in his arms. Clansmen all seemed able to handle me as if I weighed nothing.

Morgunn carried me to a seat by the fire where all eyes soon turned to me. If I were one to squirm, I would certainly have done so.

He settled into his seat, a crude wooden stool which I nevertheless thought of as his throne. He squared his shoulders, and started speaking in a clear voice.

'Sili, I wanted you here this morning because the Clan spent the last couple of days debating your situation and that of your baby daughter.' He paused. I made sure my face showed nothing, but I held my breath.

'I have decided to invite you to remain indefinitely under our protection,' he continued. 'You will eat by our fire and sleep under our roof, and we will guard your life and your daughter's as if you were one of our own.'

I stared at him, speechless. The silence stretched uncomfortably.

Morgunn looked sideways towards Efalaa, as if for reassurance. She seemed unsure of what to do next.

'Do you accept my offer, Sili?' said Morgunn, a note of annoyance creeping into his voice.

Vidris was pink with what I presumed was anger, and Leodurr watched me sadly.

Morgunn waited for my answer. I was taken aback; I hadn't thought it possible such an offer would ever come. Quickly, I saw Efalaa's hand behind it, and looked around at the assembled faces. Steon seemed worried, and Vidris stared daggers at me.

I willed my voice to remain steady as I said the only words I could say in the circumstances.

'I accept your offer, and I thank you, Morgunn Ulfborn.'

The faces around the campfire relaxed and broke into smiles of various levels of sincerity.

Efalaa beamed, obviously relieved.

'For the Clan,' she called out.

'For the Clan,' they all replied.

I was not sure whether I too was expected to say those words now, so I kept quiet. Veiti passed me the grizzling baby for me to feed.

As I received the child into my hands, a wave of anger came over me. I had been offered permanent shelter. There was no longer a reason for me to leave and return to who knew what fate in New Bodie.

By this act of charity, the bird riders had hollowed out my plan to return to the life I had lost. They had destroyed the future I had chosen for myself.

I hid my feelings as best I could but felt my eyes brimming with tears. Hopefully, they would think these were tears of joy and not of rage. They had delivered the worst blow they could have: I felt like a prisoner again.

Steon gave me a strangely penetrating look and, despite my efforts at composure, read something on my face he did not like. All the others - apart from Vidris - smiled and greeted me warmly, making my stomach churn.

'Now you need to give your daughter a name,' Efalaa said excitedly.

'I haven't thought about that at all...' I demurred. In fact, I'd never thought I would need to speak that baby's name.

As I stared into the fire, I struggled to come to terms with what had just happened. They probably imagined I was thinking of girls' names.

'What was your mother called?' offered Efalaa trying to be helpful.

'Siliana, like me,' I replied.

Efalaa looked surprised. 'Oh, is that your full name?'

'I never use it,' I said.

'That wouldn't work,' she said gently.

I looked at her blankly.

'Her Clan name would be Siliana Silianaborn,' Veiti

98

explained with a laugh. 'We can't do that to the poor little treasure!'

This was received with a general chortle. Everyone apart from me carried on eating breakfast. I passed bowls of nuts and cooked apples left and right without helping myself. Leodurr gave me a mug of thyme tea. I stared at the steaming liquid and noticed the ripples caused by the tremors in my hand.

I struggled to bring myself back to reality. I had to appear normal and happy to be given permanent hospitality. I couldn't let the Clan suspect I still planned to leave.

'What was your mother called, Efalaa?' I asked after long minutes of silence.

Efalaa smiled with her whole face and stole a glance at Morgunn. He took her hand and squeezed it.

'Vona. My mother was called Vona,' she replied in a strangled voice. 'It's from the Old Language word for "hope".'

'Then I will call my daughter Vona. Vona Siliborn.'

Veiti showed all her pretty white teeth. 'A good Clan name, how lovely!' she exclaimed.

Aalma clapped her hands happily, 'A Singer's name!'

Leodurr patted my shoulder. Morgunn hugged Efalaa tight; she was laughing through her tears.

My choice of name had obviously delighted the Skyriders. If the girl was to grow up here, she might as well have a name that meant something to them.

Efalaa hugged me. 'Thank you, Sili,' she whispered in my ear. 'This is such a gift.'

A few hours after the cheerful welcome I had been given, the atmosphere in the Orchard Camp changed. I worried that the Skyriders had noticed my lack of enthusiasm and taken offence.

15

S teon

I had rejoiced with the others when Sili was welcomed into the Clan. Morgunn had offered her our protection after all. This was not the same as making her a full member of the Clan, but I wasn't sure anyone else had noticed the difference.

Sili had shown genuine surprise, but her happiness had seemed a little forced. Her eyes had remained cold, perhaps even angry.

I couldn't deny that Sili would be an asset to the Clan. She was clever – her choice of name for her daughter showed how skilled she was at manipulating people – and her Outsider's blood could help our bloodlines now that there were so few of us.

However, she would have to be kept in check for a while.

It was part of my job to ensure that everyone in the Clan lived by the rules.

As I went into the birds' shed to fetch Frid, I walked into Vidris.

'Hey, watch out!' she said rudely. I guessed she was furious about Morgunn's decision. It was painful to her that Morgunn should have been swayed away from the beloved Clan's traditions.

Maybe she didn't take kindly either to Efalaa's place in his life. She hadn't spoken a word against the Chief, but she had poured soup on Efalaa's lap, and not so accidentally dropped an armful of firewood onto Leodurr's feet. Neither rose to the bait, and Vidris had left in a temper to go and look after the birds. No doubt they heard everything she had to say on the matter.

I hadn't yet mentioned to Morgunn the Raiders Sili and I had seen. I wanted to check the perimeter before giving him my report. I was just flying out of the Camp when I saw Efalaa riding Mila and waving at me with insistence. We both landed.

'Thank you for what you said yesterday in Sili's support,' she started.

'I only said what I thought.'

She looked at me doubtfully.

'I'm not as easy to influence as Morgunn Ulfborn, sweetheart.'

She ignored the friendly barb. 'Do you think I did the wrong thing?'

'Are you asking the man or the Guardian?'

'The one then the other.'

'The soldier says we've allowed a stranger into our midst, and we have to be watchful. The man says it was the only honourable thing to do. Our ancestors wouldn't congratulate us for upholding their rules against simple humanity.'

She remained thoughtful and gave me a long look.

'It's not as if we have hordes of Outsiders at our doors asking to join the Clan,' I added to lighten the mood.

Finally, she smiled. 'One Outsider every three hundred years or so should be manageable, don't you think?'

'Rest easy, chickling. I'm standing watch,' I concluded jokingly.

Her eyes crinkled at the sides, and she gave me one of the prettiest smiles I'd ever received. For the first time, I could fully see why Morgunn had gone so far out of his way for her.

We both returned to our duties. She flew north and I continued on my way south.

It was already mid-morning. The temperature was still below freezing, but the skies were clear. I carried out my reconnaissance flight towards the River where Sili and I had seen the Raiders.

As I approached the Hedge, a nagging fear grew in my mind. All the signs pointed to one conclusion, and I had overlooked them. When I flew over the boundary, I already knew what I would see.

Indeed, the Raiders were still there, at least a hundred of them erecting tents and fences. Their camp was set in between the two waterfalls that formed part of our natural defences and stretched on either side of the river gathering at the foot of our twin mountains.

I flew in circles over the Raiders' shabby camp, missing my fellow Guardians with such longing that I was almost overwhelmed. It took all my courage to push my dark thoughts away. I was a Guardian, and alone or not, I had a job to do.

Many had tried and failed to breach the Territory. The Hedge was as thick as the birds wingspan. The waterfall to the west was three hundred feet tall and the one to the east was twice the size. Both would prove impassable. As children we dared each other to stand underneath the deafening roar. The water was so strong it could knock you unconscious and peel off your clothing. A child had died there, generations before us, and we were under strict instructions never to approach the falls alone.

The Raiders would soon find out just how impregnable our borders were. We controlled the air, and we were armed.

I hurried back to the Orchard to give my report to Morgunn. He took the news of the Raiders' presence calmly, as a Chief should, and decided not to share it with the others until evening assembly.

When he stood at the beginning of dinner, his face stern, the silence around the fire was deafening.

'Steon has informed me of the presence of group of Raiders camping outside the Hedge, by the River Mouth.'

Efalaa, who was sitting in her usual place on Morgunn's left, stiffened and her face lost its rosiness. Morgunn didn't need to look at her to feel her reaction, and he reached out his hand to her. She didn't take it.

Morgunn continued. 'It is possible that they're only making use of the fresh water of the lake and have no idea that they have set up camp on our doorstep.'

Efalaa frowned, unconvinced. Aalma narrowed her eyes. Vidris looked at me, and I beckoned for her come and sit next to me. She sat so close that I guessed she would have preferred to sit on my lap, as she would have done a few years earlier. I wrapped my arm around her shoulders.

Gauging the mood around the bonfire, Morgunn adroitly involved me in the conversation.

'Steon will now explain what I have asked him to do.'

I stood up, but kept my hand on Vidris's shoulder.

'The Chief has ordered me to keep watch on the Raiders' camp from the Watch Tower. We mustn't tell them where we are, so no flights for any of you until further notice. I will monitor the situation and report to Morgunn at breakfast, lunch and dinnertime so you can all be kept informed. We are in no danger. This is an inconvenience, not a threat.'

Despite my reassuring words, faces remained grim. We had lost so much already, few of us still believed in lucky outcomes.

Morgunn was the only optimist. 'They will be gone in a couple of days. I can't imagine a worse place to camp in winter. The winds sweep the Lowlands in every direction.'

When Efalaa got up to go to bed he followed her. Even though they weren't touching, they walked as one.

I flew to the Hedge for a swift reconnaissance. Like us the Raiders were sitting around their campfires. I counted five fires, and they were well stocked and blazing. I wondered how much firewood they had brought with them. The Lowlands around the Hedge were a desert, they wouldn't be able to replenish their supply.

I decided to return to the Orchard and get a good night's rest before starting my watching duties at dawn the next day.

Unfortunately, I lay awake thinking about what needed to be done, and no amount of discipline could help me sleep. Eighty or so Raiders wandering the Wastelands in the dark didn't worry me in the least. But a contingent twice that large setting up camp around the only weak point in our natural defences was a matter of deep concern.

Leodurr snored softly, oblivious. Someone went to the latrines. I must have fallen asleep for a moment because I didn't hear them come back.

I was also concerned about Sili. I remembered her face as she finally accepted Morgunn's invitation into the Clan. She hadn't looked happy. I couldn't understand why her face showed such negative feelings now that she'd had her way. Had I misunderstood her? If she had indeed manipulated everyone to her own ends, why did she look so upset?

I would never understand her, and to me she would forever be an Outsider with strange customs and values. Yes, she would be an asset for the Clan, but at what cost? Guardians had never before had to watch one of our own.

I wished I could share my doubts with my fellow soldiers. Isveg would have listened. Erlen would have known what to do.

When I did sleep, I had a dream of the nine of us Guardians training together in a sunlit forest, and the relief I felt at seeing them alive was overwhelming. I choked on my happiness and walked on a cloud. I woke up berating myself for my sentimentality.

The best thing I could now do for my fallen comrades was to honour their memory by being the best Guardian I could be. I would be all that they had been: strong, reliable, caring and fierce. Never mind that I was the last of my kind, one Guardian was better than none. I was born to serve, and serve I would.

Exhausted and nervous, I went out of the sleeping hut to clear my head of the last tendrils of the dream. The air was so cold that the back of my throat hurt. Dawn was not far away, and I decided to start the morning fire and make some tea for Veiti and Vidris who were the early risers.

❧ 16 ❧

S ili

Leodurr brought me a plate of nuts and cheese with a mug of nettle tea in which the leaves still floated. It was unusually poor fare. Perhaps they already regretted the food they gave me. I was too tired to think about it. I fed the baby and slept the day away.

No one woke me for evening assembly. Veiti brought the child for me to feed at bedtime then swiftly took her away. I could still hear hushed voices by the fire and felt so betrayed and alone I cried.

I woke in the middle of the night, overwhelmed by a feeling of dread and urgency, a premonition of great danger. The fear was so real that I was too frightened to move. I lay under the furs like a child afraid of ghosts.

Then, the reality of my situation struck me. I couldn't rely on people who could withdraw their help whenever it suited them. I couldn't afford to become too comfortable or too grateful. There was no choice; I had to leave before I lost the will to.

So I summoned my courage, stole Veiti's fur coat, a water-skin and some dry food and went on my way without delay. I hadn't walked unaided in many days, and I felt as if my legs had been replaced by twigs.

I went into the birds' shed but found Vidris sleeping there. I could not take a bird without waking her up. This thwarted all my plans, but the need to escape had become so strong that I decided to leave regardless. If they did track me down, I could still refuse to come back, and if they did force me to take the baby with me, I could threaten to let it die.

I hurried down the mountain flank in the direction of the river, each step uncertain. The cold air burnt my lungs. The moon was full and threw long-fingered shadows of the trees on the icy path.

Walking alone through the Wastelands in the middle of winter was a foolhardy plan, but that was better than becoming the mother of the child I had birthed.

I headed for the Watch Tower Steon had shown me. From there, I could make my way down the hill to the edge of the Clan's territory. If Efalaa had found a passage through the Hedge, I probably could too. I was smaller than her again.

I walked for an hour downhill, stumbling on my weak legs. The morning light was just breaking when I reached the Watch Tower. To rest my already weary feet, I sat in the same chair as I had with Steon.

The view was eerily familiar as I looked out to the Waste-lands beyond the Hedge. I had to rub my eyes. Tiny flickers of light littered the bleak landscape. I forced myself to think clearly and did my best to ignore my fears, but there was no other explanation for the picture forming in front of me.

These were the same torches Steon and I had counted

that night, closer together and brighter than before. Each tiny light must have had several men associated with it.

The torches had formed a thick line around the mouth of the river. Now, they stretched like a crescent moon along high wooden fences that encircled a portion of land on either side of the waterfall.

The Raiders had come back in greater numbers. Perhaps as many as two hundred. I couldn't be sure. If I went out of the Territory the same way as Efalaa had gone back in, I would now walk straight into the Raiders' camp. Back where I started.

As I watched in dismay, I noticed bright flames were being carried out of the Raiders' camp towards the brambly hedge that served as the Clan's boundary.

The Raiders were setting fire to the only obstacle that separated them from me. Fear ignited my body, and my blood burnt through my veins.

My thinking now clear, I saw only two options. Run back to the Clan and raise the alarm or make my way unseen to the opposite end of the Territory in order to find a way out there.

Both paths could lead to death. The Wastelands would be crawling with Raiders' scouts and patrols, and the Clan would not take kindly to my desertion.

I well remembered the last time they had looked at me as an enemy. It was the night when I arrived on the back of Efalaa's bird. I would have done much to avoid a repeat of that experience. But the safer course of action was still to throw myself on the Skyriders' mercy again.

Walking back up the hill was much harder than my journey down. Soon I was bleeding again, and my head swam with every unsteady step.

❧ 17 ❧

S teon

Veiti was the first to notice Sili's absence when she took the baby for her dawn feed.

'She's gone,' she said as she strode past me and into the foodstore. She re-emerged looking pale and hurried towards the house Morgunn was now sharing with Efalaa. She rapped her knuckles on the door.

Morgunn appeared, half-dressed and half-awake.

'What?' he said not too kindly.

'Sili's gone,' replied Veiti.

'What do you mean "gone"?' he said.

'She's left.'

It was the second time I'd heard the news, and I still couldn't believe my ears.

'Did you check the latrines?' I tried.

'No, but she's left, I'm telling you!' Veiti repeated.

Efalaa poked her head out of the door over Morgunn's shoulder.

'She can't have left now we've let her in,' she argued.

Veiti lost the last of her patience and raised her voice.

'She's taken food and a waterskin! She has left, and she's abandoned her own daughter!' she shouted in a shrill voice.

'She's left Vona?' cried Efalaa.

'Look,' said Veiti, pointing to Vona in her arms. 'I was looking after her last night... She left her behind. I can't believe I spoke in her favour!'

Without a word, Morgunn went back inside the hut for the rest of his clothes.

Aalma came out of her house, and Leodurr poked his head out of the sleeping hut. We all looked at each other, bewildered. Wearily, I returned to the main hut to fetch my things. I knew what Morgunn would say as soon as he came back out of Efalaa's house. I fastened my cloak, pulled on some gloves, and waited for my orders.

'We have to find her,' Morgunn said, the exasperation clear in his voice.

'Not again,' lamented Aalma.

'At least this time, she can't be in labour,' I said.

'I'll go with you,' called Efalaa behind me.

'No,' said Morgunn to Efalaa. 'You're not going. I won't put you in harm's way for her.'

'Why would I be in harm's way?' questioned Efalaa. Morgunn ignored her.

'The birds are all here,' said Vidris. She'd already harnessed Frid and was leading him out of the birds' shed.

'Go towards the River,' Morgunn told me, 'She will have heard about Efalaa coming in that way.'

'Yes, Chief,' I said.

'If you can't find her in the next hour, come back. We have more important things to do.'

'Steon, wait for me,' called Efalaa.

I didn't.

'Why are we even looking for her at all,' I heard Vidris say, as I was taking off. 'She's the one who decided to betray our hospitality and sneak away in the night!'

As I flew south, anger rose in my throat. I could overlook much of Sili's strange behaviour – she was an Outsider after all – but I couldn't forgive her for abandoning her newborn daughter into our reluctant hands.

As instructed, I returned to the Orchard an hour after dawn. I had searched the greenwoods from the air and on foot, but I'd seen no sign of Sili.

My thoughts kept returning to the boy and his father I'd met by the canyons. This made Sili's actions even more unacceptable.

I found the others sitting around the morning fire. Morgunn sat on his Chief seat, and Vidris was looking at him with concern. He was still seething. They had finished breakfast, but someone had saved me some flatbread and boiled duck eggs. Aalma passed around mugs of sage tea.

'New mothers can make strange decisions sometimes, especially at times of great stress,' she said kindly.

'Well, she's only been one of us for less than a day. If she wants to throw her life away, I'm not going to stop her,' replied Morgunn.

'Morgunn!' said Aalma, shocked, and I thought I could hear my own mother. She too, would have taken exception to our Chief's rash words.

My time and efforts to find Sili turned out to be wasted when she returned on her own, just as I was preparing to fly out again to check on the Raiders.

'Where have you been?' I snapped at her.

She walked past me as if I wasn't even there, the dark

mass of her hair trailing behind her. She was wearing a travelling cloak.

'Did you have a nice walk?' Vidris asked her sarcastically.

'Yes, thank you,' replied Sili without missing a beat. Aalma stared Vidris down. Anger made the veins in Morgunn's neck stand out.

I too was struggling to keep my irritation at bay.

Sili planted her small frame in front of Morgunn and addressed him boldly, despite the murderous look he gave her.

'The Raiders have settled by the Hedge,' she announced. 'Many more of them. Too many to count.'

'Are you trying to say that you were out inspecting our borders, instead of deserting your own child?' Vidris bit back unrepentantly. 'We have a Guardian for that, we don't need you to do his job.'

'I saw them from the Watch Tower, they're at the River mouth, as you call it,' Sili continued undeterred.

'Shame that our only Guardian was busy in the greenwoods looking for you,' sneered Veiti.

'I haven't finished,' said Sili coldly.

At that point my dislike of her threatened to turn into hatred. I cursed Efalaa and Leodurr for their sentimentality. I cursed myself for my weakness, and I even thought unkindly about Morgunn allowing his feelings for his wife to influence his judgement.

Sili finally revealed her hand. 'The Raiders are setting fire to your Hedge.'

'What?' shouted Morgunn.

'They started at least two hours ago. I came back to warn you as fast as I could, but I'm bleeding.' She parted the folds of her cloak and revealed clothes that were soaked in blood.

'Oh, darling!' exclaimed Aalma.

She and Efalaa ran towards Sili to help her back to Veiti's

hut. Vidris and Veiti, each cradling a baby, looked on disapprovingly.

Morgunn was already leading Eko out of the birds' shed.

'Now is not the time to squabble,' he said. 'We all need to go and defend the Hedge, or those left alive will wish they were dead.'

The women stood rigid.

'Vidris, go fetch Oxi and Mila,' ordered Morgunn.

As usual a word from him brought Vidris back into line. She handed Leif to Veiti and the next minute, the reins for the remaining two birds were in the Chief's hand.

'Sili, you'll be looking after the babies,' he continued.

'No, not my son!' objected Veiti, outraged.

'You're coming with us,' Morgunn said to her. 'We need everyone.'

'No! I'm not leaving him with her,' she spat. 'He's the Clan's only child now,' she added, forgetting the generous words she had spoken about little Vona only the day before.

Morgunn gave in and took the cloak from Sili's shoulders before fastening it around his own.

'Very well. Get ready to escape north if we're unsuccessful. Those who can will pick you up, and we'll regroup at the Cave.'

'You're scaring me,' said Veiti.

'The Territory is about to be invaded,' I answered. 'It's time to worry and hurry.'

Morgunn nodded his approval. It took less than a minute for the others to equip themselves, and we all stood to attention around him.

I spared a second to be grateful to the Elders for the traditions of diligence and discipline they had instilled in the Clan. When a situation required obedience and speed, the Chief spoke and all sprung into action. It must have taken Veiti all her courage to set her will against Morgunn.

Now, she stood outside the circle, a shadow of her usual self.

'How's the wind?' Morgunn asked me.

'In their favour.'

'The plan is to put out the fire, then kill them to the last man,' said Morgunn fiercely.

'Our best chance may be to soak the ground, Chief,' I suggested.

He gave me a nod and continued. 'Leodurr, you take Mila. Vidris and Aalma on Oxi, and Efalaa and I will go on Eko.'

The Hedge was a short bird ride away. Even the smaller birds could carry a pair of us over that distance provided the riders' weights were carefully matched.

I fetched our meagre arsenal from the sleeping hut. We had a couple of spare short daggers and three slingshots. I also had my own long knife. Efalaa and Morgunn had bows and hunting knives. It would have to be enough.

I armed myself and called Aalma. She was ready and tying her arm braces. I gave her a dagger and handed Efalaa two slingshots which she tucked into Eko's saddlebags with a supply of pebbles that were used for hunting foxes and wolves.

Morgunn and I clasped arms. 'Long life,' I said. These were the words Guardians said to each other before going into a fight.

'Long life, soldier,' he replied.

'For the Clan,' said Morgunn.

'For the Clan,' we all called out.

As the four birds took flight together, the sound of so many wings flapping in concert reminded me of the past.

Morgunn and Efalaa took the lead, with Oxi and Mila flying on either side of me. Despite the tension, I laughed when I realised Vidris had a shovel slung behind her back.

She saw me and shouted, 'It'll be a lot more useful than your arrows to fight the fire!'

Of course, she was right.

I went into battle full of righteous anger that some scabby Raiders had dared to try and breach our perimeter.

⚜ 18 ⚜

S**teon**

The Raiders had piled kindling underneath the outer layers of the Hedge and had already lit their fire. After two days of dry weather, the low branches were starting to singe, and the acrid smell of burning green wood and leaves filled my nostrils.

Twenty men or more were standing fully armed by the scorched bushes. They wore light armour of metal-reinforced leather and carried themselves as men used to fight. I considered our position. Leodurr, Morgunn, Efalaa and I could engage them on foot outside the Hedge, but we would be seriously outnumbered, and if we died, the others would be left unprotected once the defences burnt down. There was no point in attacking them.

In order to win that battle, we only had to put out the fire. Then, we would be safe behind our impregnable thorny walls again. Our best strategy was to dam the river and flood the area. The slope would then direct the water to the fire as surely as the acorn falls off the oak tree.

I shouted to Morgunn who was flying in circles with Efalaa behind him. 'Dam the river, flood the ground.'

He nodded and signalled for everyone to land on our side of the Hedge.

Working swiftly, Leodurr and I created a barrier at the wider part of the river with stones, sticks and foliage. It was soon breaking its banks. The others created channels by kicking at the soft ground with their heels.

Because of the lay of the land, the east side of the slope would soon be covered in the river overspills. Yet the west side was still vulnerable to the fire.

We left Aalma to maintain the dam, and the remaining five of us flew over the Hedge to the area where the fire damage was the most important.

The twenty raiders who had gathered there were waiting for the brambles to burn down before attacking their tangled roots. They had a few axes between them, but not a single shield or helmet. Not for the first time, I wondered if they knew who they were dealing with.

'Stones only,' Morgunn shouted to us. 'Keep your arrows.'

Efalaa, Morgunn and I flew in circles over them, pelting them with our sharpest stones. Leodurr, who didn't have a slingshot, had to make do with dropping handfuls of pebbles at a time. Judging by the reactions of the men below, this was just as efficient. I knew better than to underestimate my opponents, but the sight of the Raiders running this way and that away from our Master Farmer's little stones was rather satisfying.

Most of the men retreated to their horses.

Vidris had now landed and was putting the fire out by shovelling soil onto the flames. She worked quickly and was already making a difference. Morgunn and I landed between her and the retreating Raiders to protect her while she worked.

We hadn't noticed the five men who had sheltered under the bushes until they came out to attack Vidris. We sent the birds back to safety in the sky and stood our ground.

I flung my dagger into one of the men's stomach. The blade was sharp enough to go through his leather jerkin, and when he pulled the blade out the wound started bleeding profusely. His blood loss would make him inaccurate in a few minutes and unable to fight shortly after that. I could have finished him off but chose to concentrate on our able-bodied opponents.

Morgunn charged at one of the men, grabbed him around the waist and threw him over his shoulder. The man landed heavily with a thud, winded. While his opponent was disoriented, Morgunn knocked him out with a punch to the temple.

I engaged the third Raider in a knife fight which ended swiftly when I sliced the tendons at the back of his knee. He fell to ground holding his leg, moaning in pain.

I tackled the man I had wounded in the stomach by putting him in a stranglehold, until he collapsed. I retrieved my dagger and wondered briefly whether he was dead or had just fainted.

Morgunn was fighting against the remaining two who were trying to bring him down. I rushed to his aid and evened the odds. The one closer to me fell, and I pinned him down with my weight and proceeded to punch him until his nose broke, and his face turned into a mess of bloodied snot. I'd never done that to anyone before, and I would not do it again out of choice. This seemed such a crude way to fight.

Morgunn had the last Raider's arm pinned behind his

back and was about to break it when we noticed several more men were running towards us to help their friends.

Efalaa landed in between us and them and, without fear or hesitation, she rushed the man heading the rescue effort. Somehow, she managed to stab him in the neck. I don't know who was the most surprised, him or me. She didn't pause before slashing at the next man. The others hung back, watching her with dismay.

Morgunn snapped the arm of the man he held and ran towards Efalaa, his hunting knife aloft.

'Wait,' I called after him. 'Let them return to their camp and carry their wounded with a message.'

'What message?' asked Morgunn.

'The message will be clear to their leader.'

Morgunn grinned and pulled Efalaa back towards the Hedge.

'Come, sweetling,' he said. She looked at him with outrage. He added with a twinkle in his eye, 'Come, you'll only get your clothes dirty.'

At that she chuckled and allowed him to lead her away. They whistled for the birds, took a running jump and leapt onto Eko's back.

I picked up my bloody blade and wiped it clean on the unconscious man's shirt, while the injured men watched. I called Frid and calmly straddled him before flying off. The Raiders seemed even more awed by my slow manoeuvre than by Morgunn and Efalaa's gravity-defying stunt.

Leodurr carried on stoning the retreating Raiders, and Efalaa couldn't resist shooting a few arrows at those in her range. Her aim was deadly accurate. She had brought down five already. I'd always thought of Efalaa as an inferior Hunter and an even worse fighter, but I had to admit she was now capable of doing the same job as a fully trained Guardian.

I circled the area to review the situation. We were

unscathed. The men Morgunn and I had fought by the Hedge were limping back to their camp. Leodurr had downed three men with his stones. They were bleeding from head wounds but unlikely to be dead. Efalaa had killed six Raiders. The man I had wounded in the stomach would take hours to die. I wished I had snapped his neck.

Vidris was finishing putting out the fire, and Aalma kept the water running freely in dozen of rivulets down the eastern side of the mountain. The battle hadn't lasted more than twenty minutes, and we had complete victory. Leodurr flew back to the Orchard Camp to reassure Veiti and Sili that all was well.

We cleared an area by the scorched bushes and took the time to pile up the dead. We divested them of their weapons and everything else that could be useful, then we used the kindling they had brought to set fire to their bodies.

An hour after our desperate ride to the Hedge, we were back home, washing the blood and dirt out of our weapons and clothing, elation and relief painted on all our faces.

In stark contrast with the general good mood, Sili sat by the firepit with her fragile little daughter against her chest and threw uncomfortable glances at those walking past. Her position within the Clan had become much worse because of her ill-advised walkabout.

While we fought Outsiders off our doorstep, she was a reminder of the threats that came with allowing strangers into your house.

❦ 19 ❦

S ili

The Skyriders returned victorious and loaded with weapons and clothing looted from the Raiders they had killed.

I was sitting by the fire with the baby on my lap. Veiti hadn't spoken a word to me while the others were gone. I couldn't blame her.

They landed in a tight group a small distance away from the huts. Leodurr had told us we were safe, but I was impatient to hear the details. Nevertheless, I kept my face smooth.

Veiti threw one arm around Morgunn's neck in congratulation and kissed his cheek. He kissed her back, their earlier disagreement entirely forgotten.

As Efalaa walked past my seat, she squeezed my shoulder and looked down at me with an air of sadness.

'If only you hadn't left, Sili. Morgunn had just allowed you into the Clan,' she said. 'Didn't you trust us?'

'I don't want to be where I'm not welcome,' I replied sharply.

'What are you saying? You were welcome. We'd taken you in. You needn't have taken our initial reluctance so badly. You should have given us more time. It was a big step for us all to take. We are the last of a long line of Clanspeople. They were worried about betraying the memory of our dead.'

'I didn't realise that.'

'You should have talked to me.'

'Well, I didn't, Efalaa Vonaborn,' I replied and turned away from her.

Nobody paid me any attention after that.

This discreet shunning was the reaction Efalaa had expected for herself when she returned to the Clan after her long absence. She had feared the silent treatment to which I was now subjected. It ruffled me more than I would have expected. Although I had acted out of sheer self-preservation, I knew I had done wrong. It was one thing to admit it to myself, but entirely another to admit it to them. In all honesty, I doubted anyone expected me to repent or apologise. I would never have done so anyway.

Still unsteady on my feet and with my womb in throbbing pain, I returned to Veiti's hut. The walk to the Watch Tower and back had left me utterly exhausted. More than anything now, I needed to sleep. I couldn't plan my next move without a clear head.

I retired to my bed and laid the baby next to me. She didn't cry for a feed, so I concluded that, after finding me gone, Veiti must have fed her herself that morning. I snuggled under the furs and fell asleep immediately.

I woke up briefly halfway through the day, and my stomach called for food, but I was still too tired and unwilling to risk being refused lunch if I joined the others by the fire. The baby grizzled, and I let her latch on to my breast before going back to sleep.

I was lost to the world for the rest of the day.

That night, Efalaa broke my long fast by bringing me my dinner in bed.

She smiled at me, and I knew I still had a friend. I almost broke down in tears but managed to keep myself and my face under control.

She sat and detangled my hair while I devoured a bowl of pigeon breast and mushroom stew. This was the best meal I'd ever had in the Skyriders' camp. The orange mushrooms lent their delicate flavour to the carrots and dark green leaves that floated in the stock. My stomach was so grateful the thought of apologising to the Clan seemed a lot more palatable than before.

I was about to thank Efalaa when the baby started to wheeze. We exchanged a puzzled look. Efalaa composed her face swiftly and spoke words of reassurance.

'Newborns make all sort of strange noises. Don't worry.'

The child fussed, and Efalaa picked her up.

'She must be hungry too,' she said.

Trying to hide my reluctance, I put the baby to my breast, and moved the conversation toward the events of the day.

'Do you think the Raiders will go away now?'

Efalaa's face darkened, and she didn't reply.

'I agree,' I said. 'No chance.'

She raised her eyebrows in silent resignation.

'What are they after?'

She shrugged.

I wondered if she'd shared with Morgunn how deeply upset she was at the return of the Raiders into her life. I took her hand.

'We're safe here,' I said.

'For now,' she whispered.

I thought of what Steon had said about the Hedge having never been breached. He'd obviously done as poor a job of reassuring Efalaa as he had of reassuring me.

The child spluttered, and our attention turned to her as she breathed hoarsely through her feed.

Efalaa said, 'I'll ask Aalma to have a look at Vona.'

'I'm sure it's nothing,' I replied. 'Such a pretty name, isn't it?'

'You don't need to sweet-talk me, I'm already on your side,' she said, and for the first time she sounded annoyed.

I gave her a sheepish smile.

'Will they ever forgive me?' I asked, changing the subject again.

'Yes.'

'When?'

'When you make amends.'

'I was afraid you would say that.'

'What else did you expect?'

'Nothing. Shunning is the best I could hope for.'

The baby gave a weak cough, and we both looked down at her flushed face.

'Don't be so greedy, little chickling,' said Efalaa tenderly.

I rolled my eyes at yet another bird-related term of endearment. I would never get used to those.

The baby abandoned her feed and returned to her wheezing. Efalaa stroked her head before gathering up my dinner things.

I was still so tired that I went straight back to sleep after she left.

Early the next morning, Veiti came to see the baby. Her breathing sounded worse.

'Aalma will rub some unguent on her chest, she'll be fine in a couple of days,' said Veiti.

Her tone was cheerful, but I caught a hint of unease. Veiti was constantly worried about Leif's health, and I easily dismissed her fears.

Efalaa returned, this time carrying my breakfast. It was acorn porridge, and I crinkled my nose. I washed the foul mixture down with a dark tea that tasted strong yet not entirely unpleasant.

The child didn't even wake up when Efalaa changed her linen. The only sign that she was still alive was her laboured breathing. As she reattached the successive layers of clothing, Efalaa's face lost its usual expressiveness and froze into a forced neutrality. She handed the baby back to me and left with a quick 'see you later'.

Efalaa's swift exit worried me more that Veiti's concerns. The Skyriders clearly thought the child was ill. For the first time, I took a careful look at her.

She was very small and thin-limbed with a patch of blond down on the crown of her head. The wrinkles of her face had smoothed. Her ears were minuscule and perfectly formed, as were her hands, with each finger tiny but strong.

She did struggle to breathe. After another small feed, she fell asleep again. I tried to wake her up to drink some more, but her eyes and her little pursed mouth remained stubbornly closed.

Soon after that, Aalma entered the hut with her healing supplies. She examined the child by placing her ear on the tiny back, listening to the workings of the tiny lungs. She applied a mixture on the baby's chest and deftly swaddled her in a square piece of woollen cloth.

'Keep her with you for now,' she said. 'She needs her mother to hold her.'

'I'm going to get some more sleep,' I replied.

Aalma furrowed her brow but said nothing and placed the child in a cocoon of furs by the side of my bed. I turned over and tried to escape into a mindless slumber, but the sound of the baby's struggle for breath was too disturbing.

Eventually, I picked her up and cradled her in my arms. Despite the swaddling cloth, she was cold to the touch, and I had to wrap us both in another fur before her temperature started rising again.

Sleep eluded me, and I sat while the child wheezed through every breath against my chest.

Her eyes had lost some of their puffiness. Her snubbed nose looked too small to be of any use, and a few strands of golden hair escaped out of the fur onto her forehead. A blonde child. I couldn't remember anyone in my family being blond. She would look like Veiti's daughter one day, but her nose was definitely mine.

I hoped she wouldn't be ugly like her father must have been. The Raiders all looked disgusting, their men scarred and stubbly and their women dough-faced and dull-eyed. The thought of their hands on me and their dirty, crude bodies inside mine revolted me still.

I put the child back down into her furry cradle and faced the wall.

❧ 20 ❧

Steon

Sili looked up slowly when I entered the hut without knocking. She looked pale. Within seconds, she was wearing her scornful expression, the one she reserved for me.

'How is Vona today?' I asked.

Sili scowled as I said her daughter's name. I thought for an instant she wouldn't deign to answer me, but she replied curtly, 'Fine, thank you.'

I could hear the child's raspy breathing, and I gave Sili a dubious look.

'Do you want me to call Aalma?'

'We're fine, thank you for your concern,' Sili said with a condescending tone.

I smiled at her and left. What I wouldn't give to wipe that contemptuous smirk off her face. Sili needed a lesson. She needed to be taught no one was above anyone else. We all were born, we all fought for life, we all died. Equal.

I was due to relieve Morgunn at the Watch Tower after breakfast, but the morning was unusually mild and the sun shone, so I stripped down, stood in the stream outside the bathhouse, and splashed myself merrily with the chilly water.

Leodurr sat by the sleeping hut cleaning the weapons we had taken from the Raiders. There were several short swords and three of the typical Raiders' spears. The spearheads were the sharpest pieces of weaponry I had ever seen.

It was funny how we'd all started to do each other's jobs. I'd spent the autumn farming, Morgunn was now guarding, and gentle Leodurr was cleaning weapons. I was the son of a Farmer and a Guardian and so was Leodurr; but for a Chief's decision, our positions could have been reversed. Not that Leodurr would have made a good Guardian, he was far too kind.

I was pleased with our loot. I slept better thinking of those extra blades that had landed in our laps. Once the Raiders were gone, they could be melted into cooking pots. You could have too many weapons, especially for our reduced numbers, but you could never have too many cooking pots.

I was brought back to reality by the shadow of wings darkening the ground. I looked up expecting Efalaa, but it was Morgunn, radiating a fierce energy that made my hackles rise. He landed so close to me that my braids flew.

'They haven't left,' he said in a breath.

I didn't need any further explanation. I pulled on my clothes over my wet body and ran toward the Orchard calling for Vidris to fetch Frid. She stepped out of the birds' shed, bucket in hand, looking alarmed.

'Find Efalaa,' Morgunn said to her. She dropped her bucket and harnessed Oxi.

I was already laying a saddle on Frid's back.

'You might need your boots,' said Morgunn, smirking at my bare feet despite the crisis.

We arrived at the Watch Tower tense and alert.

'I'll do a reconnaissance flight then come back and report,' I offered.

Morgunn nodded. 'Be as discreet as you can.'

'I'll fly against the sun; they won't see me.'

I took off and soared so high that even to my trained eye Morgunn was now just a dot. I approached the area where the Raiders had settled. When I arrived between them and the sun, I lost some altitude and hovered for less than a minute before returning the same way I'd come.

'More men than before.' I said to Morgunn. 'They've put up more tents and dug a second line of fences. They have about twenty horses. Obviously a sort of cavalry attack force, rather than an escape plan. They also have piles of sticks that might be arrows or firewood but more probably arrows. Their camp is tidy, they seem organised, and they are cooking.'

Morgunn listened with narrowed eyes.

'I can't be sure, but I don't think there were any women,' I continued. 'They're here on a military campaign. They're not settling down permanently. Or at least not yet.'

None of this sounded good. Morgunn and I were both quiet while we mulled this information over. I came to a conclusion before him.

'One, their cavalry is essentially useless against us as they will soon find out. Two, arrows are a poor weapon against high-flying birds who can gain altitude at will. We can hit them with the slingshots from a height that they can't reach with their arrows. Gravity works in our favour and not theirs. Even if an arrow found its mark, it would have lost the power to pierce the birds' feathers. They won't even feel a scratch. However, if we shoot at them, our arrows will gain velocity as they travel down and will do more damage than if shot from ground level. Three, we can set fire to their tents. They will take serious hits, and we can do that all day without tiring the birds at all.'

'It seems almost too easy, doesn't it?' Morgunn said.

'I don't think they have thought this through.'

'How do you think they found us?'

'They might have followed Efalaa's tracks. They're camping very close to where she went through the Hedge. There is even a chance they might try to get inside the Territory the same way she did. I only checked the Hedge on the inside the night she returned. I should have looked on the other side as well. I'm sorry, Chief, it was my mistake.'

Morgunn dismissed my apology. 'We had no birds, remember. We couldn't have inspected the outer edge that night. I should have sent you to check the next day, but because of Efalaa, I didn't think of it. It was my mistake, not yours. I give the orders.'

Out of respect for him, I didn't point out that he'd only been a Chief for a few months and that I, an experienced Guardian, should have known better.

'She must have left all sort of footprints and broken twigs,' Morgunn continued. 'Especially in the state she was in.'

'She said she crawled under the Hedge for a long time.'

'She is smaller than most of their men. They might not be able to fit through the same gaps she did.'

'Let's just hope so.' He rubbed his face with both his hands. 'Just how much trouble is this girl going to cause me?' he wondered aloud.

I raised my eyebrows in sympathy and patted his shoulder.

When we returned to the Orchard, our camp was bustling with activity. Vidris hadn't found Efalaa yet, and I caught Morgunn's look of fear.

'She has Mila, she's not on the ground,' I said to reassure him.

Nevertheless, he pulled himself back onto Eko and went to search for Efalaa himself.

Again, I wished everyone could stay in one place. How was I supposed to protect them when they kept flying off in all directions?

❧ 21 ❧

S ili

At midday, I returned to the Watch Tower with enough supplies to stand guard for days.

I hung a large fur at the back of the platform to cut out the chilly winds, and stacked apples, flatbread, nuts and fresh cheese in the wooden box that served as a larder. The night would be bitterly cold. The only upside was that, at that temperature, the food would not spoil.

I settled into one of the chairs and prepared for a long watch. The difficult part of night watches is normally to stay awake, but that evening I had no such problem. Nervous energy ran through my body, and I struggled to sit still.

At dusk, I used the last of the light to check the Raiders' positions again. They had gathered around their fire pits. I could hear the hum of their conversations. They were lively but not rowdy. Clearly, this was not a party. These men were an army, not some part-time pillagers.

When I returned to the Watch Tower, Efalaa was there.

'I've spent the day flying around the perimeter,' she said. 'I haven't seen anyone, Raiders or not, for miles around. This is their only camp.'

'They've realised this is our weakest point.'

'It's not weak,' she said, 'And we're not weak either.' Her words touched a nerve.

'We're not weak, sweetheart. We're just outnumbered.'

We exchanged a look of perfect understanding.

'Why are they even here?' I wondered aloud.

'Sili and I escaped and killed several of their men. Maybe revenge?'

'Who would bring so many men to lay siege to a territory like ours in pursuit of two runaway captives?'

'From what I heard, their leader Torston is a very strange man.'

'Strange in what way?'

'Unpredictable. Irrational. Cruel.'

I didn't like the sound of that. This was not the kind of man Erlen had taught us to fight. I felt woefully ill-prepared, but there was no longer a Master Guardian to turn to. After our team effort against the Raiders who'd tried to burn the Hedge, I had started to miss my fellow Guardians a little less. Now, again, I felt helpless without them. I did my best to hide my feelings from Efalaa and returned to the business of planning our defence.

'When you go back to the Orchard, you must tell Morgunn to reinforce the defences upstream from the Waterfall. If they somehow make it through the Hedge and up the cliff, the River will lead them straight to us.'

'How can we guard the River with only eight of us? And that's counting two nursing mothers,' she asked.

'That is for Morgunn to decide.'

She gave me a pained look. 'He used to be so happy. Now he frowns all the time.'

I didn't know what to reply to that, and I watched her fly away with a lump in my throat.

The man himself seemed cheerful enough though when he visited me later on that evening.

'Hello to my one and only Guardian!' he greeted me with a bright smile. 'I've brought you some hot food. It tastes of nothing, I'm afraid. Efalaa cooked it.'

His good mood was infectious.

'As long as it's hot, I'd eat it even if Leif the Lucky had made it. I'm frozen.'

'Don't you want a fire in there?' asked Morgunn, pointing at Berjast's clay chimenea in the corner of the watching platform.

'Good old Berjast,' I said. 'What a treasure this chimenea is!'

Morgunn took his hand off it as if he'd been burnt. His face became so ashen I thought he would faint. I reached out to steady him.

'Hey there, elskan, are you alright?'

His mouth was hanging open. I shook him.

'Morgunn, what's wrong?' I asked louder.

Eventually, he came out of his daze. 'Yes, I'm fine, sorry.'

'What happened?'

'Nothing, it's fine,' he insisted although it obviously wasn't.

'Talk to me.'

He hesitated for a second, then shook his head. 'It's not my story to tell, brother.' After a while, he added, 'Don't ever talk to Efalaa about her father.'

'Was she very upset at his passing? I didn't realise they were close. She always seemed... distant.'

His tortured expression returned.

'Just don't,' he managed.

'Yes, Chief,' I replied formally, in an attempt to put his mind at rest. I stared at the chimenea for some explanation to Morgunn's strange reaction. None came to mind.

'I won't make a fire,' I said to change the topic of conversation. 'I'd rather not make myself a target tonight.'

'They couldn't shoot you from so far away,' he argued.

'No, but they would know where we are. And they would know we are manning only one guard post.'

'Right,' said Morgunn staring at his feet. 'After our victory, I keep forgetting how outnumbered we are.'

He paused.

'Couldn't we light fires in all three Watch Towers on this side of the mountain?' he asked.

'It would only be worth the firewood if we thought they could be deterred by our numbers. But they're here not knowing how many of us they face. They may be expecting hundreds of us. We can't fake that.'

He lowered his head, his good mood entirely gone.

'Still we pushed them back once, we can do it again,' he said resolutely.

If he hadn't been the Chief, I would have left him to his optimism, but he was, and he couldn't afford any overconfidence.

'There are many areas around the perimeter where we couldn't flood the ground,' I warned him. 'The Hedge could still burn down enough for men to sneak through. We were lucky, that's all.'

Morgunn struggled for something positive to say. I took pity on him.

'Efalaa fought well,' I said, interrupting his uncomfortable thoughts.

His face broke into a smile at the sound of her name.

'She killed five or six of them,' I continued. 'I knew she was a good archer, but I didn't realised how well she could do in a knife fight.'

'I taught her myself,' he said proudly. 'But I can take no credit for her knack for violence. Remember when she nearly broke my nose at the Cave on the day she left.'

'Our quiet little Singer,' I chuckled. 'It makes you wonder about breeding for skills, doesn't it. By right, Efalaa should never have even touched a weapon.'

'And now she's doing the job of a Guardian. 'There was a hint of sadness in his voice. I understood him. It takes years of training to get used to your loved ones getting in harm's way. We Guardians knew that well.

'A Guardian does not kill unless she has to,' I reminded him.

'They were burning down the Hedge, I'd say she had to. Wouldn't you?'

'I don't know. Neither you nor I killed anyone.'

'We might live to regret we didn't reduce their numbers when we had the chance.'

'Perhaps.'

Morgunn's cheery mood was now entirely gone. This was a difficult time for optimists. 'We must keep watch day and night and do surveillance fly-overs to keep track of their numbers and activities. I'll relieve you at sunset,' he declared.

'Yes, Chief.'

Then, he turned on his heels and went down the ladder with a quick 'good luck'. I saw him fly towards the Raiders' camp instead of towards the Orchard.

He was more worried than he let on.

The next morning, it was Efalaa who came to take my place at the Watch Tower.

'You missed breakfast,' she said, 'But I've brought you some fresh eggs, the ducks have started laying again.' She turned towards the chimenea. 'Do you think we can use this to cook them?'

I watched her carefully, but the object of Morgunn's distress was just a lump of clay to her.

'Don't,' I explained again. 'It will attract the wrong kind of attention.' I pointed towards the Raiders' camp.

'Oh, of course, sorry. Raw eggs for you then.'

She settled on one of the high seats and wrapped her travelling cloak closer to her.

'When shall I come back?' I asked.

'After midday, if you don't mind, elskan. I'll need to hunt for some birds or rabbits on my way back to the Orchard. We can't let our supplies run low, especially not now.'

She rested her feet on the funnel of the chimenea and turned her clear eyes towards me. I resolved to never utter Berjast's name in her presence or in Morgunn's. I had warm feelings towards the two Hunters. They were brave and funny. Their relationship that had surprised us all was now the beating heart of the Clan, and we were all the happier for it.

I returned to the Watch Tower after a few hours' sleep and lunch. I sat for long hours through the afternoon, scanning the horizon. I thought about Isveg. What I would have given to have her in the seat next to me. I missed her body and the cadences of her voice as we chatted endlessly about our uneventful life in the Clan.

I thought about my mother Gaia, and my father Hilden. They had been distant parents, and if not for Erlen Durrborn, I might have been an unloved child. It was the Master Guardian who had brought me up, taught me, and inspired me to be my best self.

They could all rest peacefully in their stony graves.

Seven of us were still here, watching, fighting, hoping, and somewhere among the apple trees, a little Clansboy and a little Clansgirl heralded the next generation.

22

S ili

As I watched the baby sleep, I couldn't resist thoughts that would have been best left alone.

I had always enjoyed sex. In my days in New Bodie, I had had my share of lovers. After my many miscarriages, I'd become convinced I could never conceive and had made the most of my barrenness.

I was not picky. A decent face and a muscular body, and I was ready to give a man a try. I had some good surprises as well as some disappointments. Mostly, the sex was good and the parting easy.

I didn't know that coupling could hurt as much as it had during my time with the Raiders. Of course, being beaten and kicked is no one's idea of foreplay. None of those uncouth, cruel men ever gave me even half a chance to ready myself for them, and penetration was always excruciatingly painful, like a knife to the gut.

For serial rapists, they were remarkably unimaginative. They went for the hole between the legs, thrusted until they were satisfied and passed me on to the next man. I did my best to think about something else until they were done, and never gave them the satisfaction of my tears. I supposed women's screams and pleadings enhanced their experience, and I made myself as boring a victim as possible.

As the days went by, I had fewer and fewer takers. Until only the ugliest and the most unwashed ever bothered with me. Tungor, the man I had killed in the small woods with Efalaa had been one of the last in my honour guard and was probably the child's father, although he wasn't blond.

When I thought of him, I wondered why I hadn't yet snuffed the life out of that child. By the sound of her laboured breathing, my intervention might not be necessary.

Steon came in at that moment, and interrupted my thoughts. He said nothing but sat down heavily by the door. He looked at the child and not at me. His face was softer than usual, and his eyes showed a longing that made me uncomfortable.

I decided to wipe that expression off his face.

'I'm not sure I want her to live,' I said to provoke a reaction from him.

'I know,' he replied. He met my eyes, and I saw his look of tenderness was not entirely gone.

I wondered whether he would step in as the baby's father after I left. He would be a decent father. Strong and protective, perhaps even kind. If she lived, the girl had a chance of happiness here.

It was during that night that everything changed. Having slept so much during the previous day, I was not tired any more, but the evening assembly was finished and the camp quiet.

So, out of boredom, by the light of a single flickering torch, I watched the baby's minuscule fingers curling and uncurling. She was grabbing at my clothing but found no purchase until her tiny fist closed around a strand of my hair. Her hand stopped searching, and she held fast. In that instant, when she claimed me as her own, I finally acknowledged that she was mine.

I watched her lips parting in her sleep, as if she was trying to form words. No sounds came out of her mouth other than her raspy breath. I wondered what she would be saying if she could speak. Then, I realised it could only be one thing.

I knew what she wanted to say. Every child's first word.

I went cold.

'Mama,' she mouthed again, and this time I heard the word in my mind, clear as a bell.

My heart splintered into a million pieces and was immediately rebuilt. A brand new heart, full of love and wonder. A heart grateful that, out of my long ordeal, I had won this perfect little person whose mother I was.

Only then did I measure how chokingly much I wanted my child to live and call me mama one day in her own voice.

23

S^{teon}

The Raiders had done nothing more than sit around their campfires since their failed attempt at burning the Hedge. The dawn found them breakfasting and fetching water out of the River mouth.

Following orders, I flew over the wintry landscape around our Territory for a couple of hours before heading back to the Orchard. I had seen no other Raider groups and nothing moving in the frosty Wastelands.

The temperature was lower than it had been in years. I returned to the Camp frozen to the bone despite my travelling cloak. I couldn't remember the last time I had felt the cold through my clothing.

Leodurr was putting away breakfast. Morgunn handed me a bowl of porridge, dried berries and nuts.

'Seen anything?' he asked.

'No, the day is clear. Not a single person for miles.'

He smiled, obviously relieved. Vidris made me a pepper-mint and nettle tea. The warmth of the drink brought some feeling back into my fingers.

After breakfast, I went to visit Sili and her daughter. I worried Sili was planning something. I didn't know what, and it unsettled me. Little Vona was one of us now, and as such, she was under my protection just as much as Leif.

I found Sili looking sad and scared. It was the first time I'd ever seen those emotions on her face. She did not scorn me, she didn't say anything, she just sat with her baby pressed tight against her chest. I thought there might have been a new tenderness in the way she held her, but I couldn't be sure. The very air of the room was sad.

'Come outside for a while,' I said to Sili, as I lifted her up.

'It's too cold out there,' she replied meekly.

'The breakfast fire is still burning, you will be warm enough.'

'She won't be,' said Sili, but she didn't fight me when I led her outside and sat her by the fire.

I draped my travelling cloak around her shoulders and across her lap.

'Now she can no longer feel the cold,' I said.

Sili nodded and stared at the ground. The baby snuffled.

I went about my business all day. I stood guard for hours at the Watch Tower but the Raiders kept building up their camp and cooking. Morgunn offered to take my place through the afternoon, and I spent the rest of the day helping Leodurr in the fields and Veiti with the gathering. We couldn't afford people sitting around and doing nothing. We all had to work for our food.

I thought of Sili a lot that day, and I worried about her baby. I didn't do anything about it though.

That evening, as Morgunn and I returned to the Camp, Veiti ran towards us. 'Vona is dying,' was all she said.

It was like a punch in the face. Morgunn ran towards the hut, and I followed closely.

The small house was crowded. We pushed past Efalaa and Aalma to see what was going on. Sili was hunched in a corner, her eyes wild. She held the child to her breast and wouldn't let anyone approach them. Aalma had four deep gashes across her face where Sili had scratched her, and Efalaa was bleeding from a bite on her wrist.

Morgunn saw Efalaa's blood and forgot all about Sili. He led his wife out of the hut to clean her wound and bandage it.

I was the first to reach Sili. She was screeching through her teeth like a cornered animal. She attacked me and managed to land a punch in my face, but I pinned her down easily, passing the child to Aalma. The Healer went out to fetch some remedies, tiny Vona bundled in her arms. She wore a deep frown.

Sili started howling like a feral beast. She tried to get up, but I tackled her back down. Morgunn reentered the hut, and he spoke softly to Sili.

'Aalma is going to do all she can. You can trust us. She is one of us now, and so are you.'

'Go away! Let go of me! Let go,' she yelled, twisting and turning furiously to escape my grip. 'Bring back my daughter! Bring back my child!'

Morgunn didn't understand the part of Sili that had wished her daughter's death was now writhing in horror, guilt and shame. He wasn't well acquainted with the worst of human nature. He couldn't understand the darkness in which Sili was wandering.

Efalaa also tried to reach Sili with kind words and reassurance. She fared no better than Morgunn, and Sili turned hysterical, slapping everyone within reach.

'Leave her to me,' I told them. 'You're just making her angrier.'

'Don't hurt her,' said Efalaa, and I raised my eyebrow at her until sheepishly she apologised. 'Sorry, I know you wouldn't hurt her on purpose...' Seeing she wasn't making the situation any better, she took Morgunn's hand and pulled him out of the hut.

Once the door was shut, the atmosphere in the dimly lit room changed. I held Sili tightly around the chest and let her kick and twist as much as she liked. Eventually, she exhausted herself and started crying silent tears.

I didn't release my hold until the fight had completely gone out of her. Then I held her still, but with less strength, and I rested my back against the wall behind us. She reclined in my arms and looked dejectedly towards the door.

We waited for Aalma to return with news. She didn't. Eventually, Sili cried herself into a slumber, and I decided it was safe to leave her alone for a few minutes while I checked on little Vona.

I found her clinging to life in Morgunn's arms, air wheezing in and out of her tiny lungs. She was so perfect, so delicate. How could the child of one of these brutes look so unspoilt?

Veiti was crying and holding on to her son. Many babies died in the Clan. A third of those born didn't make it to their first birthday. We all knew parents who had lost a young child. Many of us had lost young siblings. Aalma had lost dozen of babies during her time as a Healer. Dying babies were not uncommon, but every single little life vanishing into the ether deeply hurt us all.

Aalma, dull-eyed, was preparing yet another potion by mixing a green powder in some warm water. The smell went up my nostrils and opened my airways. Hopefully, it would do the same for Vona. She was turning blue again, and Morgunn slapped her back, as I had seen Aalma do before.

Her breath returned, ragged and thin. Morgunn looked towards Efalaa who was sitting by him and smiled at her encouragingly. His faith in Aalma's powers must have been greater than mine. Then he passed Vona to me and went to crouch near our weeping Gatherer. He whispered in her ear words I couldn't catch. She nodded but kept crying.

'I just can't take another loss,' she wept, echoing everyone else's feelings.

I hugged the little girl against my chest, willing the air in my lungs to pass into hers. I felt completely powerless.

Aalma rubbed the fragrant paste she'd been preparing under the minuscule snubbed nose and on the tiny chest. For a couple of minutes, it seemed to help, and we all breathed a sigh of relief. Then, the laboured breathing returned, worse rather than better.

I could do nothing but hold the child against my heart and hope. I felt a fierce desire for a child of my own, a healthy child, strong and vital. This realisation brought tears to my eyes, and Aalma laid her head on my shoulder.

'We need to return her to Sili,' she said. 'Only a mother's touch can save her now.'

As in procession, we filed out of the sleeping hut and towards Veiti's house.

We woke Sili up, and she blinked several times before understanding the situation. She took the baby out of my arms and held her against her chest. This time she had no words of insult for any of us and no punches. I sat next to her and put my arm around her.

Sili stared at nothing as if she wasn't really there, as if her mind was travelling somewhere else. She didn't try to push me away, which surprised me greatly. Maybe she didn't care any more now that her child was slowly dying.

Efalaa started singing 'Sofðu unga ástin mín', one of the Clan's lullabies in the Old Language, in her beautiful voice we hadn't heard in years. Morgunn and Aalma sang the deeper harmonies. The traditional song, passed down the generations since before the First Twelve, told the story of a young homeless mother roaming the wintry lands who, out of desperation, sings her baby into the endless sleep.

'Sleep so deep, sleep so long,' sang Efalaa, 'No need to wake in the morning, Oh so sad is our song, and you shall fade before too long, to leave us loving, missing, weeping, and mourning.'

Vona breathed her last before the end of the song, and the silence returned inside the hut.

'Go away,' said Sili.

One by one, we obeyed. Efalaa hugged Sili and kissed her cheek and Vona's head. I was the last to leave. I shut the door behind me and joined the others by the fire. We spoke in low voices.

Efalaa said quietly, 'I always thought I didn't want a child. But now I know that I do.' Her voice broke. 'And I will love my child as fiercely as my mother loved me.'

Morgunn wrapped his arms around her. With their heads resting on each other's shoulder and their braids melding into a dark and blonde curtain, they shut out the world and the rest of us.

We stared at the dying flames, heartsore and helpless. No Vona Siliborn would ever sing our Clan songs now, nor cook our meals, nor make our things. Added to the loss of what was, we grieved what might have been.

I interrupted everyone's silent contemplations. 'I too have no greater desire than a child of my own.' I was surprised at my own words.

'You will have a child in time,' promised Morgunn, 'Future

generations of the Clan will need your strength and your heart, elskan.'

This was wishful thinking, but it made me feel better.

'Do you think Sili would prefer a grave or a pyre? What do they do in the Wastelands?' asked Vidris.

'She's from a place she calls the "Valley",' corrected Efalaa who was still wiping her eyes. 'I don't know what they do there, apart from killing each other.'

'It's too soon to ask Sili about any of that, my loves,' replied Aalma.

'She's probably going to want to say goodbye in her own time,' said Veiti.

'Maybe we shouldn't leave her alone,' suggested Leodurr.

'You're right, elskan, we will take turns sitting with her so that we can all show our solidarity with her grief,' decided Morgunn, and we all agreed.

'You need to know that part of her wanted the child to die; that part will fester and eat away at her if we do nothing about it,' I said.

They looked surprised.

'It wasn't ill wishes that robbed that little girl of her life, but a premature birth and weak lungs,' said Aalma firmly. 'Sili must be made to see that.'

I nodded. 'Veiti, I don't think you should go in to see her, dearie. A new mother with a healthy baby will rub salt on her wounds.'

Veiti hung her head. 'But she's my friend,' she argued. She'd obviously forgotten all about her anger at Sili when she'd tried to escape in the night.

'She'll scratch your eyes out,' replied Morgunn. 'She's a danger to herself at this point, and she is a danger to us all.'

'Really?' said Efalaa looking from Morgunn to me.

'It is my opinion as your Guardian that this woman, at this time, is capable of anything. She will try anything to relieve her guilt and her anger. She might try to hurt herself or one of us.'

'All the more reason to watch her through the night,' said Aalma.

Efalaa took the first shift at Sili's side while we ate a sorrowful dinner.

When I took the last turn of the Clan's wake, it was already mid-morning. As far as I could make out from everyone else's accounts, Sili had not moved a muscle all night. When I entered the hut, she looked over her shoulder at me, and wrinkled her nose in disgust.

I didn't speak.

'Aren't you going to tell me how it's not my fault my daughter died? Or maybe you're here to say that I will get over my loss in time? That's another popular one.'

'Would it make any difference?'

'No,'

'Then I won't waste my breath.'

'You hate me, don't you?'

'No. I like you.'

'What?' she scoffed.

'I like you,' I repeated. 'You're a fighter.'

'I'm a loser. I've lost every battle I ever fought.'

'Then you must have fought hard battles indeed.'

That gave her pause. Her expression changed.

'Yes, they were,' she answered in a milder tone.

'As I said, you're a fighter. A fighter fights the battles in front of her, not only those she can win.'

She seemed to think about that for a while.

'That's the nicest thing anyone has ever said about me.'

'That explains a lot,' I said.

'Yes, it probably does,' she said bitterly, but then she smiled. It was a thin smile, with no joy in it, but I was pleased to have made a chink in her grief.

We were quiet for a while before she spoke again.

'Are you here to prise her out of my hands?'

'No, there is plenty of time.'

She turned back towards the wall, staring into the dark corner of the room.

'Did someone ask you what you preferred?' I enquired.

'About what?'

'For Vona. Burial or pyre?'

'You don't beat about the bush, do you?' she said, irritated.

'No.'

'Pyre,' she said.

'I'll see to it myself.'

'Thank you.'

We didn't speak after that. When I got up to leave, she kissed the child then handed her to me.

As I walked away from the hut, with Vona's tiny cold body, I caught Efalaa's eye and sent her with a look to watch Sili and comfort her.

We lit the pyre after sunset and watched as the flames devoured the Clan's youngest. Sili was dry-eyed. Everyone else cried.

24

S ili

I wished the Skyriders could have put out the fire burning within me as quickly as they had the one threatening their cursed Hedge.

My insides were in flames. The loss of Vona had made way for a relentless pain, an angry, raging pain that nothing could stop. I went to bed chewing on it, I woke up with the taste of it in my mouth. Its noise was in my ears and erased most other noises. It sounded like distant howling and the frantic pumping of blood.

I wanted to kill, I wanted to maim and crush limbs. I wanted to break everything I touched. Sometimes, in the quiet of the night, I felt I would soon turn into a tornado of wrath that would demolish everything in its path. The thought of the destruction I could wreak was my only relief.

The only thing holding me back was the knowledge that a

certain great hulk of a man would put on his hateful Guardian face and break my neck without hesitation.

The Skyriders may have been barbarians, but they were extremely efficient and successful at everything they undertook. They found food even in the midst of the harshest winter in memory. They continued to improve their huts with extra insulation and kept themselves, their clothes and their things clean. They even had effortlessly defeated a Raiders' group twenty times the size of the Clan.

Morgunn was intrigued the Raiders had not yet left. They still camped by the Waterfall but had made no further attempts to break into the Territory. The Clan did not know what to think of that, and Leodurr even ventured the theory they had only been trying to collect firewood when they attacked the Hedge.

It was foolish, obviously. Raiders only did one thing. They took what they wanted from those who could not defend it. The Clan had defended itself, and it had given the Raiders pause.

Personally, I was now sure they were waiting for reinforcements.

Throughout those freezing days, I had nothing to do but sit and watch my hosts as they went about their business.

It was a source of constant irritation to see them interacting. They worked together well, they laughed, they sang, they ate, and they went to bed happy. Having little else to do or think about, I observed them closely.

I was surprised how unaffected they were by envy of other people's possessions or by sexual jealousy.

Aalma was celibate, Vidris probably a virgin and Veiti still recovering from childbirth. Efalaa had been appropriated in a move that had nearly torn the Clan apart. So Leodurr and Steon were left with no sexual partner. In any other group, they would have become enraged by enforced celibacy. As it was, they seemed accepting of it. It was astonishing to see these well-built, handsome men so respectful of their women-folk and so in charge of their disciplined desires.

Although I felt nothing but utter contempt for him, I had to admit Steon was the better specimen of male. Leodurr wore his gentleness on his face and that marred his sex appeal. Morgunn was classically handsome, smooth skinned and bright-eyed, but there was no darkness, no mystery to him. He was obvious. He idolised Efalaa, he probably had loved her since childhood. No one could ever compare in his eyes, and he would no sooner stray than chop off his own leg.

Steon, on the other hand, oozed brute strength and confidence. Much like the other members of the Clan, he knew who he was and was accepted as such. There was no uncertainty, no way to take control, no weakness to exploit. Or was there?

He was bound to be hungry for sex, and I felt like hurting a man. To make him feel sorry he'd ever clapped eyes on me. To take from him and give nothing back. To make him love me and break his heart. Instead of destroying everything in its path, my inner tornado could simply destroy a person, and that person, I decided, would be Steon.

I began by giving him studied looks and come-to-bed eyes. He looked startled but not yet enthralled. I didn't want to stoop so low as to smile at him, but I started brushing against him at every chance I had, drifting into his personal space while seemingly ignoring him.

He certainly paid me attention, but in a watchful, careful way, which was far from the loss of control I had been working towards. He kept his distances warily. Not once did he drop his guard. This started to feel like fun and distracted me from my raging anger.

He still spent time at the Watch Tower, taking random shifts there. During his guard dog missions, he was unavailable to me, and my frustration redoubled. I waited impatiently for his return, planning some sly underhand action I hoped would hook him onto my line.

When he was there, I didn't self-combust; I could direct my fire outwards, and it was a relief. I pelted him with angry looks and dismissive or disparaging comments. I tried to put him down with every single one of my actions, and he still wouldn't bend or surrender. He bore everything evenly and seemed entirely unaffected.

It came to the point that frustration at his absence and indifference became the foremost emotion I felt. I became obsessed with him and could scarcely breathe when he wasn't there.

Within a few days, I couldn't wait any more; I followed him into the forest as he went foraging. The rain had started, and the ground was nothing but thawing mud.

I pushed him against a tree and grabbed him through his trousers. He was immediately hard, and I felt beautiful victory was at hand. I tore his belt off and opened his shirt. He was now sufficiently riled that he took charge. He bent me against the tree, my cheek on the rough bark, and lifted my dress. A wave of intense relief came over me. The world righted itself. He gripped my hip with one hand and with the other held the back of my neck. I felt my excitement building.

Then he pulled away unexpectedly and said in an angry voice, 'What are you doing, you crazy woman? You're gushing blood! Why are you doing this?'

'What? A big strong Guardian's scared of a little blood?' I mocked.

'Enough,' he growled and he walked away, readjusting his trousers.

'Steon!' I called, but he did not turn around and kept

walking. I watched as the rain ran down his back. The mud sent splashes onto his legs with every step.

The tornado, which now had nowhere else to go, hit me with its full force. I was no longer in control of my actions. I punched the tree with all my strength, and the pain helped. I started yelling at the top of my voice, stomping in the sodden ground.

Feeling Steon's absence like a gaping hole in my gut, I tried to catch up with him despite the sheets of rain blinding me, and I realised I had once again strayed so far off the path that I did not know which way to go.

Fury overwhelmed me, I wanted to kill and destroy. After the gut-wrenching loss of my sacrificial victim, I settled for destroying myself. I chose the widest tree in sight and ran at full speed head first into its trunk.

The world went dark and peaceful at last.

25

S teon

I was angry with myself for letting Sili get into my head and into my trousers. I had vowed to myself I would keep away from her.

Being inside her was the most powerful sensation, but it was all wrong. She was too full of twisted feelings and tortured emotions. Nowhere close to simple.

The way she'd tried to mock me and undermine my manhood smelt of her desperation. Sili was in a tremendous amount of pain, and we needed to do something about it before she harmed someone. Or herself.

As soon as I thought these words, everything fell into place. Sili's next move would be to hurt herself. It was obvious. How could I have not seen it?

I retraced my steps in the pouring rain. I called her. No answer. She wasn't where I'd left her, skirts trussed up and rump exposed. I felt guilty about that now. I could have been more respectful about turning her down. I could have been kind. Again, it was clear that Sili wasn't bringing out my better side—nor I hers, assuming she even had one.

I looked around the bushes for a minute or two, still calling for her. She was probably stomping back towards the Orchard, rage in her heart. Despite my best efforts, my fears couldn't be stilled, and I kept looking.

I found her eventually, passed out in the ferns, her face covered in blood and her wet hair forming a dark spiderweb around her head. My immediate thought was that she was dead, and panic rose in my throat. On closer inspection, I found that she was breathing faintly. She had a deep gash in her forehead where bits of bark still clung.

I wondered whether she'd walked into a tree by mistake, but it was broad daylight, and in my heart I knew she'd run straight into it on purpose. I didn't dare move her with such an obvious head injury, so I covered her with my travelling cloak and ran back to the Orchard to fetch Aalma.

When we returned to the place where I'd left Sili unconscious, she was no longer there. My cloak was on the ground, and the collar red with blood.

Aalma and I called and called and searched the woods, but Sili didn't call back and remained untraceable.

'How far can she walk with a head wound like this?' I asked Aalma.

'The mere fact she came round and is able to walk more than a few steps is a good sign. The forehead, and particularly the brow, will bleed profusely for relatively little damage.'

'Her woman's parts were bleeding as well.'

'How do you know?' Aalma started, but quickly stopped herself. 'Oh Steon,' she said, like a disappointed mother, and I felt thoroughly ashamed of myself. 'Enough to bleed out?' she enquired after a pause.

'I'm not sure. Between that and her face, enough to feel disoriented, especially after knocking herself out.'

'I should have taken better care of her,' lamented Aalma. 'Bereaved mothers react in so many different ways. Her stoicism shouldn't have fooled me.'

'She's a tricky one,' I said to console Aalma.

'But she's one of us now,' she concluded.

'We've all failed her,' I said.

Aalma and I fanned out to cover more ground, and I cursed myself that I hadn't brought more people with me. What a useless Guardian I was proving to be. Raiders trying to break in, a woman self-destructing in front of me, and I was always on the back foot, always late.

I beat the wet ferns and the mountain laurels for any sign of Sili, but my search remained fruitless.

Then out of the silence, the call of the night owl rang out. As it was still daylight, I understood Aalma was trying to get my attention, and I followed the sound through the tangled undergrowth. Soon I reached a clearing just by the edge of a dark stone cliff that separated the greenwoods from the flank of the mountain. It was shiny with rainwater and dotted with furry patches of light green moss. The air smelt like rotting leaves and sodden earth.

Abruptly, the rain stopped, and the birds resumed their busy twittering.

I should have guessed Sili would try to hurt herself again.

Drenched by the heavy rain, with her hair like a dark river, she was standing ram-rod straight by the cliff edge. The Cliff separated two mountains that formed the Territory with a sheer drop of three-thousand feet—and certain death at the bottom.

One look at Aalma and our plan was took shape. She called and approached from the west. I sneaked round from the east.

Still and calm, Sili appeared not to have heard Aalma at all. I needed her to notice Aalma and turn towards her if I was to catch her before she lost her mind and jumped.

Aalma came into view calling softly, 'Sili, dearest, it's only me, Aalma. I want to talk to you, just talk.' Her voice was steady and soothing, and it went a long way to calming my own nerves. Yet Sili didn't turn around to look at her and only stared ahead.

Aalma did the right thing: she stopped close enough to Sili, but out of her sight so that she would have to turn her back to me to look at Aalma. Sili still stood frozen and unresponsive.

'Sili, Vona's death wasn't your fault, darling,' started Aalma again.

I frowned: gentleness and kindness wouldn't break through Sili's walls. Only violent emotions could make a dent. Telling her she was responsible, and that her daughter had died because she'd wished her dead would have got her attention better than any soothing words. It was a risky strategy though, and she may just as well have jumped as engaged in conversation.

Aalma waved her hands in Sili's direction. No response. So Aalma gasped in a convincing imitation of surprise, and fortunately Sili fell for that. She turned away just a fraction, and I was able to tackle her to the ground.

Aalma joined us in seconds. She opened a small earthen jar and poured liquid into Sili's mouth while I kept her jaws open. Sili tried to spit, but the fight had gone out of her. Fighting my way through a tangle of unbraided hair, I was able to hold her mouth shut until she had no choice but to swallow.

I kept her pinned down until she relaxed under my weight. I started to pull myself upright, but just as I got to my knees, she tried to make a run for it.

'It doesn't act that fast!' Aalma warned me too late. Sili only managed a few unsteady steps before I caught her again and threw her roughly on my shoulder.

As we walked back to our camp, her body went limp. She weighed nothing. It reminded me of carrying Efalaa home through the forest as Morgunn and I scrambled up the incline by the light of a single torch.

We returned to the Orchard, soaked and caked in mud, with Sili still fast asleep down my back. Aalma took her into her house, and Vidris went to make herself a bed in Veiti's hut. Efalaa gathered some dry clothing for the three of us while Aalma checked and cleaned Sili's wounds.

Once Sili was warm and comfortable, we ate around the fire. Aalma and I didn't reveal the full story of the afternoon's events, but we informed the Clan that Sili, maddened by her grief, had tried to harm herself.

Veiti was in tears, and Leodurr looked sad and shocked. Efalaa bit her bottom lip. Morgunn stood and spoke.

'Many in the Clan have had to deal with the sorrow and guilt of losing a child,' he started. 'This ordeal came for Sili at a time when she was already weakened by the loss of her father and of her home and the abuse she had suffered at the hands of the Raiders. No matter how brave and strong she is, we've all failed Sili by not taking the full measure of her trauma and distress.'

Around the fire there were nods and murmurs of agreement.

'But no one ever tried to kill themselves over it, did they?' argued Vidris.

'We know our lives belong to the Clan, they are not ours to end. Outsiders are different,' replied Morgunn. 'We need to do better by Sili now,' he continued. 'She is our guest, and we must support her just as well as we support each other.'

'What can we do?' asked Leodurr.

'She needs rest and probably sedation for a few days,' said Aalma. 'Her body needs to recover before her mind can. After that, she will need constant supervision and some simple chores to keep her occupied.'

'She needs to forgive herself,' I added.

No one spoke after that. We ate our acorn cakes and white cheese with a beetroot soup that reminded me of blood. Aalma stirred lashings of wild honey into our sage tea to help us over the shock of Sili's attempted suicide, but the mood around the fire remained heavy.

The clothes Aalma, Sili and I had worn were still wet despite hours of drying by the fire. Leodurr and I hung them in the main hut to keep them out of any further rain. The smell of the forest still clung to the fabric, bringing back memories of Sili's distress and of her body around mine.

Even the flashing images of her bloody face and limp body were not enough to curb the hunger I felt for her. I knew that what had happened between us wasn't about sex. It was about power and desperation. It was Sili's last call for help before bashing her head against a tree. I wondered why she hadn't gone to Efalaa or Aalma for help.

Most of all, I wondered who Sili was underneath the layers of trauma. Was there a shy, kind, brave girl like the one who'd hidden behind Efalaa's cold exterior? I didn't think so.

Sili was all fire. Proud, angry, spiteful or cruel, she always burnt bright. Her love would be as scorching and dangerous as a naked flame. I started to doubt I could stay away from her.

26

S teon

Sili was still in her enforced sleep when the Raiders' reinforcements arrived from the east in a long unbroken line that stretched from the horizon.

'They look like ants,' said Morgunn as we flew over the Lowlands watching their progress from the air. 'How many do you think?'

'Two hundred maybe?'

'Plus a hundred already camped within shooting distance of the Hedge...'

'If you count only those of us who have been trained to fight, we are outnumbered a hundred to one.'

'So Master Guardian, what can we do? We can't defend the Hedge against three hundred men. Eventually they will hack their way through it.'

'We hit them from the air with anything we can think of.

Rocks, arrows, manure, scorpions, anything. Day and night, relentlessly, until they leave.'

Morgunn didn't think much of my strategy, but neither of us could think of anything else to do. Neither his training nor mine had included battle plans against hundreds of armed men.

We met the others back at the Orchard. They were already sitting down for lunch, a thin bone broth with winter nettles and melted butter. It was hot if not filling. The weather had been cold for so long now that Leodurr could no longer grow anything in the fields or in the vegetable patch. We were relying on Veiti and the Hunters to feed us, and we kept whatever meat was available for our dinner.

Morgunn had no choice but to tell the Clan the Territory was again under attack. They took the news calmly. It didn't come as a surprise.

'If they think this is a siege, the Raiders are mistaken,' Morgunn said. 'We have control of the air and all the food we need right here. Whoever leads them has to feed three hundred men three times a day, and we all know how little there is to hunt or forage on the Lowlands.'

Efalaa, Morgunn and I set off soon after that with our leather slingshots and bagfuls of sharp rocks. We picked their men out one by one until the birds were too tired to fly. The Hunters' aim was deadly accurate, and I did better than I expected. We left perhaps forty men injured.

Our opponents adopted the only defence they could. Most hid in the tents and those who couldn't force their way under the canvas sat on the ground in circles with their shields above their heads.

In between our volleys of stones, they shot arrows at us. The birds avoided them easily by gaining altitude and the shafts fell back on the ground, useless.

As night fell, their numbers were not significantly diminished, and our stones were too small to go through wood or canvas. Our hard work inconvenienced them as little as a heavy hailstorm.

Frustrated with our lack of progress, we returned to the Orchard.

Sili was too dazed to help us but the seven of us sat up by the campfire and whittled arrows through the night. We dispensed with the fletching and hardened the tips over the coals. By dawn, we had produced more than a hundred arrows. They were primitive but the Hunters insisted they were useable.

Efalaa, Morgunn and I slept for a few hours before resuming our campaign against the Raiders' camp.

We found that our arrows, no matter how hastily made, did pierce the canvas and caused enough damage inside to bring many of the men out into the open. I targeted the tents while Morgunn and Efalaa's perfect aim brought down those foolish enough to step outside.

Eventually though we ran out of arrows and had no choice but to fly back to the Orchard. We spent the rest of the day raiding the wood stock for any stick long, light and sturdy enough to be turned into a shaft. We cut, sliced, peeled and whittled until our fingers bled.

There was a feeling of disappointment around the fire that evening. Soon we would run out of wood dry enough to fashion and shape. No one mentioned it, but we all knew it. What we knew also was that while we made and shot arrows, we were not hunting or foraging, and the foodstore looked more and more bare.

Morgunn sent Vidris to the Watch Tower with instructions to fly over the Raiders' camp at midnight and at first light. The poor girl left with a travelling cloak, her only comfort through what promised to be a long, cold watch. Aalma fed and watered the birds in her place.

The rest of us sat around the fire, but no songs were sung that night. I went to bed early. Erlen used to say 'When all else fails, sleep,' and I followed his advice.

I flew out at first light to check the perimeter of our Territory. I found nothing but chilly winds from the north and dark clouds bringing a storm.

Breakfast was being served when I returned to the Orchard, and Sili stepped out of Aalma's hut supported by Leodurr. She looked gaunt and frail, and a large bruise stretched across her forehead and into her hairline. The wound would leave a scar.

After a few steps, Leodurr realised she couldn't walk, and he carried her to the seat closest to the fire. His kindness was rewarded with the ghost of smile and a pat on the arm.

Sili's hands shook so much she struggled to feed herself. I thought about helping her but decided to stay out of it. I was sure any offer of assistance would only earn me an angry outburst. Aalma was looking at Sili's struggle too and made the same decision as me.

Vidris arrived as Leodurr and I were clearing away the breakfast things. Efalaa was in her undergarments, knee-deep in the stream despite the bracing cold, bravely washing off the grime of the previous day. I was about to join her; there was no time to warm water for a bath.

'Nothing to report, Chief,' said Vidris, sounding like a Guardian's Apprentice. 'When I left they were having break-fast. They don't look like they're going anywhere.'

I was unsurprised, but there were a few anxious murmurs. Morgunn squared his shoulders, and said, 'As long as they do not breach our defences, they're harmless. They can breakfast all they like, we will just carry on with our lives.'

'Why are they even here?' asked Efalaa. 'That's what I don't understand. What do they want from us?'

'Efalaa is right,' said Aalma. 'What have we got that they may want? We have no riches of any kind...'

'Beautiful women are valuable in the Wastelands,' Leodurr said.

The women looked at each other with a mix of incredulity and fear until Sili broke the silence.

'That's not what keeps them here.'

'What do you mean?' asked Morgunn sharply.

'They can get women anywhere. They have seen your birds and what you can do with them. That's what they want, and they're not leaving without them.'

Gasps and shocked exclamations filled the air. Everyone talked at once.

Morgunn was quick to recover control of the situation. 'Quiet.'

In the eerie silence that replaced the noise, his voice seemed too loud.

'How do they propose to get them?' he asked. 'Our defences are impregnable.'

'They're only thick bushes,' said Sili dismissively to the shock of her audience.

The fear I saw in the assembled faces prompted me to intervene.

'The Hedge has never been breached,' I said firmly.

'There is a first time for everything,' replied Sili. She paused. She sounded too exhausted to talk. 'But that's not what they mean to do.'

'What, then?' shouted Morgunn, 'And how do you know so much about their plan?'

'I don't know anything, I'm just thinking about it from their point of view.'

'So what are they thinking?' interrupted Efalaa.

'What's happened so far can mean only one thing. They have something you want,' said Sili.

'They have nothing we want!' Vidris said. 'Nothing that would make us give away our birds. And as Steon said, the defences have never been breached.'

'What's happened so far means only one thing,' declared Morgunn, 'That they are used to attacking settlements and taking what they want. It's their way of life. They are doing the only thing they know. When they realise that they cannot take from us, they will leave to attack a weaker prey.'

'Chief, may I speak?' I said.

'Yes, Steon, you may.'

'Chief, Erlen used to say "Know your enemy". It would be helpful if Sili could put names to some of the Raider leaders' faces.'

'Sili's seen enough of those Raiders. Don't make her do that,' interrupted Efalaa.

'Efalaa, and Vidris too, if you speak again without asking, I will send you away.' Morgunn scolded. 'Sili may be in the habit of speaking without permission, but we do not have to adopt the lesser ways of the Wastelands folk.'

Chastened, the two girls closed their mouths.

'I'm not from the Wastelands,' said Sili as if to herself.

'What would this achieve?' Morgunn asked me, returning to our previous conversation.

'If we know who leads this particular group, Sili may be able to tell us about his character, and we may be able to anticipate their decisions or understand their motivations.'

'Organise it. Sili, you will fly with Steon over the Raiders' camp and see whether you recognise anyone.'

'Sili is terrified of flying,' objected Efalaa.

Sili was silent for a long moment, and I became concerned she would refuse. If she defied Morgunn yet again, I didn't like to think about what he would do. She must have calculated the same and nodded her begrudging obedience.

'For the Clan,' said Morgunn.

'For the Clan,' came the usual reply, but voices and faces were anxious. We needed some good news soon.

Vidris took Frid out of the birds' shed and harnessed him. I checked my weapons.

Sili, still supported by Leodurr, approached Frid and me with a stony face. She was wearing leather trousers that were too big for her and the cuffs of her shirt were covering her hands. She looked like a little girl wearing her mother's clothes.

I took some of the binds that were keeping my braids together and fashioned some arm straps for her. I was able to criss cross the leather several times before running out of length. She watched me carefully but said nothing.

'I know you don't like flying, but you'll be safe with Frid and me.'

'No use talking about it, let's get it over with,' she replied, impassive.

I straddled Frid then pulled her up.

'Do you want to be at the front or the back?' I asked. I was surprised to feel her shaking like a leaf, because her face betrayed no fear, only mild boredom.

'Front,' She replied. 'I won't see a thing otherwise.'

I settled her between me and Frid's neck. I could have rested my chin on top of her head, but I made sure I was touching her as little as possible. Her loose hair tickled my neck.

'You don't have stirrups. Rest your feet on my shins.'

'Great,' she said dejectedly.

As we took off, I heard her sharp intake of breath, and I held her tighter than I would otherwise have done.

27

Sili

Taking off was the worst part of flying. It was no more terrifying than landing, but the latter signalled the end of the ordeal rather than its beginning.

Steon's hold was so tight I could hardly breathe. Despite the discomfort of being pressed so close to him, it made the whole experience slightly less traumatic.

Every few seconds, the reality of my situation and the distance between me and the ground would hit me afresh, and it was all I could do to bite down my terror.

We were flying over the Hedge when I became so light-headed I feared I would faint. I could not stop a whimper of fear.

'I know you're scared, but you're in no danger,' said Steon behind me.

'Words make no difference,' I replied.

'I know,' he said. 'Makes a difference to me to tell you.'

'Does it bother you that I'm scared?'

'Very much.'

'You don't like scaring people, do you?'

'I hate it.'

'I'd noticed that about you.'

'I know you have. Even tried to use it against me, didn't you?'

'Yes, I did,' I couldn't help chuckling.

This made me feel so much better I was able to look down at the camp, and scan the faces and the clothing of the men below. They looked up at us. They could see us as well as we could see them. One of them shook his fist at us and shouted, 'Whore!'

'Most of them are from the camp where I was held,' I said, a shiver running down my spine.

'Can you see who's leading them?'

'Not yet, let's keep circling. These are foot soldiers, they will eventually call their masters.'

As predicted, a man came out of the central tent, covered in shiny armour and flanked by two bodyguards and two officers. I recognised him immediately, and my stomach clenched.

'That's Torston,' I said. 'We're all as good as dead.'

'What? Because of this man?' Steon scoffed. 'He doesn't look that menacing. How can he even stand with all that metal hanging off him?'

'He leads hundreds of Raiders. He's a very powerful man,' I retorted.

His presence in this temporary camp indicated a large scale military operation. Whatever they wanted, they wanted very badly.

'Where is their food?' asked Steon.

'They keep it in the main tent.'

'I can't see any women.'

'They're here on business, not for fun.'

'Maggots,' said Steon through his teeth. 'Have you seen enough?'

'Oh yes.'

'I'll take you home.'

'It's your home, not mine.'

'Nonsense,' he said. 'It's your home too now.'

We veered right, Frid leaning precariously into nothingness. Steon pushed my weight left along with his, to compensate for the bird's movement. It was one thing to straddle a bird in flight, but this was beyond what I could take. I started screaming, and despite Steon's insistent shushing, I couldn't stop.

Eventually, he covered my eyes with his gloved hand until I was able to control myself enough to replace the full-throated screams with pitiful whimpers.

'We're just going over the Hedge now,' he said. 'Nearly there.'

My stomach threatened to empty itself when we started losing altitude, but the anticipation of the solid ground under my feet helped me through the descent. I clamped my mouth and swallowed my fear in silence.

We landed neatly just outside the Orchard Camp.

Steon glided off Frid's back and presented his arms for me to jump into. My fear had curbed my pride, and I would have had no qualms about accepting his help, but I found I simply couldn't move. I stared at him wide-eyed, unable to even form a word.

He sighed, then pulled me off the bird by my clothes and deposited me feet first on the ground. I thought my knees might give way, but by sheer willpower I was able to stand unaided.

The others quickly gathered around us, and Efalaa put her arm around my waist.

'Did you see anyone?' she asked, breathless.

'Torston is there,' I replied through clenched teeth.

She gasped. 'Anyone else?'

'Garrod and Jeb, his usual lieutenants.'

Leodurr placed between my hands a scalding mug of sage tea. I drank a few careful sips, relishing the hot liquid's sweetness, a rare treat that loosened my tongue.

'Most of the men are from the camp where we were kept,' I continued. 'They're loyal to Torston – or at least scared of him – and they're used to fighting. The others must have been recently drafted: they weren't wearing any armour. Some poor village boys newly recruited at the tip of a blade. No doubt they'll be on the front line.'

Morgunn took this information in his stride. 'No need to change our strategy. We watch them; if they attack the Hedge, we push them back. Otherwise, we go about our business. We still need to eat.'

'What if they settle here long term?' asked Veiti.

'What is there for them except a steppe exposed to the winds?' argued Morgunn.

'The River Mouth is not that bad a place to stay,' replied Efalaa. 'They have fresh water, and fish.'

'We could poison their water,' I said.

All eyes turned to me.

'How?' asked Morgunn.

'The rot of animals will contaminate the water and make them ill.'

'It will make us ill too if we're not careful,' objected Morgunn.

'Not if we hang the carcasses off the top of the Waterfalls,' I explained.

'Will that be enough to kill them?'

'Some of them may die; most of them would be weakened.'

'Good, do that,' he ordered. 'Take Steon with you.'

'I can't fly again.'

'Yes, you can,' said Morgunn.

'It can't be today,' interrupted Efalaa, rushing to my defence. 'We need to kill a couple of animals and let the meat spoil first. Sili and I will take care of it in a couple of days.'

I nodded, and Morgunn let my small rebellion pass.

'Setting fire to their tents will also make them reassess their situation,' Steon contributed.

'Very well, you and Efalaa will set fire to their camp tonight as soon as there are enough men in the tents.'

'Sili said the food was kept in there,' added Steon.

'Big mistake,' said Morgunn, and he winked, and just like that, the tension dissipated, and smiles returned to the assembled faces. He had given us our courage back.

Morgunn was not the same kind of leader that my father had been, but I couldn't imagine any of us ever slitting his throat.

For the next three days, the bird riders set fire to the Raiders' tents every night at different times. The men below kept soaking the heavy fabric, but with the help of some sheep fat, Steon and Efalaa never failed to set fire to something or someone.

This must have shown the Raiders they were vulnerable and their lives in our hands. The others kept expecting them to pack up their camp and leave. I knew better. Men like Torston do not back out nor accept defeat, once their minds are set on a goal.

In the Orchard, frustration was mounting.

'Why don't we just kill them all?' asked Vidris at assembly one night. This was a reasonable question I had refrained from asking myself.

'Most of these men have no choice but to remain where they are. I'm sure that they would rather return home than be slowly poisoned all day and be shot at all night with flaming arrows,' Aalma said quietly.

'They have no such scruples when they attack defenceless settlements and kill everything they cannot carry,' I reminded them.

'We are not killers,' said Morgunn simply. 'We defend ourselves, that's all.'

Efalaa and I exchanged a swift look. I remembered how she'd executed the man who'd chased her into the woods, and she remembered how I had sliced Tungol's artery in front of her. I caught Steon staring at us.

The following morning, Steon came back from his reconnaissance flight saying that three men were standing between the Raiders' camp and the Hedge with a white flag.

'Ah, finally,' said Morgunn gleefully. 'Let's go hear what they have to say.'

'Don't,' I said before I could stop myself.

'Why?' Morgunn asked, half-irked, half-intrigued.

'What could they possibly have to say to you?' I argued. 'Nothing that you'd want to hear. They'll only try to bargain with you.'

'They have nothing we want. We only want them gone.'

'Why do they want to talk to you then? They're not going to say "sorry to have bothered you, we'll order the retreat now", are they?'

Efalaa laid her hand on Morgunn's arm, as if to recommend patience.

'Maybe they want a ceasefire while they pack their things?' proposed Vidris.

Steon looked dubious but kept his opinion to himself.

Morgunn took Efalaa's hand off his arm gently.

'Don't worry, sweetling,' he said to her, 'we'll just listen to what they have to say.'

Then he turned to the rest of us. 'Steon, saddle up. Vidris and Efalaa, you will cover us from the air. Stock up on arrows and stones.'

They all obeyed. What a mistake they were making.

❧ 28 ❧

S teon

Morgunn, the girls and I equipped ourselves with the armour we'd taken from the first group of Raiders.

Efalaa crinkled her nose at the leather breastplate that Morgunn was fastening around her. 'It still smells of them,' she said, and Morgunn turned pale.

'Better with than without,' he nevertheless argued.

'What's the plan?' asked Vidris.

'You two will cover us from the sky,' Morgunn said to the women.

'Why?' questioned Efalaa.

'They might try to capture you,' I answered in Morgunn's place.

Vidris frowned, but did not dwell on my words.

'I don't trust Frid,' she said to me instead. 'He's still traumatised. If he gets frightened while you're on the ground, he might try to fly home and leave you behind.'

'Really?' I couldn't imagine a Guardian's bird to be easily unnerved.

'It's not worth the risk. Why don't you ride Mila?' offered Efalaa. 'She won't leave until I tell her to.'

'Yes, that's best,' decided Vidris, already behaving like the Keeper she would become.

'Long life,' said Morgunn to the three of us.

'Long life, Chief' we all replied, and we took off to shouts of 'For the Clan' from those left on the ground. We flew over the wintry forest still white with morning frost. The morning was so beautiful, the air so crisp and fresh I was tempted to rally to Morgunn's optimistic view that the Raiders would be leaving soon.

As we came into sight of their camp, there was a flurry of activity among the men below that raised an alarm in my mind. They moved together in a well-rehearsed sequence. They'd been preparing for our arrival. My optimism disappeared.

'Be careful,' I shouted to Morgunn and the girls. 'Make no mistake, we're in danger.'

'Be on your guard,' he answered, and Efalaa and Vidris's faces took on the same fierce look Isveg and Saaria would have worn in their place. I was the only Guardian here but not the only fighter I thought with a pride tinged with sadness.

Torston, easily recognisable by the heavy jewellery he was wearing, appeared out of his tent.

Morgunn signalled for us two to land a few paces from the three men with the white flag who were our welcome party. We sent Eko and Mila to safety high in the air with the girls.

Morgunn drew out his long knife and I unsheathed my dagger. Efalaa nocked her arrow.

The men in front of us appeared unarmed, but we knew they had archers inside their camp, and I was ready to bet they'd calculated their position so that we would be within shooting range.

Torston arrived on horseback, flanked by four uniformed bodyguards.

He was surprisingly young and fresh faced. He couldn't have looked more different from the scraggy, hairy, unkempt bunch that were his foot soldiers.

He smiled at us warmly.

'Ah, the fabled Skyriders,' he said pleasantly, breaking the eerie silence. 'Welcome, welcome. I am glad you decided to come.'

He dismounted from his beautiful chestnut horse unhurriedly. Then, turning towards us, he put his hand over his heart and bowed.

'Please call me Torston,' he said in a voice that sounded like singing.

Morgunn took one step forward, and I followed him, careful to stand just behind his shoulder. He was an inexperienced leader, but by no means a weak man. The way he held himself, steady and calm, made me proud.

'What are you doing here?' He said to Torston with narrowed eyes.

'Oh, let's not rush anything,' replied Torston placatingly. 'First, I beg you to forgive me, but I didn't hear your name,' he said, cupping a hand to his ear. His face wore a grin that could have passed for a smile.

Morgunn clenched his jaw, and for a moment I thought he wouldn't answer. 'I'm Morgunn Ulfborn,' he said flatly.

'Are you the leader of the Skyriders?'

'Yes.'

'Very good, very good,' smiled Torston. 'How pleasant to meet you.'

I could not help but be intrigued by this man and his strange manners. His every word and expression seemed calculated. He was silent for a moment, and his demeanour changed.

'Do you think you are better than me, Morgunn Ulfborn?' His tone was now as frosty as the ground. There was a collective holding of breath. Morgunn stared but said nothing.

'Do you think you are better than me?' Torston repeated louder. Behind him, his stony-faced guards did not move a muscle. 'Is it because you have a big man behind you?' he insisted. 'Is that why you think you are better than me?'

'I don't steal from people and I don't rape women,' answered Morgunn finally, 'so yes, I think I am a better man than you.'

Torston smiled again, but his eyes were cold. 'If one is to believe every single rumour spreading through the Wastelands, then you are a baby murderer.'

'What?' said Morgunn in astonishment.

'Yes, you, mighty Chief of the Skyriders. You,' mocked Torston. 'Everyone knows why there are so few of you, you kill the babies that you don't want.' He turned towards the small crowd at his back. 'Am I speaking the truth, you all?'

'Yes,' came the reply. 'Murderer! Baby murderer! Monsters!'

'What do you want from us?' asked Morgunn over the noise.

Torston shushed his men, with a finger over his lips like a playful child. They immediately obeyed, and the silence thickened.

Morgunn stood, his face expressionless, waiting for Torston to speak.

'We want some of the beautiful things you have, don't we, my friends?' he replied finally. He winked at the men behind him.

'Yes,' they answered with one voice.

'And you're here to take them?' asked Morgunn.

'Do not believe every lie you hear, Morgunn Ulfborn. We are not Raiders but traders. We want to trade with you, barter, whatever you will call it. We are not as uncivilised as you think. We are not common thieves. We even have brought gifts for you as a token of goodwill.'

Morgunn didn't react.

Torston turned to a scared young man on his left. 'You, prepare the presents for our kind hosts.'

The tension in the air was palpable.

'Please accompany me to my tent, young Morgunn Ulfborn. I would like to offer you some refreshments. I have ale fit for a king such as yourself.'

'No,' said Morgunn.

'Bring your bodyguard if that would make you feel safer,' Torston shot back with a hint of mockery that was lost on no one.

'I'm not afraid of you,' countered Morgunn.

'So are you afraid of my ale?'

A snigger ran through the crowd of Raiders behind Torston.

'I don't drink with rapists.'

'No reason not to drink with me then.' Torston said pleasantly. 'When a man offers you a drink in good faith, young chief, you have to accept it. Or maybe your father hasn't had time to teach you proper manners.'

Morgunn flinched. My heart sank a little, and Torston gave us a wolfish smile.

'Oh, forgive me. I see I caused you hurt. Would it be that you have been recently bereaved?'

Morgunn remained silent. Torston looked pleased with his little victory over the Chief, but he changed the subject.

'Those birds are truly beautiful,' he said, looking up and

shielding his eyes against the sun. 'Magnificent animals. May I touch them?'

'No'

'Don't worry, young Chief, I don't suppose they will fit in my pocket.' That got a strained laugh from his men. 'Where did you acquire them?'

'Over the sea.'

'Oh, I see you like a joke, Morgunn Ulfborn,' replied Torston with a cold laugh. 'But you do not fool me. I know that you breed these beauties. I know that!' He laughed – merrily now – looking around at his men who hurried to laugh with him. 'Where are those gifts? I'm getting older here,' he added comically, but no one laughed this time, not even the men standing around him.

The servant eventually returned with an armful of objects wrapped in cloth, and a veiled captive, small enough to be a woman or a girl. Torston took the parcels and casually punched the back of the boy's head. Then he unwrapped the first item which turned out to be an ornate metal cup, engraved with crosses.

'Please accept this gift, Morgunn Ulfborn as a token of my friendship.'

He held the cup within reach of Morgunn. When Morgunn didn't take it, Torston tutted.

'Manners, young man... this is getting awkward.'

This got an increasingly forced laugh from his followers.

Morgunn obviously didn't know whether to accept or refuse. I feared he would look at me, and weaken his position. I breathed a sigh of relief when he held out his hand, but Torston put the cup into Morgunn's palm only to pull it away again with a girlish giggle.

When his fingers closed around nothing, Morgunn's face turned angry for the first time.

'Only joking,' chortled Torston, and he put one knee to

the ground to present the cup again to Morgunn from that position. I'd never seen such an arrogant display of humility. Morgunn grabbed the object quickly.

As he pulled himself up to his feet, Torston said conspiratorially, 'Now it's your turn to offer me something. That's the way it works.'

'Is that so?' said Morgunn with feigned interest. 'I thought you burnt people's fences, marched into their villages and took whatever you liked. I thought *that* was the way it worked. Obviously something else my father omitted to teach me.'

'How remiss of him,' replied Torston, studying Morgunn with one eye closed.

'I have nothing to give you,' Morgunn declared.

Torston clucked his disapproval. 'Looking at these lovely animals above you, I would say that's not entirely true.'

For the first time, Morgunn met Torston's eye. Without a word, he held out the cup and dropped it at Torston's feet. There was a ripple of fear in the Raiders ranks.

'You do not like my gift, young Morgunn? I am surprised. Many men died defending it. I myself find it most beautiful.'

Morgunn started turning on his heels.

'Not so fast, my friend,' interrupted Torston. 'I still have a present you may like.' He clicked his fingers, and two men brought the prisoner forward before lifting the hood that covered her head.

She was a dark-haired woman with a round face, dirty and scared.

'This is Kasha. Some of your group who were guests of mine for a time might remember her.' He looked up at the women flying overhead. 'Kasha here will die tomorrow at noon, if you do not hand your birds over to me, Morgunn Ulfborn, Chief of the Skyriders.'

Morgunn stared at Torston, but didn't reply. I was relieved

he didn't look to Efalaa and even more relieved Efalaa made no sound that indicated her recognition of the captive.

Morgunn's silence stretched a second too long and started to sound like hesitation. I swallowed my discomfort. After a long pause, he spoke evenly.

'Lord Torston, we protect our own, but we care nothing for Outsiders. You have my answer.'

'Very well,' said Torston. 'Here is mine.'

He reached for Kasha and held her by the shoulders. He pulled out his gem-incrusted dagger, and in one fluid move that spoke of long years of blade practice, he cut her throat with a spectacular spray of blood.

The look of horror on her face froze me to the ground. Then she fell like a sack of potatoes, heavy and undignified. Her blood flowed freely from a wound so deep I could see her breathing tube. A bloody puddle spread outward towards us.

My stomach churned, but I succeeded in keeping my face expressionless.

Neither Morgunn nor I dared to look up at the women in the sky. I desperately wished I could have put my hand across our young Keeper's eyes. Little Vidris didn't need to see the horrors of the outside world yet. I had failed in my duty to her.

Without moving my head, I glanced sideways at Morgunn. He was engaged in a staring contest with Torston. His young face showed nothing but indifference and mild distaste.

'You must see, Lord Torston, that killing your own people inconveniences you more than it does me.'

Torston's eyes glinted, but he contained himself. When he spoke again, his tone was neutral. 'Tomorrow, at noon, I will kill another of your friends' acquaintances. A young girl by the name of Una.'

The pool of blood spreading outward across the frozen

ground had finally reached the tip of Morgunn's boots. He looked down in perfectly feigned disinterest and took one step backwards.

'Another such execution is unlikely to capture my interest.'

'I might well have another surprise for you,' said Torston in his studied sing-song voice.

'Are you planning on killing one of your horses, or maybe setting fire to your own camp?' said Morgunn mockingly.

'No, something much closer to your heart.'

In answer to this, Morgunn gestured at the distance between Torston and himself.

'This is a close as you will ever get to my heart, Lord Torston,' he said. 'You will not break our defences, and neither will you have our birds. Good day.'

I raised my dagger, ready to strike. Morgunn turned on his heels and gave a short two-tone whistle. Eko dropped to the ground like a stone and swooped him off back into the air. The manoeuvre had taken less time than a breath.

Even I was left open-mouthed. I had never seen a rider do that before, and I allowed myself to enjoy the look of undisguised awe on Torston's face.

I took advantage of the stunned silence to call Mila to me, fully aware I was unable to display the same birdmanship.

'You're the bigger man, yet you ride the smaller bird. If you ever fancy some respect, remember I can use a strong warrior like you,' said Torston, as I calmly climbed on Mila.

'And you ride no bird at all,' I riposted before taking flight.

Within seconds, I was in the air with Morgunn, in a frantic ascent that brought tears to my eyes.

I expected arrows to be shot at us, but none came. I supposed they didn't want to harm the birds they so coveted.

The four of us rode hard towards the Hedge, and as soon

as we passed it, Morgunn signalled for us to land by the Watch Tower.

I arrived last. Efalaa and Vidris had already dismounted. They were both pale and their rigid jaws told a long story. Morgunn rubbed his hands over his face several times.

'Torston is bound to see this Una girl is more useful alive than dead,' I started to reassure the women.

'Her life was never in our hands,' declared Morgunn.

Efalaa looked up at him. He set his face in a stubborn frown and avoided her gaze for a moment. Then he looked her in the eye and spoke with some ill-humour.

'He could have killed her anytime since he captured her. She's lucky to have survived that long.'

'Una helped me escape, and I left her behind.'

'Then that's on you,' interrupted Vidris angrily, 'not Morgunn.'

Efalaa flinched, and Morgunn gave Vidris a murderous look.

He laid a hand on Efalaa's shoulder, and she didn't shake it off. Either she could forgive him anything, or she was cleverer than I had given her credit for.

'Say we do attempt to rescue her; say we succeed,' said Morgunn. 'What happens next? Torston has camps full of innocent women and children he can slaughter on our doorstep, one after the other—toddlers, babies, pregnant women.'

Efalaa looked horrified and gazed at him with tears in her eyes. Vidris stared at her feet. It was too late to lead her away from the adult conversation. The earthquake had cut short her childhood, and the Raiders had taken her innocence. I took her under my arm and held her close. She started crying silently.

Morgunn continued to speak to Efalaa in a sensible voice.

'If we show him we care, he will kill more innocents than if we hold our nerve and don't give in to his blackmail.'

'What are the chances he will not kill Una?' asked Efalaa, looking from Morgunn to me.

I waited for Morgunn to reply.

'Better now we've shown strength and resolve,' he said after a moment.

'Still, I do not like her odds,' countered Efalaa. 'If we wanted to save her, how could we go about it?' she asked me.

'It isn't up to me, sweetheart,' I replied as gently as I could. 'It's the Chief's decision.'

'But if Morgunn asked you, could you think of a plan?' she insisted.

Morgunn raised his eyes to the sky, then jerked his chin at me in acquiescence.

'She will be under guard,' I started, 'probably inside a tent. We can't tell which one until we search them all. There are three large tents. That's three times the risk that the person looking for her will be captured and tortured until we give Torston our birds or they die, whichever comes first.'

Efalaa shivered. Morgunn put his arm across her shoulders.

'If we find her, we'll have to kill her guards, I'd say anything between one and four armed men. Then we would need to strap her on a bird or let her ride behind one of us. That's a three to four-Guardian operation with two or three pairs of feet on the ground and at least one bird landing and risking capture or death. This plan would require us to put the four of us in mortal danger, and at least three birds. If we failed, it would mean the end of four out of seven bloodlines and might well leave only one bird for the three survivors. This is my best plan, and failure would mean the end of the Clan.'

Efalaa swallowed and hugged herself pitifully. Morgunn,

who had stood so strong against Torston, now seemed about to cry.

However, it was my duty to continue. 'The only reason why we didn't get riddled with arrows today is that Torston was afraid to lose face if you girls retaliated by shooting at him. Next time we put a foot on the ground outside the Territory, he will kill us.'

❧ 29 ❧

S ili

After Efalaa left with the other riders, I performed my chores in a daze. I washed shirts in the leftover bath water and rinsed them in the stream. I was dimly aware my hands were frozen.

So many thoughts swirled inside my head, none clear enough to be put into words, but all with a distinctive flavour of heartache and self-loathing.

Aalma found me hanging the laundry. When she spoke, I realised I had been crying. She wiped my cheeks and sent me to rest in her hut until lunch. As I lay down under the furs, I had a vivid waking dream of falling off a bird into a cloudy void. My body jerked in terror, and I muffled a cry. Then the gaping hole Vona had left inside me swallowed the fear, and I could no longer feel anything but grief.

I was surprised I was still tired enough to fall asleep.

I woke up with a start to giant wings tearing the silence. Fear returned and grief retreated to the back of my mind. The sound was ominous because the riders never normally landed quite so close to the huts. Clutching my sleeping fur around myself, I rushed out to see what the matter was.

Efalaa, Morgunn, Steon and Vidris were climbing off the birds, their faces drained of blood.

'What happened?' asked Leodurr, his voice betraying our collective anxiety.

Morgunn looked ashen, and Efalaa seemed about to faint. Aalma rushed to her side, but Morgunn was quicker and steadied her with his arm around her waist.

Steon and Vidris took the birds to the shed together. He had his arm around her shoulders and was talking into her ear while she nodded sadly.

The rest of us stood around Morgunn and Efalaa, waiting for news.

'They want our birds. They killed a woman in front of us,' started Morgunn.

'It was Kasha,' added Efalaa in a strangled voice.

'Kasha?' I exclaimed. 'Our Kasha?'

Efalaa gave the slightest nod.

'That's not possible!' I cried. 'They didn't have women with them.'

'They had her. As a hostage,' answered Efalaa.

'They must have kept her hidden on purpose,' said Morgunn. 'Until it was time to blackmail us with her life.'

I managed to swallow my shock long enough to hear the rest of it.

'They've strung her up on the outer side of the Hedge,' Efalaa choked out. 'Torston said Una was next.'

'Una's there too?' I cried before biting my lips.

'We were lucky to escape with our lives,' concluded Morgunn.

'Who's Una?' asked Veiti.

'My friend,' I said simply, and I realised she was that. My friend. My poor friend.

'She helped us escape,' added Efalaa.

'Can't we go and rescue her?' asked Aalma.

'She's as good as dead,' cried Veiti, speaking for us all.

'I can't leave her,' sobbed Efalaa. 'Not her. Not again.'

The wind blew a lone snowflake onto her face where it melted immediately, leaving a wet mark among her tears. Morgunn watched her with a tortured expression.

'There's nothing we can do, sweetling,' he said eventually. 'We can't take on an army on foot.'

Of course, he was right. Even I knew it.

'We can do a low fly-by and swoop her up...' Efalaa tried.

'They'll shoot the birds,' said Morgunn.

Leodurr nodded in agreement.

'We can throw her a rope,' insisted Efalaa now clutching at straws.

One minute, my mind was racing; the next, my thoughts became very clear.

I reached out and touched Efalaa's arm lightly. She caught my eye and opened her mouth to speak before snapping it shut: she'd got my silent message.

I wrapped my arm around her shoulders and led her away as if to comfort her. Morgunn stared unhappily as we walked past him but did not intervene. He probably thought me so cold-hearted that I would try to dissuade Efalaa from helping Una out of self-preservation.

The situation had obviously caused a rift between them. He would not risk his precious Efalaa or the lives of his birds for an unknown girl from the Wastelands. I could see his point of view, and in his shoes, I would have done the same. But I wasn't in his shoes, and it was Una who had wiped the blood flowing from my violated insides once the Raiders were done with me the first time. She'd been kind and sympathetic, a ray of light in my darkest place.

She'd helped Efalaa and me escape, and I knew how Efalaa felt about having left her behind. I knew because I felt the same. I'd lost Vona, I had to accept Kasha too was gone, but I would not let Una die without a fight.

Efalaa and I walked to the edge of the greenwood, our cloaks tight around us against the intense cold. Once out of earshot, we wasted no time in idle conversation.

'The rope could work, but it takes a great deal of strength in the arms to support your own weight. We won't get a second chance. We need a foolproof plan.'

'Wait for nightfall and sneak in?' Efalaa proposed.

'We don't know where they're holding her. And they still might shoot the birds.'

'How fast can you run?' she asked.

'It's not about how fast I can run, it's about how fast a terrified Una can run. Also she may be hurt.'

Efalaa leant against the mossy trunk of a dead tree.

'The first rule of close combat is to be where your opponent doesn't expect you,' she said. 'They won't expect us in the middle of their camp.'

I tsked in irritation. 'But how do we get away?'

'We'd just need to catch a rope, tie it round our waists and let the birds fly us away.'

I sat on a stump and rolled my eyes.

'You've got too much faith in those birds, Efalaa. They're not people. What if they fly too low or get shot?'

'The birds are clever. They'd do anything for me, especially if I was in danger.'

'Mila flew away without you last time we met Torston.'

'I ordered her to go!' she replied defensively.

Tiny snowflakes penetrated the forest canopy, and swirled

around us. I sighed in discouragement, and the small cloud of my breath joined the mist rising from the sodden ground.

I wished we could ask Steon for his advice, but he opposed our course of action on principle, and there was no point seeking his help. We were truly on our own. How could we mount a rescue that wouldn't end up a suicide mission?

'We have two problems,' I counted on my fingers. 'One, we need to know where Una is, and two, we need an escape route.'

Efalaa brushed the snow off her braids and stubbornly repeated her original proposal. 'I say we sneak into the camp in the middle of the night and find her.'

What else could I expect from the girl who'd chosen exile over marriage to the man she loved but maximum risk and minimum cunning?

'We might not be able to catch her alone,' I objected again.

'I didn't see any other women in the camp when we flew over it. Did you?'

I shook my head. My unwashed hair was heavy and didn't move prettily like hers, I noticed.

'Torston only brought the two girls he knew he could use against us,' she concluded.

'I've never hated anyone so much,' I sighed. 'And I've hated a lot of people.'

She met my eyes. 'Now you can do something about it.'

As they were meant to, these words reminded me of what I'd said to convince her to fight and flee the Raiders' camp with me. That day, she'd followed my lead; it was time for me to follow hers.

I took a deep breath and brushed my fears aside. 'Let's use poison arrows and poison blades,' I decided. 'It will even the odds a little.'

Realising she'd won the argument, she gave me a broad smile.

'I will make the poison so strong', I continued, 'that anyone we so much as graze will be incapacitated within a few seconds.'

'Perfect,' she said encouragingly.

'We find Una—'

'Yes, then we call the birds to the rescue,' finished Efalaa.

'I'm still worried about how those birds are going to carry us away.'

'If you hang on to the rope dangling from Mila, she'll do the rest.'

'I'll be trusting my life to an animal whose brain is smaller than my fist.'

Efalaa looked shocked, and her mouth formed a perfect circle.

'What? You'd never realised?' I said. 'You have seen the size of their heads. Where do you think they keep their brains?' I added jokingly.

She shrugged and then smiled. I hoped I wouldn't lose her to this foolish mission of ours. The world without her would be an even bleaker place.

'I'd rather you stayed up in the sky, Efalaa, and controlled the birds. I can hang from the rope and look inside the tents from above. All silently. Then I'll sneak into the tent, kill the guards, and tie Una to one of the ropes. You'll tell the bird to fly off over the Hedge, and if she hasn't died of fright, Una will be safe.'

'If I ride Oxi and pick Una up myself, I can control Mila from a distance by voice alone. Just hold on to the rope, and she'll fly you out of the camp.'

'If we time this right, there will be minimum resistance. Three, four guards at the most,' I said.

'I wonder whether they expect us to try and save Una,' wondered Efalaa.

'Hopefully, Morgunn managed to convince Torston he didn't care about her in the least. They won't expect a risk-all rescue mission. It's our only chance.'

'This is the stupidest plan I've ever heard,' she said.

'It doesn't mean it won't work,' I replied, although I completely agreed with her.

I stood and started towards the path.

'Wait.' She rested a light hand on my arm. 'I want to tell you one thing,' she said in a small voice.

'What?'

'If you're in danger, I will land and fight with you, but if all seems lost, I will send the birds back to the Clan. I can't allow them to be taken, it would be the end of the Clan.'

I said, 'I understand,' but her simple declaration chilled me to the bone.

She took my hand and smiled sadly at our interlinked fingers. I watched the snowflakes gather, pure white on the pure black of her hair.

✺ 30 ✺

S ili

Efalaa and I made swift preparations. While pretending to cook dinner, I brewed two vials of poison which I stoppered with two long bone darts the Clan used for stitching leather. She stole and coiled the longest ropes she could find and hid them in her saddle bags.

Then we went into the sleeping hut each carrying two wicker baskets that were used for laundry and we filled them with every piece of armour we could carry. We took our loot deep into the woods and found a snow-strewn clearing surrounded by pine trees where we could equip ourselves when the time came.

At dinner, Efalaa said to Vidris, 'It's too cold for you to sleep with the birds tonight, dearie. Why don't you join the others in the main hut?'

Vidris was about to argue, but Aalma sided with Efalaa.

'Yes, come and sleep with us, little dove,' said Steon to Vidris in a tone remarkably devoid of lewdness.

After a quiet meal and an evening cut short by the unrelenting snow, we all retired to bed.

I didn't bother to remove my clothes, but considering the freezing temperature, Aalma didn't suspect anything. Unable to sleep, straining my ears to separate Efalaa's footsteps from the noises of the night, I waited for her signal. When she came, the snow crunched under her feet, and I feared we would be discovered.

We quietly slipped out of our huts into the darkest of the night and hurried towards the now unguarded birds' shed.

Our plan nearly collapsed when we saw Steon still awake, sharpening weapons by the fire. Efalaa and I exchanged terrified glances, but the noise of metal grating on stone covered the sleepy twittering of the birds we were bringing out into the cold.

We led Mila and Oxi to the clearing where we'd left our armour and weapons. I felt such all-consuming fear I hardly noticed the cold. I pulled on a leather shirt and secured it with a fabric belt that went twice around my waist.

'These still smell of the Raiders,' I remarked.

'That's what I said,' she replied.

'Soon, it will smell of their blood,' I said to lift her spirits.

She smiled uncertainly.

'I've seen what you can do, Efalaa. We can do this.'

She helped me tie a pair of small shin pads and I fastened the breastplate that covered her from neck to waist. Her thick leather belt touched the top of her floating ribs and would keep out all but the most determined blades. I secured my poison vial along my forearm, underneath the straps Steon had tied over my shirt. Efalaa attached hers to her Clan necklace.

'Shall I plait your hair?' she offered.

'No, it's fine,' I said and tucked it out of the way inside the collar of my shirt.

Efalaa pursed her mouth, but I had more pressing things to worry about than my hairstyle.

We saddled the birds in silence, and Efalaa helped me onto Mila. My breath hung in the air at each shaky release. I had known for hours our plan hinged on me being able to ride independently, and I had had time to prepare myself. My fear of flying blended into all the other fears I harboured about our mission. I took the short bird ride as a necessary evil. In the cold light of reason, falling off Mila would be a much easier death than what awaited us in the Raiders' camp should our rescue mission fail.

I sat astride Efalaa's bird and patted her neck, feeling more confident than I had expected. I was always braver when facing dangers on my own, and squarely blamed Steon for my pitiful display the day before. Had he not been there, I would have had better control of my nerves. I would prove to myself I could overcome my fears when enough was at stake.

'Ready?' asked Efalaa. I was grateful she didn't fuss over me. Her trust boosted my confidence even further.

'As I'll ever be,' I replied.

The clearing was only just wide enough to allow two birds to spread their wings at the same time. Efalaa spoke a soft instruction under her breath, and Mila shot off into the sky. I felt deep in my stomach the moment when her feet left the ground.

We were going upwards, but I felt I was falling off a vertiginous cliff. My jaws locked together painfully and for a long moment I didn't breathe. I kept my eyes on Oxi and Efalaa who were flying just ahead of us.

We were rising over the tree canopy when we heard the first shouts from the ground. I recognised Morgunn by the anguish in his voice. He called and called but made no attempt to follow us.

S teon

I woke half way through the night and could not go back to sleep, no matter how much I called upon my soldier training. So I sat by the dying fire, sharpening our entire stock of weapons, whiling away the hours before dawn. The rhythmic noise of the metal on the whetstone soothed my nerves. Snow kept falling softly. The cold was intense.

I was surprised to see Morgunn join me as the night was still dark and the morning two hours away. He seemed despondent.

'Have you seen Efalaa?' he asked.

'No,' I said. 'Maybe in the latrines?'

He hung his head before changing the subject. 'What do you think about all this?'

'I hate the idea of this poor girl ending up with her throat cut, but you're right, there's nothing we can do about it.'

'I'm glad to hear it. How's Vidris doing?'

'She's shocked, but she's taking it rather well.'

'What a coming of age,' he said.

'You know Vidris. She cares about the birds first, then she cares about you, and lastly she cares about the Clan. Anyone outside that circle doesn't matter very much to her.'

'I wish Efalaa could see things a bit more like that.'

'How is she?'

'She reacted very badly at first, but I think Sili was able to talk some sense into her.'

'Sili's been talking to Efalaa?' I spluttered.

Morgunn widened his eyes. 'Yes, she took her for a walk this afternoon. She was being kind for once. You know, comforting her.'

'You mean Sili and Efalaa walked away for a chat?' I asked again. Could he really be that blind?

'Yes, why? What do you mean?'

No wonder Efalaa was nowhere to be found. 'Don't you know these two and their death wish by now? They're planning to rescue the girl without you.'

'What?' he exclaimed, staggered.

'Run,' I ordered, for once forgetting my place.

As I followed behind him, I just had time to see Efalaa and Sili on Mila and Oxi, winging away into the darkness.

'Efalaa!' yelled Morgunn, but she was already too far to hear, or maybe she ignored him.

My blood went cold, and for a minute I could only stand there, paralysed.

'Not again,' said Morgunn, his head in his hands.

All I could think about was how desperate Sili must have been to rescue that girl. She was riding a bird on her own.

Morgunn was still watching Efalaa fly away from him in the moonlight and apparently couldn't get his brain to work.

'What happened?' shouted Vidris, running out of the main hut.

'They've taken Oxi and Mila. They're going to rescue this girl on their own,' I explained.

Vidris's jaw dropped.

'But how?' she asked uselessly.

'Get me Eko,' ordered Morgunn tersely.

For the first time in her life, Vidris refused an order from her Chief. 'No! Don't go!' she shouted hanging on to Morgunn's arm. 'You can't go.'

'Vidris, get Eko' he repeated menacingly.

She blinked rapidly, and ran off in the direction of the shed, her feet sliding on the blanket of freezing snow that covered the path.

'Morgunn, you can't go alone,' I said.

'No, I can't. You're coming with me.'

My training kicked in, and I started formulating a plan. 'If we want half a chance of surviving, we need some air cover. If we want Efalaa and Sili to survive, we need some boots on the ground.'

Morgunn listened intently. I could tell by the absence of mist that he was holding his breath.

Vidris returned with Eko.

'Get Frid,' I said to her. She opened her eyes wide but, obviously relieved that Morgunn wasn't going after Efalaa alone, she turned on her heels after handing him Eko's reins.

He smiled a sad smile when he realised she'd already loaded up two bags of stones and a quiver full of arrows. 'Poor child,' he said. 'Poor girl.'

Whatever his thoughts were, they gave him pause. His face went from angry panic to sadness, but after a minute, he shook himself. By then, the Clan were all assembled around him, waiting for his orders.

'Aalma, you're coming on Eko with me. Veiti, you're going with Steon.'

Veiti's face froze. 'What?' she said, but Morgunn ignored her.

'Leodurr, you will stay here with Vidris and Leif. If all is lost, we'll send back whatever birds we can. You are to take everything you can carry. Then the three of you will fly directly to the Hunting Cave.'

'If all is lost?' squeaked Vidris.

'What are we to do at the Cave?' asked Leodurr, uncertain.

'Stay alive, and when Vidris comes of age bring in a man from outside the Clan, old enough to mate, young enough to adapt to our ways.'

'What? No, no,' repeated Vidris, hysterically clawing at Morgunn's arm.

'Obey the Chief,' said Leodurr, raising his voice for the first time since I'd known him.

Morgunn grabbed Vidris's face between his hands.

'For the Clan, little dove,' he said in a voice full of emotion. 'For the Clan.'

'No,' she shouted in his face, pushing him away. 'You're doing it for her!' she sobbed angrily. 'Not for the Clan, Morgunn! For her!'

Leodurr grabbed her from behind and dragged her away still sobbing.

The rest of us stood and stared at Morgunn—lost for words. I couldn't believe we still obeyed him despite the madness of his plan. The Elders had succeeded in breeding such obedience in us that we were following our Chief into self-destruction.

Morgunn turned to us to give us the rest of his instructions.

'You two women will rain stones on them while Steon and

I fight them on foot. If the fight doesn't go our way, save who you can and return here. Aalma, you will become Chief if I die. Do not bargain for anyone. Save the Clan, not the individual.'

He paused for her to confirm her understanding.

'You mean "do as I say, not as I do", is that it?' she said coldly.

There was an intake of breath, and Veiti pressed her fingers against her lips, her eyes wide.

Morgunn looked as if he'd been slapped. Aalma didn't back down and held his gaze uncompromisingly. After a long pause, Morgunn took her in his arms and kissed her cheek.

'You remind me of my mother, Healer,' he said softly. 'You're right, I'll go alone. Clan, Aalma is in charge.'

He straddled Eko and took off before we could stop him.

'I'll send Eko back. Don't come for me,' he shouted from the air before disappearing into the dark sky.

Aalma's face was a picture of grief and furious anger, but she lost no time. She turned to Veiti and me. 'You two, go with him.'

Veiti was about to argue, but I'd seen what chaos indiscipline had already caused that night, and without hesitation, I yielded to Aalma's wisdom.

'For the Clan,' I said pulling Veiti onto Frid behind me.

I sheathed my dagger, and grabbed my slingshot, the only weapon Veiti had any experience with. She probably hadn't used one since her girlhood, and then only in play. While I trusted her with a blade to defend her son to the death, she wouldn't be much use from the air against the Raiders. At least she could bring Frid back to the Orchard if the rest of us died.

Veiti put her arms around my waist, and as we rose in the air she said, 'I didn't even get a chance to say goodbye to my son.'

She was too shocked to cry.

With a determination fuelled only by desperation, I replied, 'You're coming back, darling. I swear to you, you're coming back. As sure as I am a Guardian, you will see your son again.'

Faced as we were with the worst of odds, I knew this was an empty promise. One I probably wouldn't be able to keep. Perhaps Veiti knew it too. She didn't say.

❦ 32 ❧

S**ili**

The night was still at its deepest when we reached the Raiders' camp. We landed unseen in the snow-coated grasses at the furthest end. Even after the short ride, my heart was beating wildly. Despite my surge of self-confidence in the clearing, I was now less afraid of sneaking into the camp than I was of flying back.

As we lay side by side on the frozen ground, Efalaa whispered in my ear. 'She must be in one of the smaller tents. Unless they have her serving dinner in the main one.'

'Torston wouldn't have a lone woman in there. He's not stupid. It creates tensions when there aren't enough girls to go around.'

Efalaa shut her eyes in disgust, then shook her head and carried on. 'We can't get her out of the central tent anyway. We might as well slit our own throats.'

'Alright, small tents then,' I replied. 'As Steon said, probably two or three guards.'

'They wouldn't need three men to keep control of Una,' she countered. 'Hopefully, she will be alone.'

'Either way, I'll have my poisoned dart at the ready. I'll start with the tent closer to us. If I come out with her, your job is to get us on the birds and fly us away. Otherwise, you'll go round the camp, and I'll try the second small tent.'

'I have a better idea,' she started. 'I'll fly you into the camp and set you down right next to the tent.'

'How?'

'I'll dangle you underneath Oxi. Her blindness makes her very obedient.'

'As long as I don't have to ride...'

I took my life into my hands again and trusted my fate to a foolishly brave girl and two stupid birds.

It went better than I had hoped. Efalaa fashioned a loop at the end of one of the ropes, and I was able to sit in it with my legs dangling on one side. The rope cut into my flesh, but it was better than supporting my weight with my arms only.

I landed silently on my feet close to the first of the smaller tents. I listened for any noise. It sounded empty, but I told myself Una was very quiet and might be asleep.

I took a deep breath to calm my trembling and opened the tent. A man stood up and looked at me with a puzzled expression.

'What are you doing here?' he said roughly.

My heart was in my mouth, and it wasn't hard to feign the fearful respect Raiders expected of their captives. I'd done it so many times before.

'Orken sent me to keep you company,' I replied, mentioning the name of one of the sergeants I had seen on my reconnaissance flight with Steon.

'Oh,' he said with a puzzled frown, 'I didn't know you girls were here.'

'He said to be discreet. Torston only means to reward his best fighters.' I looked up at him briefly to judge the effect of my words. His distrust instantly melted under the compliment.

As I stepped closer to him, he started untying my lengthy belt.

'What are you wearing?' he said with surprise.

His look of suspicion changed to astonishment when I stabbed him in the neck with the poisoned dart. He only had time to blink before he fell on the ground, dead.

It was only then that, by the dim light of the smoky torch, I noticed another person in the darkest corner of the tent. The shape was far too large to be Una.

A man in rags knelt with his arms tied to a wooden bar that hung high above his head. The position must have been excruciating painful, but he was calm and breathed evenly. He wore a blindfold that hid most of his face. I was about to dismiss him as one of the many Raiders who displeased Torston and leave him to his fate when I noticed his hair.

It was dusty and dirty but braided in elaborate ways that made my heart skip a beat.

This man was not a Raider.

I swallowed my fear and knelt closer to him. His body tensed, but he did not recoil.

'Are you a Skyrider?' I whispered close to his ear.

His face in no way indicated he'd even heard me. He was filthy, with dirt incrusted deep into the tiny wrinkles of his skin. He'd been beaten and cut in many places, and most of his fingers hung at unnatural angles. I touched his braids lightly, and he ignored my touch.

I could not afford the seconds I was spending worrying

about this prisoner, but I couldn't help but ask one last question.

'Are you Ollo?' I whispered as close as I dared get to his ear.

There was an involuntary tensing of his muscles which I might not have perceived had I not been so close to him.

'Ollo?' I said again.

'Why would you call me that?' he replied in a hoarse voice.

'The Clan have been looking for you.'

'The Clan?'

'Morgunn, Efalaa and Steon. They're alive. Veiti, Aalma, Vidris and Leodurr too.'

'Veiti?'

I untied the blindfold and his blue eyes found mine. They were full of hope.

'Yes, she's had her baby,' I replied.

'Veiti's alive?'

'Yes, alive and well. You must come with me. Can you ride?'

'Of course I can ride. Cut me loose.'

I sliced the ropes in a half-daze, my heart beating a stampede at my discovery. I removed the ropes around his ankles, as I didn't think his fingers were up to the task, and attempted to pull him up. It became clear he could not even stand. He rolled onto his side and rubbed his legs with the heels of his hands to bring the blood flowing back into his lower limbs.

He was far too large for me to lift him, but after a minute he managed to stand shakily on his feet. His first few steps were weak and stumbling, but he garnered his pride and marched toward the exit like a king off to war.

The whole scene had taken no more than two minutes. He peered through the opening of the tent.

'Where's the bird?' he asked suspiciously.

I threw my arm out of the tent, and waved up. Within a second, a rope appeared in front of my face. I tied it round Ollo's waist, and helped him sit in the loop.

'What about you?' he said.

'I have something else I must do. Go!' He didn't wait for me to ask twice. He grabbed the rope in between his teeth and tugged.

Without delay, he was hoisted up into the dark.

The excitement of my discovery faded swiftly, and I realised that now my ride was gone, I had probably just sealed my fate and Una's. Death or another rape-baby if I was lucky.

Quietly, I slipped out of the tent and hid behind a pile of wood. From there, I crawled to the horse pen and wondered whether I could get away with stealing horses again. I needed to find Una first, or all of this would have been in vain.

I looked anxiously in the direction of the Territory. Just as I feared I would never return there, it started to feel like home.

🐾 33 🐾

S**teon**

I'd never before flown through such a cold night. My body was warm, but my face felt as if slashed by blades. Veiti and I followed Morgunn on Frid.

Then out of the darkness came a shout in a woman's voice. 'No!' she called, 'No!'

We were flying straight towards the sound, and as she passed the light of the dim moon, we realised it was Efalaa waving at us with an ardour most unlike her.

Only she wasn't saying no. She was yelling 'Ollo!'.

Efalaa came out of a cloud into the moonlight screaming, 'I have Ollo at the end of my rope! He's alive.' Morgunn hadn't seen or heard her and was still flying at full speed towards the Raiders' field camp.

'Land!' I shouted back to the Hunter and took Frid in a steep descent. Veiti, behind me, was calling 'Ollo! Ollo!'

It was indeed him dangling under the bird that turned out to be Oxi. He fell to his knees then shoulder-rolled back onto his feet. I jumped off Frid and ran towards him, but somehow Veiti was already there.

She threw herself at him, and he held her in silence, his hands awkwardly away from her body. Frid was clucking happily and dancing around them. Efalaa slid off Oxi and just as my arms closed around Ollo, she dragged my attention away from the incredible reunion.

'Sili is still looking for Una inside the camp. I don't know what Morgunn is doing,' she said. She was gripping my hand anxiously, as close to pleading as I'd ever seen her.

'Take Frid back to the Orchard with Veiti,' I said to Ollo.

'To the Orchard?' questioned Ollo.

'I'll tell you en route,' said Veiti pulling him away.

As soon as they were gone Efalaa pointed at Morgunn, who was now shooting at the central tent with fire arrows, lighting a giant bonfire in the middle of the Raiders' camp. A riderless bird flew in circles high above the smoke. It looked like Mila.

'Go and help him, I beg you,' said Efalaa.

'What are you going to do?'

'Try and swoop up Sili and Una with Oxi.'

'The bird can't carry the three of you,' I objected.

'I've got Mila circling over their camp,' replied Efalaa.

How she expected me to help Morgunn on foot was beyond me, but Guardians ask no questions when the safety of the Chief is jeopardy.

I ran towards the Raiders' camp, armed with a bow without arrows, my dagger and my fists. I would be lucky to make it back alive.

As I neared the spot where Morgunn was flying, I saw Raiders were shooting back at him while trying to contain a group of horses that had broken loose. From above, Morgunn noticed me and dropped a quiver at my feet. I knelt and aimed for the crowd that was shooting at him. I spared a second to check Efalaa's whereabouts and saw she was still circling over one of the smaller tents, raining stones on the men below.

Then without warning, she landed inside the camp.

'No!' I yelled.

'Efalaa, no!' Morgunn screamed too, but she was already stabbing men left, right and centre, her back to the opening of the small tent. Seconds later, Mila flew off without her, but another shape could be seen across the bird's shoulders.

Morgunn landed Eko in the mayhem and immediately sent him back into the air. He drew out his hunting knife and killed two men in as many swift moves. The others stepped back for an instant, and I took the opportunity to join Morgunn in the crowd that was building around him.

❧ 34 ❧

Sili

I found Una in the second tent. Only one man was guarding her. I killed him with a scratch on his bare arm. Una jumped to her feet in amazement.

'Sili! I thought you'd escaped! What are you doing here?'

'I'm here to rescue you,' I replied, and my words sounded empty and vain.

'How?'

I had no idea how, so I grabbed her hand and pulled her behind me. 'Let's go.'

'Where?' she asked a in frightened voice.

'Home,' I said.

I waved my arm out of the tent, and Efalaa jumped off Oxi before I could take another breath. Energy pulsed through my veins, and all my senses were heightened. I smelt the fear and sweat on Una's skin, and I smelt the excrement released by the man I'd just killed.

In an instant, I was back in the sewers on my fateful birthday, and I lost track of time. I heard noises all around me, clear and sharp over the dull beating of my heart.

Efalaa was protecting us with her body and fighting two opponents at once. She had her dart in one hand, and her dagger in the other. A man was staring from her to the dead man at her feet, uncertain whether to fight or run.

She called Mila to her, and I tied Una onto the bird's back, in the same way as I had myself been tied, with perfect recall as to what knot to use.

'Mila, go,' I said to the bird, but she didn't obey.

'Mila, home!' ordered Efalaa. This time the bird flew off and was soon no bigger than a sparrow against the lightening sky.

'Call Oxi,' I begged Efalaa.

'She can't land, she's blind. She'll only get herself killed or captured.'

'How are we ever going to get out of here?' I despaired aloud.

'We'll kill them all if we have to,' answered Efalaa.

Her fierceness rekindled my courage. I stepped forward to stand next to her, and dipped my dart into the vial.

'Away,' I growled at the man standing in front of me, my minuscule weapon aloft. 'If you want to live, run!'

He didn't. I stabbed him in the leg, and in the space of one breath he fell, mouth open, dead.

The next man ran.

'Let us through, and we won't kill you,' shouted Efalaa. Back to back, her walking forward and me backward, we moved through the men who were threatening to swarm us.

'They've got poison blades,' one of the men closer to us said.

'They're women, you gutless pigs,' sniggered another. 'I've had that one twenty times. She's not poisonous!'

This attracted some laughs, and some of the men narrowed the distance between them and us. Efalaa flung her dagger at the man who had spoken, and it went through his eye. He had time for a gurgled scream before collapsing on himself.

'Yes, we're women, but now he's dead!' barked Efalaa over the roar of surprise.

Inch by inch, we made our way closer to the horse pen. Half the horses had already escaped since I had opened the fence, but we only needed two. Even one horse would do. We were five steps away from the enclosure.

❧ 35 ❧

S teon

Dawn was breaking on the Lowlands, revealing a bloodbath.

I covered Morgunn while he shot at the archers. They were no match for him who shot rabbits from the sky. This soon evened the fight. Our opponents were no longer so cocksure, they chose their moves more carefully, and the pace of battle slowed.

We ended up in a standoff with three burly men. This wasn't their first fight. I was just thinking we needed a strategy to win against them when Morgunn tapped my waist, and whispered 'Five.'

Relieved, I prepared to crouch. I knew what he would do next. All the Guardians knew this move. Even Clan children rehearsed it for fun. We used this tactic against Outsiders, mostly when Clanswomen were involved.

The trick was for the weaker looking fighter to stand

behind the stronger looking one. Normally, the shorter or thinner one, or the female in a mixed fighting pair, would act scared and harmless. When ready to strike, they would tap the waist of the man in front of them and announce a number. Then both fighters would count to the number agreed. Once the countdown was done, the one in front would crouch, and the one behind would leap over them to attack not the opponent straight in front of them, but the one to the side of their weapon hand. Morgunn was right-handed, so I prepared to crouch then stab the man on my left.

The manoeuvre went as expected. Morgunn jumped out from behind me and killed his opponent in one blow. I tackled mine to the ground and stabbed him in the neck. I didn't wait to watch him die and went for my next victim. Morgunn had already wounded the man in the middle, who was bleeding out and still wondering what had just happened.

The Raiders were obviously unused to finding such resistance. Their fighting skills were no match for ours.

Morgunn and I were finishing yet another assailant when we heard a bird overhead. We didn't need to look. It was Eko's cry, and as if he were a true Guardian's bird, he landed bravely in the middle of the fray to protect his rider. I pushed Morgunn onto him. He tried to resist, 'Come with me,' he said.

'Ollo will send Frid back,' I replied.

'We don't know that.'

'Yes, we do, and Chiefs don't die to save Guardians. Go!'

He took flight without any further discussion, but didn't leave me to fight alone.

'Grab,' he said to Eko.

This was a little used command, and I was not sure the bird would know what to do. I breathed a sigh of relief when

Eko went claws first towards the man closest to me, grabbed him, pulled him high into the air until Morgunn said, 'Drop.'

The man fell onto one of his comrades, killing them both.

Some of the Raiders started running away from the bird, and I was able to wound the two men next to me. I slashed one deep on the cheek and his flesh flapped open. The other one was not wearing any armour, and I stabbed him in the gut.

As Eko swooped down protectively towards me again, the remaining Raiders retreated towards the camp.

This was not a good idea, as it would increase the numbers facing Efalaa. I debated whether to follow them to fight with the women, but I saw from a distance what Morgunn was doing. He had already landed next to Efalaa, and was striking all within arm's reach.

Eko joined Oxi in circling uselessly over the camp. Morgunn had thrown away the lifeline I'd given him by putting himself and his bird in the middle of the battle again.

✿ 36 ✿

Sili

Morning had broken and the entire Raiders' camp was in chaos, squealing horses running wild around the tents.

Over the tense silence that surrounded Efalaa and me, we could hear the roaring of Torston and the hushed answers of his lieutenants.

'Where is the girl?' he yelled first. Someone answered she was gone. 'Bring out the man then! Now!' he ordered.

The next thing I heard was the strangled cry of the man bearing the news that Ollo too had escaped. It sounded like Torston had started killing his own men. This was a timely diversion for Efalaa and me, as many of the men facing us turned their attention to towards their leader.

We were almost touching the horse pen when Morgunn leapt off Eko next to us. As soon as he was on his feet, he went berserk and started ploughing through the crowd of men still surrounding us.

'Sili, get on a horse,' he ordered.

I obeyed immediately. I dropped my dart and scrambled over the corral fence.

The horses were terrified, and they could feel my fear. One of them had a bridle but no saddle. I pulled it towards me, and it went up on its hind legs, snorting. I had no time to change my mind. I jumped on its back and held on for dear life. I shut my eyes, there was no more I could do.

'Efalaa, on Oxi,' I heard Morgunn shout as my horse pushed its way through the crowd.

'No!' she yelled back.

'Don't worry, I'm coming with you,' he said.

'She can't land, it's too dangerous for her,'

Morgunn replied something I could no longer hear.

As my horse cleared the gate and nearly threw me off, I thought he shouted 'Grab!' but I couldn't be sure.

I was already galloping towards the Hedge. I passed not far from Steon but could not stop the horse to pick him up. All I could do was to scream his name, as the wind whistled in my ears and the snow absorbed the sound of the hooves.

As I got close to the Hedge, I let myself slide off the horse, which galloped on towards the whitened desert of the Wastelands. I landed heavily on my shoulder and lost consciousness. When I came round, my bones were unbroken thanks to the thick cloak that had broken my fall, but fear had rendered my legs useless. Whimpering and on my hands and knees, I crawled towards the charred bushes that separated me from safety, hoping I might find my way through.

I remembered telling Morgunn the Hedge he so trusted was nothing but thick bushes. This time, I saw it for what it was: an impassable wall. Layers upon layers of blackberry branches were knitted together, like wicker baskets. The resulting mesh was so dense I could not see the light through them. This was obviously not where Efalaa had come through. There was no way in.

The reality of my situation finally appeared to me. I had defied the Chief's orders and put his wife in mortal danger. I was no longer pregnant, and I had no child waiting for me in the Skyriders' camp. The Clan didn't have to rescue me again. Especially now they had another Outsider to feed and breed with, prettier and more amenable.

I was no more than two hundred yards from the Raiders' camp, alone, with no weapons and no horse.

🎕 37 🎕

S teon

Sili rode past me, in a cloud of dark hair, screaming my name in that unusual way of hers, 'Ste-on!' Stupidly, my first thought was that next time she would appreciate the comfort of a bird ride.

I looked behind me, and saw Morgunn on Eko with Efalaa hanging from his claws, flying over the Raiders' fences, closely followed by Oxi. They only managed a short distance before an exhausted Eko deposited Efalaa back on the ground.

The Raiders started shooting arrows at them from inside their camp. Efalaa tried to run and jump onto Oxi's back, but the blind bird took fright and rose back into the air without her rider.

Morgunn landed next to his wife. They ordered both

birds to stay in the air and started running together towards me in a zigzag mimicking the prey they normally hunted.

I finished the last two of my opponents, and with weary legs and my shirt soaked in blood, turned around and ran to meet Efalaa and Morgunn. They were already being swamped by a pack of Raiders.

Used to doing everything together, and knowing each other's strengths and weaknesses, the two Hunters were fighting well and courageously, but they would not survive unless I reached them soon.

My lungs were on fire, and I could only see a red mist in front of my eyes. I forced my legs to keep running but felt my strength ebbing away. They were too far. I couldn't afford to stop even for a second, but the sane part of my mind told me I wouldn't be able to fight when I got where I was going.

At least I could still die with them, maybe even save one of them. I hadn't saved anyone from the Quake, I could still save the Clan's Chief. Then I thought Morgunn would never forgive me if I saved him instead of Efalaa.

I kept running. I felt I was dying, but I kept running. I would be lucky if there were even one of them left to save. I would be lucky to get there at all.

As despair crept into my heart, a huge shadow fell in front of me, and I heard a bird's war cry above my head. It was Frid.

Shrieking furiously, he landed on top of a group of men and pinned them to the ground. He started stabbing at their faces with his beak that soon turned red with blood. I was so stunned I stopped running.

I couldn't believe my eyes. Frid was fearlessly attacking all within his reach with claws and beak. An archer took aim at him, but Efalaa put her last arrow through his throat. Then she slung her bow across her chest and seized her dagger.

Ollo jumped off Frid's back and started fighting the men

around him. 'Long life, brother,' he shouted in my direction. His moves were unusual, and I remembered his broken fingers. As I got nearer, I saw Raiders' spear blades had been strapped to each of his forearms. He was wielding them with precision and a total absence of restraint.

I heard Morgunn shout, 'You want my bird, take my bird! You filth, take my bird if you can. Here is my bird, take him if you dare!'

The battle was getting to him. As he grew more careless, I needed to become more careful. One stride after another, I was closing in on him.

The birds too looked spent and shrieked in fear and exhaustion. It was a testament to their regard for us that they were still flying overhead.

Efalaa's aim seemed more and more inaccurate, but I watched in disbelief as Ollo unleashed a violence of which I never knew him capable. He was mowing down the men surrounding Efalaa and Morgunn as fast as he could walk. Retreating men were speared in the back. Wounded men pleading for mercy were executed with the same relentless grace as those brave or foolish enough to mount a frontal attack.

I was near collapsing when I finally reached their group. I caught my breath and stood in between Morgunn and the melee.

'Run for your lives,' I wheezed at the Raiders who were still fighting. A couple of them heeded my advice. The others were skewered by Ollo or stabbed by me.

Just when it looked like we had won, Torston did the only thing he could.

His cavalry burst out of his camp, swords drawn and arrows nocked. This was worse than my worst nightmare. It didn't matter how many we had killed, plenty were still coming at us.

We had three birds for four fighters. That could have been enough if they hadn't already carried so many extra riders. Oxi, the smallest bird we had, was only used to Vidris's weight, but she had lifted Efalaa as well as Ollo outside the Camp, and could now only just keep herself in the air.

'The birds can't carry us all,' cried Efalaa.

'You go, sweetling,' said Morgunn.

'Of course not,' she answered.

'Let's run for the Hedge,' shouted Ollo, 'The birds can lift us over it at least.'

'For the Clan,' I shouted. When I turned and ran, Ollo, Morgunn and Efalaa followed me.

The Hedge that had protected generations after generations of the Clan was now standing between us and safety. The Raiders' horses were closing in on us.

What could Aalma do if our four bloodlines died with us? Only gentle Leodurr would be left to father the Clan's children.

My body just couldn't run any more. I was about to collapse.

I would never have children, I would never even see Leif grow.

The best I could do was to die a true Guardian, protecting our Chief, shoulder to shoulder with Ollo and Efalaa.

As we neared the Hedge, I saw a small shape, lying prone on the ground against the bushes to the east of where the four of us were heading. I recognised Sili's clothing and called to her.

Efalaa saw her too and changed course without hesitation.

'Is she dead?' I shouted to Efalaa.

Over my shoulder I saw the Raiders' cavalry had now split in two, some still following our party and a splinter group heading straight for Sili.

Efalaa kept running towards Sili.

'Efalaa, it's too far!' yelled Morgunn, but when she ignored him, he followed her.

Sili had heard us, and she turned to meet us.

The Raiders were nearly upon us, galloping at full speed.

My chest was on fire. My breath was coming in gasps and no air was getting into my lungs. My legs and back in agonising pain, I fell to my knees, and Morgunn dragged me up as he ran past me.

I thought for an instant of staying down, before remembering I was a Guardian with a job to do, so I scrambled to my feet and somehow continued running.

When we reached the Hedge, I looked at the birds above us. Eko was injured and struggling to stay aloft. Oxi seemed at the very end of her strength and Frid, who had carried two riders back and forth to the Orchard, shook with tiredness.

'The birds can take Efalaa and Sili, but not us,' said Morgunn.

'There must be a way,' argued Efalaa.

'Wait for us on the other side,' insisted Morgunn, and he whistled for Eko, who landed heavily next to him.

The riders were fifty paces away.

I noticed Oxi still had a length of rope attached to her harness and called her to me.

'Eko can't fly over,' said Ollo. 'He'll just land his rider right in the middle of the Hedge.'

'This is our last chance. We can't fight so many men on horses and survive. Efalaa, get on Frid now,' shouted Morgunn. He grabbed her by the waist, but she resisted.

'I'm not leaving you.'

Sili sat on the ground hugging her knees, her eyes fixed on the approaching Raiders.

She saw me watching her and looked into my eyes. 'I'm not going back alive' she said. 'Give me your blade.'

I hesitated no longer than a split second before passing it to her handle first. I turned my attention to the knots on Oxi's harness, grateful they were Efalaa's and not Morgunn's intricately tight work.

In the distance, we heard a familiar bird cry.

Efalaa shouted 'Mila!' just as the bird landed in the middle of us.

I grabbed Sili under her arms and threw her onto Mila's back.

'Up,' ordered Efalaa, and Mila shot up and cleared the Hedge. Sili's terrified screaming rang in our ears.

'Land,' called Efalaa an instant later and then 'To me.' Mila obeyed and was immediately back by her mistress. Efalaa clambered onto her back and ordered her bird to grab Morgunn. The three of them went over the Hedge in the blink of an eye.

Ollo and I were the last ones on the side of the Raiders' cavalry. They were now so close we could see the expression of thrilled anticipation on their faces.

Ollo still had spears for hands and couldn't climb on a bird unaided.

'I have a plan,' I said to him, and I gathered the last of my strength to push him onto Frid's back.

We had no choice but to trust the bird would find somewhere in his heart the strength to lift his master's considerable weight over the thorn wall.

As Frid's desperate shriek rang out, my weary fingers grabbed the lengths of rope I had attached to both Eko and Oxi's harnesses, and I shouted 'Up'.

I thought I could already feel the horses' hot breath when the two birds straining together pulled me into the air and above the Hedge.

❧ 38 ❧

S^{ili}

Steon was last to reach safety inside the Territory. He landed in a heap with two birds next to him and sat there for a moment, winded.

The rest of us shouted for joy that we were all still alive. We could hear the horses snorting on the other side of the Hedge and their riders roaring in frustration.

On impulse, I went to Steon to help him up and was surprised when he took my hand. I braced myself to lift his weight, but he pulled me down towards him instead and, laughing, bundled me into his lap to kiss my cheek.

I was mute with surprise at his familiarity. For the first time, he had treated me with the spontaneous affection he normally reserved for Clanswomen.

We scrambled to our feet together, only to be dragged into a crushing group hug. I laughed when I saw Ollo holding his arms above our heads for fear of stabbing us with the strange contraptions strapped to his wrists.

'What happened to your hands, brother?' asked Steon.

'They've been improved,' Ollo laughed, 'By the Raiders and then by Aalma!'

Steon embraced Ollo, happy like a child.

'How were you even there, elskan? Did they get you after the Quake?' said Morgunn.

'Soon after that,' answered Ollo. 'I don't know how many days they kept me in a cage underground. I saw nothing, Chief. I heard nothing. Except women crying and my own screams.'

Efalaa muffled a cry, and Morgunn put his arm round Ollo's shoulders.

Steon's happiness vanished. 'We'll make them pay,' he said, his face unrecognisable with anger.

Ollo looked into Steon's eyes then said quietly, 'I'm here, brother. It's all the revenge I need.' After a pause, he added, 'I owe it all to you, little bird.'

I didn't realise he was talking to me until all eyes turned in my direction.

'Thank you for my life,' he said simply. 'What's your name?'

'Sili.'

He looked at me with round eyes. 'Silly? That's your name?'

'It's not spelt the same,' I started, but when I took in their bewildered faces I simply concluded, 'Yes, Sili, that's my name.'

'How did you even know who he was?' asked Efalaa suddenly.

'The braids.'

'At first, I thought it was a trap,' said Ollo, 'But when you said Veiti and Morgunn and Steon were alive, I could hardly believe it, but I knew it wasn't a trick.'

He said to Morgunn, 'This Outsider gave me her ride out of that hell, Chief. She risked her life for mine, like any Clanswoman would have.'

'I hear you, Guardian.' Morgunn looked at me, not entirely mollified. He still had to address Efalaa's second betrayal and the challenge to his rule. In the same circumstances, my father would have spilt blood. I wondered what price Morgunn needed to exact to restore the balance of power between him and his Clan. I watched him with wary eyes and waited for his next words.

Surely, he couldn't demand my life now I had found his lost Guardian.

The others were unaware of the tension between us.

'Oh, Ollo,' said Efalaa, 'You're alive! And we got Una back.' Then she gave Morgunn a sideways look of pure happiness, and his anger melted instantly. He grabbed her and twirled her around. She held his face and kissed him. Suddenly, he looked like a much younger man, unburdened by power. They looked into each other's eyes and smiled.

I felt this might well be the end of their discussion about our rogue rescue mission.

Uncontested rulers could afford to be kind, and Morgunn was brave enough to forgive.

The birds had already gone above and beyond the call of duty, so we all started up the mountain on foot. Mila was the only one with the strength to fly still. The others waddled behind us along the path, twittering.

It wasn't long until we met Veiti running towards us down the hill. She flung herself at Ollo, oblivious of the lethal weapons at his sides.

'I was at the Watch Tower, I saw you all run towards the Hedge. I thought I was going to die of fear.'

'We all thought we were going to die,' chuckled Morgunn, wiping sweat from his brow, despite the freezing cold, but Veiti only had eyes and ears for Ollo.

'I was so scared you wouldn't return, that I would have got you back only to lose you again,' she cried and hung from his neck as Ollo kissed her.

Morgunn and Efalaa exchanged a look that was just as loving, but made no move to touch.

Steon, who seemed even more exhausted than the rest of us, was lagging behind. I turned to wait for him, and he smiled.

'They're not leaving,' continued Veiti. 'They're piling up the corpses on huge pyres.'

'They're probably just honouring their dead before going home,' said Morgunn—ever the optimist.

Ollo shook his head. 'We have escaped, but we haven't beaten them. That's why they're still here.'

❧ 39 ☙

S teon

I struggled to pull myself up the Watch Tower's central ladder. Veiti unstrapped Ollo's blades from his arms before helping him up onto one of the tall chairs. Morgunn was already sitting on the other.

Veiti and I passed around food from the larder and fresh water. Efalaa expertly lit a fire in the chimenea.

We were all stunned at our last-minute escape, but none more so than Sili, whose blank face was white as milk. All her energy seemed focused on whatever thinking she was busy doing.

'There were nine Guardians in the Clan again today,' said Ollo, looking at each of us in turn. 'All of you fought well. The First Twelve would be proud of you.'

His words brought a lump to my throat.

'And of you too, soldier,' said Morgunn, patting him on the back. 'I cannot imagine the hardship you have endured.'

Ollo shrugged dismissively, but his expression spoke of weeks of torture. Some of his scars might not be as visible as his broken fingers.

There was another round of quiet hugs while we savoured our miraculous victory.

Morgunn eventually broke the silence.

'Veiti,' he said, 'see whether one of the birds will carry you to the Orchard. You need to reassure Leodurr and Aalma that we are all alive and well.'

'Yes, Chief,' she answered and with a kiss to Ollo, she left.

When he spoke again, Morgunn's voice was colder than I had ever heard it.

'Guardians,' he started.

'Yes, Chief,' Ollo and I answered in unison.

'I want these Raiders gone; I want it known throughout the Wastelands that hundreds of Raiders picked a fight with ten Skyriders and lost.'

'Yes, Chief,' said Ollo.

'Yes, Chief,' I added a little late.

'But why?' asked Efalaa. 'They can't hurt us, they can't stop us from going anywhere we like. We've won.'

'We'll never know peace again if they stay,' warned Morgunn. 'How long until they cut through the Hedge? And then what? There's only ten of us able to fight, and that's including an Outsider and a child.'

Efalaa looked down. I had secretly agreed with her objection, but I could now see Morgunn was wiser.

'I will not have these people at my door for another day. They must go and forget where we are.'

As Morgunn made to climb down from the tall chair, a thin voice cut through the silence.

'They're going nowhere while Torston is alive.' Sili had

come out of her stupor to speak those words, and once she had, we all of us knew them to be true.

'He hasn't lost until he leaves, and he doesn't want to lose. He doesn't care how many men die.'

'He will if the numbers are high enough,' replied Morgunn. 'With four birds and four archers, we can kill fifty of them every day.'

'And he can bring fifty more. They don't even need to be soldiers,' Sili retorted, looking up at Morgunn through the heavy strands of her loose hair. 'He'll raid villages and bring farmers, craftsmen, then any boy strong enough to use a bow.'

'Then we will kill them. We defend our own. These men can defend themselves.'

'Is that how we are to live now? Caring only for ourselves?' Efalaa stood up to him.

'There is a way to get rid of them,' said Sili in a half-whisper.

'How?' said Morgunn.

'Cut off the head, and the body will fall: Torston must die.'

'He's surrounded by his bodyguards in an armoured tent,' I pointed out.

'We can't, but his bodyguards can,' replied Sili.

'Why would they?' asked Morgunn.

'To save themselves.'

'What about his lieutenants? Why would they turn against him?' The Chief was still dubious.

'For survival, or power,' replied Ollo. 'You only know loyalty, Morgunn Ulfborn. The world is cruel beyond the Hedge.'

'Sili may exaggerate how easy it is to break soldiers' loyalty to their leaders. Betrayal is all she's ever known,' argued Morgunn.

'And you overestimate the love foot soldiers feel for those

who send them to their deaths every day without mercy,' retorted Sili.

I frowned. Ollo saw me. 'Torston is nothing like Erlen Durrborn, long live his memory,' he said. 'They do not love Torston like we loved Erlen.'

'His men will cave given the right opportunity,' promised Sili. 'When they're more scared of him than of us, they will betray him. My father was killed by his own men because they feared him, and he didn't fear them.'

❧ 40 ❧

Sili

Morgunn gave us one evening to celebrate our escape from the Raiders' camp.

Still weary and dirty from the fight and the walk home, we gathered around the bonfire, making tea, warming food and sharing out the bowls and spoons.

Una stood a few paces behind us in complete silence. She threw awed looks at the assembled Skyriders.

'Make room,' said Morgunn.

She went around the circle to sit next to me. Leodurr set a mug of tea in her trembling hands. Vidris fetched her a blanket.

Una hadn't yet found any words to greet or thank us.

'Are you alright now, little lady?' Steon asked her kindly.

He'd never been so kind to me, and I felt a swift outrage I managed to push down my throat and shake off.

She looked at him doe-eyed and nodded timidly.

'My name is Steon,' he said, and he offered his hand, which she held by the tips of her fingers.

'Una,' she said.

'Oh, I know that,' he laughed gently. 'We've been talking of little else but you in the past two days.'

She smiled prettily, obviously relieved and pleased. To have one of the scariest Skyriders treat her with such consideration and friendliness reassured her greatly.

She was able to murmur 'Thank you' and smile at the assembled faces.

The meal finished, the others started taking turns in the bathhouse to wash the battle off their skins, but Leodurr and I sat with Una while she finished her food. It was her third helping.

'This is delicious, thank you so much,' she said to Leodurr, who nodded kindly, bouncing Leif gently on his knee. Una looked from the baby to the man in utter wonder.

'I can't believe it, Sili. This morning I was a good as dead. And now I'm here.' Her laugh was a happy trill. Leodurr's eyes wrinkled at the sides, and he laughed with her.

'That's the Skyriders for you,' I chuckled. 'No end of wonders.'

'I couldn't be more grateful,' she assured Leodurr, who nodded again. 'They didn't bother feeding me since we left the Southern Camp. I realised it was a one-way journey. When they took away poor Kasha, I gave myself up for dead.'

Her amber eyes welled up at the thought of our friend, and so did mine.

'They cut her throat,' Una said in a low voice to Leodurr. He listened intently and his brow furrowed in sympathy but he didn't speak. They both stared at Leif's little fist around Leodurr's forefinger.

Leodurr was never a talker, but I had never seen him so quiet. I wondered what was going through his mind.

Veiti, fresh and relaxed after her bath, came to fetch her son out of Leodurr's arms.

'Come on, Leif the Lucky needs his bed,' she crooned.

'Good night, little lambkin,' said Leodurr to his child.

His kindness was a stab in my heart. No one would ever call my daughter by one of these silly pet names that seemed to burst forth every time a Skyrider opened his or her mouth. The ocean of my grief stretched to the unreachable horizon. You could drown in a grief this wide and deep, even if you only dipped in a toe. With a sharp intake of breath, I wrenched myself back to reality.

'Would you like to wash too?' I offered to Una for something to say.

'I could do with some clean water and a comb,' she replied shyly. 'I don't want to start my new life looking like some wild thing.'

'You look just fine,' volunteered Leodurr, and Una smiled prettily at him.

As I led her away to the bathhouse, she looked over her shoulder at him.

'This is like a fairytale, Sili. They're all so kind and so handsome. More like gods than men.'

'You have a high opinion of the gods, Una. I myself have never found them quite as fair as the Skyriders.'

'Are we their prisoners?'

'No,' I smiled. 'The worst that will happen to you is that they will ask you to leave.'

'Ask me to leave?'

'Don't worry about it now. We'll have plenty of time to talk about that once the Raiders are gone.'

'Do you think we're safe here?'

'Have you not seen their Hedge?' I asked. 'It's never been breached.'

Her look of relief changed into surprise when I opened the door to the bathhouse.

'I wasn't expecting this,' she confided, taking in the two large wooden tubs and the round pebbles heating in a metal firepit.

'It works,' I said. 'Fill the tub from this pipe, then you use the tongues to drop the stones into the water. A dozen will heat the bath to the right temperature for me.'

'I can't remember the last time I washed with hot water.'

I waited while she bathed.

'They have soap,' she marvelled.

On our way back to the huts we met little Vidris. 'Come,' she said to Una, 'I've made you a bed next to mine in the birds' shed.'

Una raised her eyebrows at the mention of the feathery monsters, but she was too polite to comment on what the Keeper thought a perfectly good offer.

She followed meekly as Vidris led her away, her arms full of furs borrowed from the others. Thanks to Vidris's generosity, Una would be the only one to enjoy a warm night. Again, I felt a twinge of envy at the wholehearted welcome the new Outsider received, in such contrast to my own experience. Then again – unlike me – she was grateful and delighted with everything she saw.

We ate and sang late into the night. For the first time since the Quake – unlike me – the Skyriders didn't feel guilty for being alive.

❦ 41 ❦

S teon

I returned from my early morning surveillance flight to find breakfast was already finished. Veiti had kept some food for me, and she was sitting talking to Una.

'Hello, cousin,' she said to me, 'is the west side of the greenwood still frozen? I'm after some cattails from the river banks.'

'I don't know how thick the ice is, but it's still there,' I replied.

'Are you sure you don't mind looking after Leif?' Veiti asked Una. Then she frowned. 'Do you have much experience with babies?'

'I do,' said Una very quietly.

The Gatherer and I had expected a longer answer, and we shared the same look of uncertainty. But Una reached out to the child and cooed, 'You don't want to go to no frozen river, do you little one?' She added, this time to Veiti, 'He can stay with me, I have nothing to do, and I'll be glad of the company.'

Veiti kissed her son, thanked the girl, and left them with me. While I ate my cold porridge, Una stole terrified glances at me from under her lashes.

'I'm not going to hurt you,' I said.

She shook her head vehemently as if the thought had never entered her head.

'You're safe,' I insisted. 'No one will touch you. We don't hurt women here.'

She nodded vigorously, keen to agree with me in all things. This was going to be a long conversation.

'Tell me about Torston,' I asked and a shadow fell on her face.

'Lord Torston is a powerful man.'

'I'm asking you for your opinion, not what people say of him.'

'He controls the Raiders of the South, and at least three camps I know about.'

'What kind of a person is he?'

'He's cold and calculating, and he wants everyone to know how important he is,' she stuttered.

'What else?'

She looked at me uncomprehendingly and fear threatened to silence her again. 'You know him better than you realise,' I said. 'How long were you his captive?'

'Two years,'

She shivered.

'Have you no coat?' I asked.

'No, sir.'

'Would you like a blanket perhaps?'

'Only if one can be spared.'

I crossed the few steps that separated us from the

sleeping hut and returned with my bed fur, which I laid on her slender shoulders.

'Thank you, sir. You're very kind.' She folded the sides carefully across Leif's lap.

'Now, about Torston,' I started again. 'What are his habits? What does he spend his time doing?'

'He's on raids most of the time. When he comes back, he takes all the loot into his tent, and lets only his favourites have some of the less good things.'

'The others get nothing?' I asked, intrigued. 'Nothing at all?'

'Only food and women,' she replied with a flinch.

'What kind of things do you believe Torston prefers out of all the spoils he takes?'

'He likes weapons best, I think. He has a collection of swords and daggers.'

'Does he have many clothes, for instance?'

'Yes, lots. He even keeps those that are far too big or too small for him. He tries them on when no one is looking.'

Her mouth curved into a pretty grin. Whatever fearsome power Torston believed he had, there had been at least one frightened little girl in his camp who thought him a ridiculous man.

I chuckled. While Leif chewed on my finger, I continued my investigation.

'What do you think his men think of him?'

'They're afraid of him.'

'All of them?'

'Maybe not all, but most. He kills many of his own men himself.'

The thought made my skin crawl.

'For what kind of reasons?'

'Disrespect, disobedience, theft, laziness...' She shrugged. 'Anything really.'

'Does he have friends or family amongst the group?'

'His son left last year, with a few of the men. He and Torston had an argument, and Pil had no choice but to leave in the night. He doesn't have any other family.'

'Who are the other powerful men in the group.'

'Jeb and Garrod, they command smaller groups when they go on separate raids.'

'Have Jeb and Garrod ever disagreed with Torston?'

'They would not be alive if they had. If you want the Raiders to return home and leave you alone, you have to kill Torston and Jeb,' she volunteered. 'Garrod would certainly become the leader, and he's been whispering about returning to the Southern Camp.'

I laughed. 'I should have just asked you what to do rather than waste my time with all these questions!'

Her face broke into a lovely smile. I couldn't imagine Morgunn ever sending her away. She was so young, she could start as an Apprentice in any vocation, and her blood was brand new. I could already hear the passionate defence Efalaa and Veiti would mount on Una's behalf. If I was allowed a say, I wouldn't be slow to support them.

❧ 42 ❧

S^{ili}

Morgunn decided to fight back to the Raiders and finally rid ourselves of Torston and his men. The next morning Vidris, Efalaa, Veiti and Aalma flew out on the four birds with bags full of stones and poisoned arrows in their quivers.

'Don't speak, just kill,' said Morgunn. 'Taunts breed anger, silence breeds fear.'

I didn't normally share the Skyriders' devotion to their young Chief, but in moments like these, I had to concede Morgunn Ulfborn was a leader I could follow.

The women returned an hour later, bags and quivers empty.

'How many did you kill?' asked Morgunn.

'Twenty-two,' said Efalaa.

'That's not enough,' he said as he walked away.

Efalaa watched him go. 'Sometimes, I don't recognise him,' she whispered sadly.

'That's what evil does. It leaves a stain even on the victims. But I'd rather be a bad person than a captive,' I said to console her.

'Me too.' She still looked sad.

The women reloaded their quivers and carried on their guerrilla war. Three more times they flew to the Raiders' camp, shot some arrows through some bodies, set fire to what they could.

Morgunn was getting increasingly unnerved by Torston's lack of reaction. Eventually his patience ran out. 'What do we have to do to get rid of these men?' he shouted in exasperation.

Steon and Una exchanged a pointed look, and the Guardian said, 'Chief, you want to hear what Una has to say about this.'

Morgunn stared at Una with curiosity, and she shrank back against Vidris next to whom she was sitting. 'One of Torston's lieutenants, Garrod, wants to go home. Many of the men are secretly on his side,' she murmured.

'And Torston keeps all the goods for himself. His men are ruled by fear, not reward,' Steon added.

Morgunn was quiet.

'It only takes a spark to start a fire,' I said to him.

Una and Morgunn spent the rest of the evening whispering to each other, their voices swallowed by the crepitating of the bonfire.

The next morning, Morgunn decided to return to the Raiders' camp himself and bring the situation to a head. Not everyone supported this plan.

'It is what he wants,' warned Ollo. 'We cannot guarantee your safety. He will go to any length to kill you.'

'I can't continue to sit here and skin rabbits while these

men are on my doorstep. I want you both in full armour by noon,' the Chief answered. 'Vidris, saddle up the birds. Sili, you're coming too. I may need you to put names to faces.'

Panic rose in my throat, but I was flattered Morgunn needed my insights, and pride won over fear.

As the sun reached its zenith, we rode out, Ollo on Frid, Steon on Eko, Morgunn on Oxi, and me again on Efalaa's bird.

It was a clear day, and the Raiders saw us arrive from miles away, but Torston didn't come out to meet us. Morgunn circled over the camp for long minutes, calling for him. Finally, he came out of his tent armoured like an armadillo.

'I have nothing to say to you, Skyrider.'

'Nor have I you, Raider, but I want you to hear what I have to say to your men.'

'Why would they want to listen to your empty words?'

'Let them decide if my words are empty,' riposted Morgunn, and while Eko floated aloft on the air currents, he spoke to the men assembled below in a powerful voice that came from deep in his gut and seemed to get louder the further it carried.

'Men!' he shouted. 'Or should I say lambs, for so easily you bend your necks to your shepherd's knife. Trusting, innocent lambs, fresh from their mothers' teats.'

Torston froze in disbelief. Morgunn continued.

'He says go and off you gambol out of your scorched tents towards our poisoned arrows. He says and you die. Or with luck, you live another day to drink bad water and eat poor food, shivering under your tattered canvas and waiting for our arrows.'

Torston came out of his trance and opened his mouth to speak, but Morgunn drowned out his voice with his own.

'What has he done to deserve your sacrifice? He does not share the spoils. He doesn't protect you or risk his life for yours. Is your life worth less than his? Why do you give your life for his? Is he your loving father? Your true-born son? Your loyal friend? Is he some kind of god with power over you? No, he's just a man who breathes, eats and sleeps just like you.'

Below, Torston was issuing rushed orders to his followers.

'Is his blood not the same colour as yours? But you wouldn't know about that, would you, my lambs? Your blood is all over the plain, but where is his blood? I've seen your blood, my lambs, not his. I'll tell you where his blood is: safe in his selfish veins.'

Morgunn paused, and a clamour started among the men around Torston.

'Quiet!' shouted Jeb on the right side of his leader.

Morgunn went on, his voice carrying over the din.

'I heard you Raiders were tough men, skilled fighters and conquerors. Men flee and women cry at your approach. But you're not conquerors now. Now *you* are the crying virgins, hiding under splintered shields, being shot at by girls, a laughing stock throughout the Wastelands. And why?'

'Shut up,' yelled Orken, pushing at some of his recruits. They moved back a few steps, but there was nowhere to hide from Morgunn's booming voice.

'Torston will spend to the last drop of your blood because he wants to sit on a bird like mine. A bird that wins battles and travels to the sea in a day. That's what Torston wants. A bird like mine, or two, or three.'

'K-Kill him,' stammered Torston, his face puce with fury. Several of his guards nocked their arrows, but none released them.

'Perhaps you too can ride a bird one day. Oh what a proud day that would be!' Morgunn added sarcastically. 'All the sacrifices you've made, the friends you've lost. Your blood on the ground finally rewarded—'

The first arrow tore the air, and missed Morgunn by an arm's length.

'You too can ride a bird like mine,' he continued, 'One day. Perhaps. If your shepherd allows it. Perhaps, you too can glide amongst the clouds, free and safe from the strife below. Who knows? Perhaps Torston will be kind. Perhaps he will let you have one of the beasts of wonder. One of the birds that make men like gods. Maybe you will be one of the lucky few. If Torston is kind. If he shares.'

Several more arrows flew in the direction of Morgunn. He avoided them easily. I started worrying Oxi couldn't see the projectiles and might get hit in Morgunn's blind spot. I kept my eyes on the archers, ready to warn him of any danger.

Ignoring the cries of Torston's sergeants who desperately tried to herd the soldiers away from us, Morgunn continued his improvised speech.

'But your shepherd is not kind, is he?'

'Enough!' bellowed Torston. 'Shoot him again!' Garrod stood motionless and silent next to his leader. His quiet betrayal went unnoticed.

Another arrow flew through the air, but it never got close to Oxi.

Unperturbed, Morgunn went on. 'Torston doesn't share, does he? He wants your life, your blood on the plain, so that his blood can stay in his veins. So that he can ride like a god among men. So that he can parade on a bird that you, my lambs, will never touch, let alone ride.'

Torston grabbed one of his bodyguards by the hair, pushed him to the ground and sliced his throat. The man died with a look of astonishment on his face, and a murmur of dismay rippled across the camp below us. Jeb and Garrod each took a step back, effectively pushing Torston to the front of the crowd.

'Look at this man at your shepherd's feet. His blood

soaking the ground. It could have been you. Not for you the freedom and the safety, not for you the glory and the spoils. You are here to die when Torston says die.'

Morgunn pointed to me.

'You see this woman at *my* side, riding a bird high against the sky. Many of you may know her. She was his captive for many months. She too went hungry. She too feared for her life. And look where this woman is now. Is she cowering under your shields and tents? Is she taking orders? No, she isn't. Because she was brave, and while she was still heavy with child, she didn't let fear keep her down. She did what she had to do to escape. This woman that you despised, she was strong enough to free herself. Are you not as brave as her?'

Morgunn shouted those last words even louder, and the wind carried them throughout the plain. The men below were now silent. Jeb retreated further into the crowd.

'Kill him!' yelled Torston to those of his guards who still stood close to him despite the bloody knife in his hand. One of the archers took aim.

'Do you hear, my lambs? Kill, says the shepherd. You kill when he says kill. You die when he says die! Like trusting, innocent lambs. Like defenceless crying virgins.'

The noise below turned into a roar of indignation.

'Unless...' said Morgunn, 'unless you find your courage— like this woman did. Shake off your little snowy fleeces. Dry your unmanly tears. Raise your hand in righteous anger and stand like men, proud and free. And shout with one strong voice: "No, shepherd. Now it's *your* time to die."'

A sound like gathering thunder built below us.

'Men, save yourselves, give me Torston's head, and you can all go home,' Morgunn concluded. He took a moment to gauge the effect of his speech on the Raiders. I too was scanning the crowd for a sign of what they would do.

I heard the twang of the bow string just before Steon launched Eko forward. Steon's cry of pain broke the spell Morgunn's speech had woven, and the Guardian slumped over the bird's powerful neck.

My shout of anguish was lost in the mayhem below. A group of Raiders broke through the ranks of Torston's guard. The man at the front, a tall soldier whom I knew only too well, ripped off Torston's shiny helmet and planted his dagger in his neck.

Morgunn' air of wary confidence had evaporated. His eyes were wild and went from the red warm blood gushing out of Torston's neck to Steon's increasingly limp body. 'Eko, home!' he shouted, and the faithful bird pierced the sky, swift as an arrow, toward the Hedge.

'Home,' I said to Mila, and for the first time she obeyed me.

✢ 43 ✢

S ili

The birds landed in a tight group by the firepit. The Guardian, who always looked so strong and vital, seemed barely alive.

'What happened?' shouted Aalma.

'They shot at me. Steon flew in the path of the arrow. It was poisoned,' Morgunn explained.

I caught one of Steon's arms and put it around my shoulders. Aalma did the same, and we dragged him towards her house.

We laid him face down on my bed furs, while Vidris undid his clothes with anxious gasps. The arrow jutting out of his back brought frightened tears to my eyes. This injury was entirely my fault. If I hadn't prepared this poison, Steon wouldn't be dying right in front of my eyes.

Vidris cut Steon's clothes with her dagger, and Aalma

started sawing the arrow shaft in swift motions. Tears were falling thick and fast onto my hands. I hadn't realised how safe Steon made me feel until I saw him there, breathing his last. Vidris and Aalma worked quickly, in the true tradition of the Clan.

'Stop crying,' Vidris said, annoyed.

'Clean the blade, Vidris,' ordered Aalma. Vidris held her knife to the torch flame until it reddened, then poured what smelt like pure alcohol over it. She passed the blade to Aalma, who cut Steon's flesh lengthways along the line of the arrow head.

She pulled the shaft in one move that sent Steon's blood gushing out. I bit down my own cry.

Aalma pressed on the wound to bring more blood to the surface. Steon gasped in pain, his face deathly pale. This was all my fault. The room started to swirl, and my eyes slowly closed. Vidris struck me in the face and brought me back to reality.

'Get out if you can't be helpful,' she said roughly.

Be helpful. I had to be helpful. What could I do to help?

'What is the poison doing to him?' asked Aalma urgently.

I recovered my focus. 'It's speeding up his heart, and it will bring convulsions. He shouldn't even be still alive.'

Vidris shot me a murderous look, but kept cleaning Steon's wound with the foul-smelling alcohol.

'They must have shot him with one of our own arrows. The best part of the poison will have killed the first victim.'

'He's burning up,' Vidris cried, her hand on Steon's forehead.

'We're losing him,' said Aalma.

'We need to remove the poison,' I said. Then, seized by sudden inspiration, I put my lips to Steon's wound and sucked a mouthful of tainted blood.

'What are you doing?' shouted Vidris.

I spat the blood on the floor and took in another mouthful.

'She's cleaning the wound,' said Aalma relieved.

Steon's blood was dripping down my chin and on my clothes mixing with my tears.

'Do it one more time,' instructed Aalma.

I obeyed.

'We need to slow his heart,' I then said to her. She checked the pulse at his throat. 'It's as fast as if he was running at top speed.'

'If we can cool him down enough, his heart will slow. It's one of the body's survival mechanisms.'

'Get water from the stream,' Aalma told Vidris. She stood and ran out.

'Let's take him outside,' I said.

Morgunn and Leodurr carried him into the camp square. Veiti and Vidris were returning with buckets full of icy water that they threw over Steon. He gasped despite his weakness. His braids were dripping bloody water onto his bare back. My mind was now working at full speed.

'He's not cold enough for his heart to slow,' I said to Aalma, 'We need to sit him in the stream and pour more water on him.'

'What about infection?' Aalma asked.

'He won't have the luxury of dying of infection if we don't do this!' I shouted, furious at her reluctance.

Morgunn and Leodurr carried Steon over the snowy bank on the side of the stream and sat him in the frigid water. Vidris and Veiti splashed more water onto him while Efalaa held a bandage to his shoulder. She too was soaking wet, but undeterred.

Steon's lips turned blue. He looked dead apart from the trembling.

Leodurr and I brought him back to Aalma's hut and laid him under the furs.

Aalma checked his pulse. 'His heartbeat is back to normal, but we need to warm him up or he will die of cold now.'

'I'll get him a warm drink,' said Leodurr, and he left.

Aalma turned to me, her face stern. 'Sili, take your clothes off now and get under the covers with him.'

'What?' I asked, confused.

'Body heat is the fastest way to warm someone up. Do it.'

As I still wasn't moving, she looked at me with a penetrating look. 'Get in there with him, it will do you both good.'

I didn't want her to explain herself further as to why this would help me too so I obeyed.

'Everything,' she added, pointing at my underclothing with reprobation. 'Skin to skin.'

She turned her back, but I had seen her smile.

As I stretched next to Steon, I shivered and squirmed at the contact of his frozen skin.

Aalma left the hut. 'I'll get you some food,' she said as her only explanation.

She was right about one thing. It felt good to hear Steon's heart still beating next to my ear. I listened carefully for any changes in rhythm. His pulse was sluggish, but still there.

I could not explain to myself the intense emotions that had taken me over since Steon's injury. Seeing him so weakened terrified me. I shouldn't have cared so much, and I couldn't understand why the world felt a better place with Steon still in it.

His skin smelt clean after his enforced bath, and his hair was still damp. The braids reached down to his floating ribs. I pulled them away from his cold flesh and arranged them on the floor, like rays of wet sunshine around his head.

I had never taken the time to notice it, but the braiding was intricate and beautiful, like plaits of golden sheaves. His chest was muscular and firm and his nipples a dark pink. Reclining as he was, he seemed a sleeping lover, not a dying man.

I clicked my fingers by his ear, but he didn't react, not even the smallest muscle twitch. I decided that he was unconscious which both made me fear for his life again and reassured me my moment of weakness in his company would remain a secret.

Emboldened by his unconsciousness, I lifted his arm and let it rest on my shoulders, then I pressed my chest to his side, and my core to his hipbone. The contact sent thrills down my spine.

Steon moaned softly. I gasped, and I stupidly pulled the fur to cover my naked body.

I recalled our meeting in the woods, and the calm I had felt as he entered me.

Our open animosity had always had undertones of lust. I hoped he would live so that I might, if only once, enjoy his embrace again.

The minutes passed, and his body remained cold. I listened for his heartbeat. It was fainter than before. I held him closer and turned my mind to solutions.

Leodurr came back carrying two steaming mugs of tea and a plate of warm food. I sat up and the furs slipped down revealing my naked breasts.

Leodurr didn't blink. Shrugging off his sheepskin jacket, he passed it to me without a word.

I covered myself. 'Aalma said he needed my body heat,' I said by way of explanation.

'Yes, I guessed this wasn't your idea,' he smiled. 'Now help me get some warm tea into him.'

We tried to pour the liquid down his throat, but Steon was too weak to drink more than a few spoonfuls.

'What news of the Raiders? Is Torston really dead?'

'I don't know, darling,' Leodurr replied gently. 'Morgunn and Efalaa have gone back to see what's happening.'

He took Steon's hand. 'Stay strong, elskan, and come back to us,' he whispered near the Guardian's ear.

I handed Leodurr his jacket back, before lying back down with Steon under the furs. What we could do to save his life? I cursed myself for my ignorance. What kind of a fool wields a poison that she cannot cure? What good had I ever done in my life? What was my contribution to the world? I'd lived the life of a spoilt child long into adulthood, my only achievements were two daring escapes and a long history of fruitless scheming.

For the rest, the only child I had carried to term had died within the week. Her loss was still a gaping wound I would have to carry every day. I had no skills, no knowledge that could be useful to anyone and certainly not to the man dying beside me.

✼ 44 ✼

Sili

I cried useless tears until Ollo entered.

'Hey, little bird,' he said kindly. 'Why are you crying? The man's not dead!'

'How's Una?' I asked, wiping my eyes and propping myself up on my elbow.

'Eating her own weight in acorn cakes,' he joked. From anyone else, that remark would have seemed callous, but he had first-hand experience of the Raiders' hospitality, and if he chose to make light of our common ordeal then I was ready to let him.

'Has everyone been friendly to her?'

'Of course, why wouldn't we be?'

'The welcome I received was not that warm.'

'I believe you arrived in different circumstances,' he said diplomatically. 'She came straight from a battlefield.'

'I did too.'

He looked at me with a mix of annoyance and discomfort. 'Let's stop counting our woes. We're all here now,' he said.

'How are you feeling?' I asked before regretting my words. I didn't think he would want to share that with me, but he did.

'Much as you would expect. Being back here is like a dream. I thought everyone was dead, and I was hoping to die too.'

'I know what that's like,' I said quietly.

He held my gaze, and I waited for his next words with some curiosity. I felt they would show me what kind of a man I had risked my life to save.

'I realise how lucky I was,' he said.

'I'm glad,' I replied.

His mouth stretched into a pained smile. 'I survived the Quake and the Raiders. Now I will have to find out why.'

'Maybe luck is one of these qualities the Clan can breed into bloodlines,' I quipped.

'I'd say that work has already been done, wouldn't you?' he said seriously. 'No one here has got to where they are without incredible luck.'

'You could see it that way, I suppose.'

He lifted the rabbit fur blanket that covered Steon and looked at his wound.

'It's looking good,' he commented.

'Are the Raiders leaving?' I asked.

'They've been fighting among themselves and looting all afternoon. The horses are gone. I reckon by tonight the camp will be deserted.'

'So you've won?'

'Yes, I believe we have.'

'I hope this victory doesn't cost us Steon's life.'

'If it did, he would deem it a fair price.'

I looked up at him, shocked. 'How can you say that? You value his life so little?'

He held my gaze. 'I love Steon, and he's my last brother. But our lives are the price we Guardians are willing to pay for the Clan's safety. If you hadn't freed me from the Raiders' camp, it is the price I would have been happy to pay.'

'No one has ever been willing to protect me with their life...' I said, surprised at my own words.

'Efalaa was.'

I had no reply for this. It was true.

'You have earned some loyal friends amongst our Clan, Sili.'

I didn't trust my voice enough to answer, so I simply nodded.

'You have earned my friendship too. And that is why I have an offer to make you.'

'Really?'

'I have heard how you tried to leave the Clan in the night, on foot, only a few days after giving birth. I understand you meant to travel back to the Valley.'

I stared at my lap in shame at the memory.

He continued. 'If you still want to go home, I will take you there myself and protect you while you regain your place.'

My first reaction was a cold wave of fear.

'Morgunn will not be happy to spare one of his Guardians,' I started. 'And Veiti will be distraught to see you go.'

'This is my debt to repay. Morgunn and Veiti will understand.'

I couldn't think of anything to say. Ollo had just offered me everything I had worked for since leaving New Bodie.

He pushed himself onto his feet with his heavily bandaged hands, and grimaced in pain. 'Thank you for looking after Steon,' he said as he reached the door. 'He will owe you too.'

❧ 45 ❧

S teon

I came round slowly to the feel of a warm body next to me. My head pounded, but the rest of me felt absent. Leodurr spoke. His presence meant safety. I tried to go back to sleep, but someone forced some tea into my mouth. Swallowing was painful. My head hurt. I'd been injured, yet I couldn't remember how.

I didn't have the strength to open my eyes.

Next, I heard Ollo's voice.

'I'll take you there myself,' he said.

Who was he talking to?

'And I'll protect you while you regain your place.'

Sili. He must have been speaking to Sili.

Indeed, the next words were in her voice. I couldn't catch them. She sounded scared.

I returned to the blackness.

'How is Steon?' Aalma said.

Why didn't she know?

'He's no better,' Sili declared.

'He's still alive, and that's the important thing,' Aalma replied.

'Why are you so cheerful? He's still unconscious.'

'The Raiders are gone. Morgunn has given orders for us to take everything that is left in their camp. I've got my eye on some pots and utensils. Don't look so shocked. I need somewhere to store my potion and my herbs!'

'What are you going to do about Steon?' insisted Sili. She still couldn't say my name properly.

'He didn't die of the poison,' replied Aalma.

Poison? What poison?

'No, I suppose he didn't.'

'And he will not die of his arrow wound.'

'Unless that becomes infected.'

'It won't, I have just the thing here.'

A powerful odour filled the small room. 'Help me turn him over,' Aalma said.

A sharp pain spread through my back. I moaned.

'Let him rest on his front for now,' she said.

The pain receded.

'I can't stop crying,' Sili said.

'Yes, I've noticed,' Aalma replied. 'If your tears were the antidote to your poison, he would already be cured.'

Sili had poisoned me? My thoughts were so tangled that nothing made sense. The only thing I knew was that I was warm, and the Clan was safe. I went back to sleep.

I woke up cold and alone, in agonising pain. I shouted for help, and the sound cleaved my head in two.

Aalma was the first to come to my aid.

'Hush there, elskan,' she said. 'I'm here.' She felt my brow, held my wrist and lifted one of my eyelids. Daylight blinded me, but I felt better for Aalma's expert care.

'Steon's woken up,' she whispered to someone who'd just stepped into the room.

'Then why are you whispering?' asked Sili.

'He needs some of my strongest potion. I have to go and prepare it. Stay with him. Keep him comfortable.'

'How?' cried Sili as Aalma left.

Sili put a wet cloth on my forehead, and the coolness gave me some relief. I tried to speak, but my jaws were locked against the pain.

'Aalma will be back, hold on,' she said in my ear. 'Do you want a drink?' She still sounded scared, and her voice was softer.

I shook my head no and grunted with the pain of it. I must have passed out.

❧ 46 ❧

S ili

Aalma's potion didn't seem to help. The poison still wreaked havoc in Steon's body. The veins on his neck were ready to burst, and he clung white-knuckled to the fur covering him.

I waited, powerless. I remembered how he'd held me while I was giving birth to Vona, and I wished I could help him.

Then I thought of the alcohol Vidris had used for the blade. That could get him drunk enough to lessen the pain.

I explained my idea to Aalma.

'I've never used this for ingestion, just disinfecting. Would it not do more harm than good?'

'People drink it all the time in the Valley. It can act as a sort of anaesthetic.'

'Let me try some more potion first.'

We helped Steon drink the mixture, and waited as the minutes passed excruciatingly slowly.

'Any better?' asked Aalma.

'No,' answered Steon, speaking for the first time.

Hearing his voice brought tears to my eyes. 'We have to do something,' I insisted. Why was I crying so much? It was infuriating.

'The pain won't kill him,' said Aalma stubbornly.

'What? You don't care that he is in agony?'

'Of course I care, but I'm surprised you do too.'

'Oh, really? Is that why you invented that stupid story about me warming him up? Because you thought I didn't care? Don't take me for a fool, Aalma.'

'You're still a young fool, Sili. A very hurt, very young fool,' she riposted not unkindly.

'Do something for him instead of wasting my time with your assessments of me.'

She snorted angrily. 'Alright, let's give him some of that alcohol as you call it. How much do you know for a fact is safe?'

She handed me the jar. I sniffed the liquid. It was amazingly strong. Practically pure. I tasted it cautiously. My whole face and throat burst into flames. I spat it out.

'Two spoonfuls should start to make a difference. Three for luck.'

Aalma helped me lift Steon and unlock his jaws. As we turned him over, I couldn't help glancing at his firm backside, covered in soft golden hairs. Had I been alone, I would have stroked it.

The wound in his shoulder was red and swollen. I poured a generous amount of liquid on it, and it ran in rivulets down his spine. He cried out.

As the alcohol went down his throat, he tried to spit it out, but I held his mouth shut. This reminded me of what he had done for me, out in the woods, when Aalma and he had found me by the cliff.

He groaned in pain, but a few minutes later, his breathing evened out. He was soon able to open his eyes a little. They were bloodshot.

'How are you feeling?' I whispered.

'The room is spinning,' he said. 'What is that awful stuff you made me drink?'

'It's called alcohol,' I laughed.

'Foul Outsiders' stuff,' he moaned. 'Can't I just have some water?'

Aalma and I exchanged a happy smile.

I made him sage tea laced with more alcohol. I tasted it, and it was not as bad as the undiluted version. He drank some more, curled his lips in disgust and went to sleep.

❊ 47 ❊

Sili

I needed to stretch my legs and clear my head. The temperature was still below freezing, and the path to the latrines
crunched under my steps.

Even inside the outhouse, I could see my breath, and my
urine steamed between my legs.

Could I ever get used to this total absence of comfort?
The food, the cold, the mud...

And what about all those pet names?

This was so far from my idea of my place in the world. So
far from my idea of what was owed to me. But it was time I
learnt the world owed me nothing, and that I should grab
happiness as it passed and hold on fast.

When I returned to Aalma's hut, she was there checking
Steon's pulse.

'We're giving you a lot of work,' I smiled apologetically.

'You did most of the work for Steon,' she replied pleasantly and fixed me with her ever vigilant, ever gauging eyes.

'They're lucky to have you,' I said spontaneously.

'You have me too.'

'I don't think I will ever be part of the Clan. You're all so close. I'll forever be an Outsider.'

'We'll see,' she said simply.

'I don't think Morgunn will let me stay if Steon dies by my hand.'

'By your hand? You saved his life.'

'I poisoned him.'

'The Raiders poisoned him.'

'I don't think the rest of the Clan will see it like that.'

'They see it exactly like me. You single-handedly rescued Ollo from the Raiders, and you saved Steon's life when he was shot in the back by one of their archers. Any other interpretation is self-indulgent guilt on your part.'

I had no answer to that.

'You didn't kill your daughter, and you didn't kill Steon. You have nothing to reproach yourself with. You may have been planning to use us and leave us, but that would have hurt yourself and not us. So you do not need to feel guilty about that either.'

I was surprised that she'd guessed my secret plans. Was I so transparent?

'I did abandon my daughter,' I managed through the stone in my throat.

'Considering your previous successes, I'd say that half-hearted escape plan of yours was no more than a cry for help. Now,' she continued, 'go to sleep. You look like a wraith.'

'What do I do about Steon?'

'As I said before,' she replied sternly, 'your job is to keep him warm and to let him know you're here.'

Now Steon had come out of his unconsciousness, lying

naked next to him felt wrong. Even in his weakened state, Steon still exuded a raw power I found appealing. Did I want to have sex with Steon? Unbelievably, throughout my stay with the Clan, I had never asked myself that question. I'd always thought about his desire for me, and how it would allow me to control and torment him.

I had half admitted to myself his presence pleased me, but I had chosen not to examine my reasons too closely. He certainly looked like a satisfactory partner. In my days before the Raiders, I wouldn't have hesitated to bed him. Here, now, things were different. Casual coupling may have been the rule in the Clan before the Quake, but I had witnessed no sexual activity since my arrival. Still, they all seemed so sexually confident and un-frustrated I wondered whether I had missed some secret trysts.

Vidris certainly looked on an intimate footing with both Leodurr and Steon, but I knew Clansmen didn't allow themselves sex with underage girls. She would become fair game on her eighteenth birthday but not before.

Steon had made it clear he could take or leave the opportunity to sleep with me. That needled me. Men wanted me, men had always wanted me, whether I liked it or not. Then I thought of the relative ease with which I had bored my assailants at the Raiders' camp. Maybe I wasn't as attractive as I thought. Maybe Steon was turning me down because he just wasn't attracted to me.

If I remained, I might have to content myself with Leodurr. Leodurr would be no fun though: he was too earnest and kind. He could never understand what was going on in my mind and in my heart. In contrast, Steon's earlier rejection proved just how much he understood me. He understood the game, and he could play it. That thought set me on fire.

Aalma moved into the main sleeping hut with Leodurr

and left me to look after Steon. She claimed to be busy pilfering what she could from the Raiders' camp.

After two days of almost constant sleep and many nourishing meals, Steon started to look more like himself. He was able to sit up and take a few steps unaided.

His first request was to wash, and Vidris heated flat stones to warm the water of his bath. Since he could not yet lift his arms to his head, Leodurr washed his hair, and Morgunn braided it while Steon sat by the dying embers of the breakfast fire.

I couldn't imagine my father touching anyone's hair let alone braiding it with such patience and skill.

I watched Steon's return to health with increasing discomfort. He moved back to the sleeping hut, but the hours spent alone with him had given me ample time to examine my heart, and I couldn't deny I wanted him more than I had ever wanted anyone. My insides burnt with a desire I could not extinguish on my own.

I was torn between my yearning for home and my desire for a man, until one night, while lying awake in bed in Aalma's house, I decided I could have both. I did not second-guess myself.

It was still hours before dawn, and the cold took me by surprise. I was only wearing my tunic, and my legs and my feet were bare. I strode into the sleeping hut and woke both men.

Steon reacted to the intrusion as to a stealth attack and reached for his dagger. Leodurr looked at me bleary-eyed.

'Everything alright, Sili?' he asked, his voice full of sleep.

'Leodurr, could you please swap beds with me? I want to talk to Steon.'

Leodurr raised his eyebrows in surprise but gave way. He grabbed his fur and shuffled outside, still half-asleep.

'What's that about?' asked Steon with clear irritation, but I didn't engage in conversation.

He was still lying on the floor, supporting his weight on one elbow. His fur covers revealed part of a naked chest. I pushed him down with my foot and although he frowned at my contact, he didn't resist. I remembered his shoulder wound too late. That must have hurt. Good, that was for keeping me awake half the night.

I slipped under the covers with him, and lifted my tunic to my waist. I settled astride him. He was as ready as I was.

'How would you feel if I had done this to you?' he asked, still annoyed, but his reluctance not extending to what I was after.

I put my hand across his mouth and took him in. Like that first time in the woods, I felt relief and completeness. I could finally breathe again. I stopped moving to enjoy the moment, eyes closed.

Briefly, I tensed, thinking of the Raiders. I searched myself for hints of reluctance or fear, but found none. Apart from the fact it involved similar body parts, there was no connection between what had happened then and what was happening now, neither in logic nor in perception.

I relaxed and opened my eyes.

'Is that it?' said Steon playfully, his earlier annoyance gone. Even his eyes smiled. He looked happy and – for once – carefree.

'Forgive me, I'd gone to sleep,' I teased.

'Oh, really?' he answered, rising to the challenge. He thrust upward once, hard.

My brain switched off, and all my energy and focus relocated to my core. We settled into a fast rhythm. When I opened my eyes, I saw him looking at me with intense concentration.

We were not having mindless sex: this felt right, deeply satisfying and reassuring.

The physical sensations ebbed away, replaced with a yearning for emotional connection and closeness. Despite the heat of his gaze, I felt we had taken a wrong turn, and our bodies were working together before our hearts and minds could.

That made me so profoundly sad I stopped moving. I was teetering on the edge of a precipice that held nothing but pain and darkness. I started crying, and my core constricted to the cadence of my crying.

Concerned, he tried to pull away, but I wouldn't let him. 'No,' I said, 'stay.'

'I should have known,' he said, desolate. 'After what you've been through.'

'It's not that,' I reassured him.

He lifted me off him and sat up, waiting for an explanation.

I dried my tears and tried to smile. I felt unspeakably foolish but couldn't muster the emotional energy to be angry at myself.

'I didn't hurt you, did I?' he enquired.

'No, thank you.'

'Thank me for what?'

'For asking.'

'Not quite what you had in mind when you came in, is it?' he smiled gently.

I shook my head.

'I must have looked annoyed, but in truth I liked it,' he volunteered.

'You liked that I forced myself on you?' I chuckled through my tears.

'Yes, that never happened to me before.'

'I'm the only crazy woman of your acquaintance?'

'You are,' he smiled. He grabbed a shirt by the side of his bed and pulled it on. He seemed ready for a conversation.

'What were your women like? Before.' I asked, surprised at my own curiosity.

'My women? I didn't own any women.'

'Your bed partners.'

'Lovely, likeable girls, and competent lovers. I also often slept with Isveg.' His voice caught, but he carried on. 'She was a Guardian too. I loved her. She was so full of life, so easy-going. She made everything simple.'

'Not like me.'

'No, not like you.'

I pushed at his shoulder in mock irritation. He laughed gently.

'You're a much nicer man than I thought,' I admitted.

'Is that good?' he joked.

'Yes, it's good.'

'What were your lovers like?' he asked in turn, and I liked the fact he didn't shy away from the question despite what he knew about my time with the Raiders.

'Good-looking and efficient.'

I thought he would start fishing for a compliment about his good looks or his efficiency, but his mind went in a different direction.

'Nothing to stir the heart then,' he said.

'No, not really.'

'Do I stir your heart?'

Again, I liked how brave and direct his questioning was. 'Yes.'

'Is that why you cried?'

'I'm not sure,' I admitted.

'I like it that you are strong,' he said, in a strange non-sequitur.

'Thank you.'

'Were you ever simple?'

'Simple? You mean was I ever not impossible to be around?'

He smiled. 'I meant did you understand yourself before everything that happened?'

'I thought I did.'

'And now?'

'I really don't know any more.'

'Are you going to stay? In the Clan, I mean. I heard what Ollo offered you.'

'You did?'

He nodded, his face betraying no emotion.

'I'm not sure,' I said.

'I don't want to go any further with you if you are not staying,' he declared.

'What? Why?'

'I can't lose another friend.'

'So we're not friends yet.'

'No, not yet. Even though it would already be hard for me if you left.'

'Would it?'

'Yes.'

'Why?'

'I'd miss you, that's why,' he answered as if it was obvious.

'I didn't think you liked me.'

'I told you I liked you right from the start. How many times do I have to repeat myself?'

'You said I was a fighter.'

'Not easily brought down.'

I hid my smile, but a pleasant warm feeling spread through my stomach.

'What could I do if I stayed?' I asked.

'You mean as a vocation?'

'Yes.'

'I think you would make a great Healer. You have poise under pressure, and you think clearly and fast.'

'I thought Healers were supposed to be compassionate.'

'We're not exactly spoilt for choice.' he laughed, 'We would be lucky to have you. Cold-hearted or not.'

'I'm not cold-hearted, I'm cold-minded.'

'I know that, I was just joking.'

'Do you want to have sex again?'

'No,' he started, and he frowned, 'not unless you promise to stay.'

'I can't do that yet.'

His face fell. 'Then I'll wait,' he said in a tight voice.

'Can I sleep here?' I asked to change the subject. 'I don't dare wake Leodurr again.'

He forgot his upset and smiled. 'You see, you have softer feelings!' he teased.

We went to sleep next to each other.

❈ 48 ❈

S teon

I'd missed all the celebrations that followed the Raiders' departure, but a mood of victory still hung over the Orchard when I eventually moved back into the main hut.

Eyes were bright and lips smiling. Una had been informally appointed as Leif's carer, and the company of the baby brought some spark into her thin face. Efalaa kept teasing Morgunn about boring the Raiders out of their camp with his lengthy monologue. He laughed good-naturedly.

I didn't share the Clan's joy and relief.

I was in great danger.

How stupid could a man get?

I spent the next day berating myself for my poor judgement and lack of discipline.

After everything I'd been through, the Quake, months struggling to survive, the war with the Raiders and a near-

death experience, I was falling in love with the most complicated woman I had ever met. A woman who had no intention
of spending her life amongst the likes of us.

I knew people fell in love sometimes. I'd seen it happen to
Ollo and Veiti and to Morgunn and Efalaa. They had paid for
their love with great pain.

That kind of love was messy, painful and just unnecessary.
I'd never thought I could be that careless.

I wondered what could be done about it now. Maybe the
best course of action would be to encourage Sili to leave. But
even with Ollo watching her back, how could she ever be safe
in the Valley? The men who had killed her father would hurry
to murder her and possibly Ollo too.

She'd suffered so much already. Did I have a right to send
her to her death just for my own peace of mind? The only
thing I could do was to ignore her, and forget what had
happened between us.

When she spoke to me that morning, I forced myself not
to hear her, and I didn't reply. She understood straight away
what was going on, and never addressed me again.

For three days, I walked past her unseeing, I went about
my work in a daze of selective hearing and slept alone.

❧ 49 ❧

S ili

Steon started ignoring me. I knew why, but I needed time to make up my mind. This was the first time in my life that change was not foisted upon me. I'd returned to that familiar crossroads. The decision whether to stay with the Clan or go home was the hardest I'd ever had to make.

Ollo moved into Veiti's house. They had been sharing a bed before the Quake, and no one raised an eyebrow when I was made effectively homeless. Aalma took me in when I came out of Veiti's hut with my belongings, a pillow and a sleeping fur.

Ollo and Veiti were an interesting couple to watch. I'd never fully understood Veiti. She seemed opinionated but changeable. The clue to that puzzle was that she had been a ship without a rudder. Now, Ollo told her what he thought, and she would immediately think the same with her characteristic vehemence. They were deeply happy to be reunited against all odds.

They were rarely seen without each other, as he combined his surveillance missions with her gathering trips, and were often away together from breakfast to dinner. It was the same for Efalaa and Morgunn who often hunted the day away.

Despite each of the couples' closeness, the rest of us didn't feel left out. There was a conviviality in the Clan's routines that brought us all together at the beginning and at the end of the day. We would all sit in haphazard groupings, knitting, making things or singing. This made everyone, even me, feel part of a whole.

Una and Vidris shared a bed in the bird shed. Vidris never tired of hearing Una's tales of woe. It strengthened her belief in the moral superiority of the Clan, and offered some solace to poor Una who had suffered longer than me at the hands of the Raiders.

Apart from Vidris who took on the role of the dominant friend and guided meek Una through the intricacies of her new life, the only person gentle and patient enough to break through Una's reticence was Leodurr. He took the time to explain the Clan's ways and tell her stories from before the Quake. It also did him good to keep those times fresh in his memory. The others were eager to forget and move on, but Leodurr needed to keep the dead alive in his tender heart.

This was the first time I shared a hut with Aalma without being ill or incapacitated. She liked her environment neat, and spent much time organising her healing supplies. I liked listening to her as she explained what everything was.

Aalma was a very smart woman. She thought clearly, and she was knowledgeable and good under pressure. Yet she managed to be unfailingly kind despite her stern manner. She was the best doctor I had ever come across and even here, in the wilderness, with rough tools and herbal remedies, she managed to save lives.

❦ 50 ❧

S teon

I returned to active duty. Morgunn had ordered constant surveillance of the Lowlands, in case the Raiders decided to come back.

He himself carried out several patrols each day, and he looked like death. Efalaa was falling asleep on her feet and Ollo was unusually quiet. They needed an extra pair of eyes.

Nothing happened on my patrol. I shot at a man, but didn't aim to kill. Sili's insights into Raiders' recruitment as well as Morgunn's speech had triggered a strange sympathy in my heart. These men below were not soldiers like me, they were farmers or makers, and their deaths would bring me no advantage and no pleasure.

In the evenings, I noticed Efalaa kept throwing anxious looks at me. Vidris too turned her attention away from Una and started watching me carefully.

Leodurr thankfully was oblivious to the situation between me and Sili. He never mentioned anything. Leodurr was a good comrade. Discreet, steady, but always friendly. He was a soothing presence. He asked nothing. His friendship was simple, just what I needed.

Day after day, I went about my chores, and Sili paid me no attention. I noticed her talking to Aalma and Morgunn at assembly, but I made myself forget her face and her attitudes. I avoided her and redirected my thoughts whenever they strayed too close to her.

I went to sleep full of longings I would not allow myself to indulge. This was less painful than the thought of losing her after letting her in to my life.

The weather improved, and the snow melted revealing yellow grass burnt by the cold. The Raiders did not return, and we scavenged everything we could from their camp. This was not the Clan's way however. Since the First Twelve, we had made everything we needed without trading or swapping or buying from Outsiders. Our pride suffered, but Morgunn declared we could make an exception for spoils of war. He said it was mere compensation for the time and effort invested in defending our Territory.

Sili was quiet. She worked all day, sat silently at dinner staring at her lap and went to bed in Aalma's hut earlier than most.

One night at assembly, she finally looked up and met my eyes. She was angry and defiant. I'd seen that look before, in the woods, just before she'd thrown herself at me. As I thought about that time, my arousal grew and I felt furious. I willed myself to discipline.

Morgunn's voice drew me away from my thoughts.

'Clan, I have decided on Sili's vocation,' he started.

I cringed. Had he not heard of Ollo's offer? Did he not

281

know she would leave as soon as he was better and able to fight?

She was about to make a fool of our Chief again. I stared at the ground. Everyone else looked up in curiosity, except Vidris who stood and left without a word.

Morgunn waited until she was out of earshot before continuing. 'Aalma and I have been discussing this over the past few days, and I have decided to make Sili Aalma's Apprentice. Sili already has some knowledge of healing, mostly acquired during her time outside the Clan. This will prove useful in developing our understanding and skills. Sili will start her training immediately, and Aalma has agreed to remain our Master Healer for another three years while Sili learns her vocation. After that, Aalma will become a Helper and Sili will be our new Healer. I am confident she will make herself and her kin proud.'

I looked up in time to see Sili bow her head in fake humility. A rush of anger went through me.

Morgunn turned to Efalaa. 'I have Efalaa to thank for finding Sili and bringing her to us. She fought for Sili to remain with us, and encouraged me to give her a place in our Clan.' Morgunn gave Efalaa a good-humoured nudge, and she laughed.

Morgunn continued. 'There is a first time for everything. This is a good day for the Clan.'

My heart sank as I listened. Sili had manipulated Efalaa and Morgunn, perhaps for no other reason than her own enjoyment. I couldn't intervene without undermining the Chief. Sili still played her stupid games toying with the hearts and minds of my Clan.

Seething, I remained silent while cheers of 'For the Clan' erupted around me.

After the noise died down, Sili stood up. I couldn't bear to look at her.

'I am grateful and humbled,' she started.

I sniggered, but she continued. 'I promise to serve each and every one of you as long as I live and I pledge you all my loyalty.'

She sounded so sincere my curiosity got the better of me, and I looked up. She was staring at me.

'If any amongst you still doubt me, I say to them: "put me to the test". I will be here tomorrow and the day after and the day after that, working for the Clan, learning your customs and doing my best to adopt them. I'm here to stay,' she concluded simply as if those words were for me.

'What about a name?' called Aalma, and the Clan replied with further cheer.

Morgunn spread his hands to ask for silence.

'I have thought about that,' he started. 'Sili has no Clan parent whose name to take. She came to us as a loose strand to be woven into the plait. Her line will start with her, and she will be known as Sili Siliborn, both the first and second of her name.'

I thought she would demand to choose her name herself, but Sili only bowed her head and thanked Morgunn with whispered words.

'For the Clan!' started Ollo, and another round of greetings followed.

Then Morgunn handed Sili a leather lace strung with two beads, and Efalaa held Sili's loose hair out of the way while Morgunn fastened it around her slender neck.

'What do these mean?' Sili asked, caressing the beads.

'This one represents you and your vocation as a Healer, and this one is for Vona,' explained Efalaa gently.

Sili brought her two hands to her mouth in time to stifle what could have been a snigger or a sob.

'We keep our dead close, Sili,' said Morgunn, patting his own Clan necklace, full of dozens of beads. 'Never forgotten.'

'For the Clan,' said Leodurr, his voice unsteady.

'For the Clan,' came the replies.

'Now, we need songs,' declared Aalma, aware our grief was about to break through.

Morgunn and Efalaa, who hadn't sung together since before Morgunn's voice had broken, took one look at each other and started the same song in perfect unison.

Let us haste to Kelvin Grove, bonnie lassie, O;
Through its mazes, let us rove, bonnie lassie, O;
Where the rose in all her pride,
Paints the hollow dingle side,
Where the midnight fairies glide, bonnie lassie, O.

Let us wander by the mill, bonnie laddie, O,
To the cove beside the rill, bonnie laddie, O;
Where the glens rebound the call
Of the roaring waters' fall,
Through the mountain's rocky hall, bonnie laddie, O.

Though I dare not call thee mine, bonnie lassie, O,
As the smile of fortune's thine, bonnie lassie, O;
Yet with fortune on my side,
I could stay thy father's pride,
And win thee for my bride, bonnie lassie, O.

Leodurr started crying silently, and Vidris returned. She sat by Morgunn and held his hand.

Several songs later, when the others started to retire to bed, I took Sili aside. 'I want to talk to you.'

She'd recovered from her emotions, and her eyes sparkled in amusement.

'The same kind of talking as we did the other day?' she teased with a sly smile.

'Let's not get ahead of ourselves,' I corrected sternly.

I held her elbow and pulled her towards the greenwoods. 'That too seems familiar,' she said playfully.

'Stop this,' I snapped.

She tried to hide her smile. Angry with myself for being rude, and even angrier she always brought the worst in me, I led her deeper into the forest where the moonlight didn't reach.

'Is this a good place to talk?' she enquired.

I backed her against the trunk of a large oak tree. She did not resist but stood where I had placed her. The condensation in the air filled the woods with wispy mist.

'So you mean to stay?' I asked.

'Yes, I've made my decision.'

'Why do I not believe you?'

'Because you do not know me as well as you think.'

'I know you well enough to be a scheming and dissembling sort of person.'

'I've had to be.'

I placed my hand on her chest and pressed her against the tree.

'How can I trust you?'

'You have to take a risk,' she said.

'I don't believe in taking uncalculated risks.'

'So we're not here to have sex?' she asked with a pout.

'No, we're not,' I replied although I wasn't quite so sure.

'Very well, then I'll go back. The night is cold and I'm tired.'

She pushed against my hand, and walked around me to return to the path. Soon, she melted into the darkness. I cursed myself, then I cursed her. In two steps, I caught up with her and grabbed her around the waist with both arms so tight her breath came out with a huff. I pulled her against me, angry yet wanting. I could not decide what to do next.

She leant her head against my arm and let it rest there gently. It snuffed my anger, and I could think and talk again.

'I don't want you to go,' I said earnestly.

'You may have noticed I'm not going anywhere.'

'Don't break my heart,'

'I'll do my best not to.'

Despite the cold, we lay down on the forest floor on top of my travelling cloak and made love slowly for the first time. Our bodies understood each other much better than our minds did, and, frantic or slow, we always found the same rhythm.

EPILOGUE

S ili

After that first time in the greenwoods, Steon went back to being careful around me. I took it as a sign of his regard. His reluctance set me apart from the other women who had been his lovers. I was sure none of them had scared him as much as I did.

Aalma taught me every morning, and every afternoon we worked together to grow or forage the plants we needed to replenish the vast collection of potions and remedies she had lost in the Quake.

Many of our pots and vials came from the deserted Raiders' camp. Some of them were made of glass, a luxury unheard of in the Clan.

Morgunn had ordered the dilapidated fences and tents be left untouched as a warning to those travelling through the Lowlands. He and the two Guardians kept up their surveillance of the Territory. Fortunately after the first assault of winter, the weather had turned mild again and the rabbits were out in force. Efalaa said it was more like picking mushrooms than hunting, and she didn't feel quite as bad thinning out their population. While still a Hunter during the day, she spent her evenings relearning all the Clan songs from what everyone remembered. Her voice was clear and beautiful, but singing often made her sad. Morgunn would then add his voice to hers until she smiled again.

All the Teachers, who would normally have looked after the Clanschildren from babyhood to Apprenticeship, had been lost to the Quake. Veiti had no one to look after Leif, but Una often took charge of the baby so she could spend the day foraging. Una was a wonderful carer, patient and kind – like my mother had been. The question of her welcome into the Clan had never even been discussed, and she'd naturally settled into the Skyriders' routine, unaware of the battles I had faced to be extended that privilege. It sometimes made me feel jealous and wronged, but I couldn't deny she was more deserving of their welcome than I had been.

Both Una and I had started drinking their 'women potion' as they called it. It tasted no different to a pleasant cup of tea, and it took me a while to believe it really had the effects they claimed. Still, after weeks without period or pregnancy, I had to admit that it worked.

Steon often worked in the fields with Leodurr; they spoke little but enjoyed each other company, as they shared the main hut.

Ollo's hands were still clumsy and caused him much silent pain. Everyday, Morgunn would send him to survey the Territory and watch out for threats. As it turned out, he never saw the next Raiders' to approach the Clan's twin mountains, not the man who would breach the Hedge.

As I ambled through the greenwoods one afternoon, I

could hear footsteps behind me. I didn't need to turn around. I knew who was following me through the leafy undergrowth that smelt of earth. No matter how windy my path or thorny the bushes, those feet trod lightly but surely behind me.

My body reacted to his presence and tightened in yearning. I pressed on through the dimly lit forest, keeping just out of reach a few steps ahead. The leaves rustled. Every now and then, a twig broke underfoot. My senses heightened, I listened. I listened with my heart, I listened with my skin. I listened for the swish of his clothes and the sounds of his steps getting closer.

I arrived at a tiny clearing in a pool of late-afternoon light and stopped, my heart beating wildly in its cage. I did not wait long. He pulled me into his warmth. My breathing was loud and erratic, but he made no noise.

I heard his heavy coat fall to the floor just before I was laid upon it. I held my breath, trembling in maddening anticipation, shivering and burning. I heard the stampede of my heart. My vision narrowed, and my attention focused inward to the saliva pooling in my mouth, to the shaking of my limbs, so weak they no longer seemed to be made of flesh.

Although I was held still, in my mind I was running at high speed through the dark woods like a crazed animal seeking safety.

As he lay on top of me, the breath I had been holding was knocked out of me, and I gasped for air like a newborn taking her first breath.

Like a newborn coming to life, I cried. With every move, my grief and my fear poured out of me, and the release of tears felt even sweeter than the tightening inside.

I choked out the pain of those cruel years, the outrage of my abused body, the relentless fear, the exhausting machinations, and the grief I hadn't allowed myself to feel. Grief for my tiny daughter, my mother, my father and for all my lost children.

Worried that Steon would stop and ask me why I was crying, I held him close to show him I wanted this as much as he did. Spurred on, he pushed me down until my chest hit the leafy ground and covered my body with his. Soon, we dissolved into the same wave of bliss.

As I struggled for breath, tears continued to fall into the crushed leaves under my cheek. He lifted himself off me with a grunt and gave me a friendly slap on the backside before straightening my dress. I lay motionless on the forest floor, absorbing its invigorating smell deep into my lungs.

Steon sat with his back against an oak tree, rear-ranging his clothes with agile fingers. Then, he turned his attention to me and watched me carefully. He did not react to my display of emotion, but he did not seem uncomfortable either. He behaved as if he had expected as much.

'Haven't you noticed I'm crying?' I asked reproachfully although I liked the fact he had not mentioned it.

'You've been wailing like a banshee, of course I've noticed,' he replied good-naturedly.

'And you aren't the least bit concerned about it?' I continued dryly.

'I've never seen you so at peace, so no, I'm not concerned.'

I turned my face away to hide a smile. He was right. I could not remember the last time I had felt so truly happy.

I sat up to gaze at him. He looked relaxed and at one with the world, his blond braids falling on his shoulders, his fingers interlinked over his flat stomach, and his long legs crossed at the ankles.

'You win,' I conceded.

'This time,' he replied and winked.

Happiness bubbled in my chest, and I started crying again.

He watched me with soft eyes.

'Your hair is a mess,' he remarked, still ignoring my tears.

'Thanks,' I replied sarcastically.

'Here,' he beckoned, and I shuffled closer to him. He took a handful of my hair and combed it with his fingers before braiding it deftly and tying it with one of the leather straps that secured his arm braces.

A few minutes later, I was sporting the traditional Skyriders' hairstyle, and several braids danced around me when I shook my head. I hadn't worn plaits since I was a child, and this was bringing back memories of carefree times. I laughed gaily, and he smiled as he tucked his arm braces into his belt.

'You look much younger,' he said.

'With my new hair?'

'No, with your new face.'

'What new face is that?'

'Your happy one.' He stroked my cheek with the back of his fingers.

'Well, you still look as old as before.'

'I feel much older after all the exertion,' he joked.

'What exertion? It was over in two minutes.'

'Oh, really?' he laughed. 'You have a complaint?'

'It wasn't long enough,' I pouted.

He didn't answer but only smiled with his whole face, and for the first time, I was sure he loved me.

I leant my back against him and watched the leaves dance in the wind. The evening was turning cold, and I gathered my knees to my chest under my dress.

Unhurriedly, he pulled his cloak towards us with his foot until I could grab it and hand it to him. He wrapped it around us, and warmth soon pervaded our improvised shelter.

'Will I get a cloak like this now I'm part of the Clan?'

'You like it?'

I nodded. 'It's like carrying a home around with you.'

'Travelling cloaks are for those who spend a lot of time outdoors. Healers don't.'

'Oh,' I said, truly disappointed.

'You can share mine,' he offered.

'It's not the same.'

'If you need one, the Hunters will make you one. If you only want one, you'll have to make it yourself.'

'I'll make one for myself then, and it'll be even better than yours,' I replied like a grumpy child.

'You have much to learn,' he shook his head sadly. I met his gaze, and he continued. 'This is not the Clan's way. We are all equal. We may not all have the same, but we all get what we need. Trust the Clan to provide for you. Learn to become our Healer and in return, we will feed you, shelter and clothe you. We will love and treasure you, and we will never turn our backs on you. This is the bargain we offered, and this is what you accepted.'

'What about bearing children? Is that part of the bargain?'

'You know it is.'

'With whom?'

'Only Morgunn can answer this question, but because of your new blood, any man could father your child. Well, probably not Leodurr because he has Leif now.'

'And probably not Morgunn, because he has Efalaa.'

'I'm not sure, Healers and Chiefs often breed together. They need similar traits.'

'But he will lose Efalaa's blood if he doesn't father her child. She'll let no one else near her.'

'Life is long, we'll see,' he said.

'So you or Ollo?'

'Are you saying you would like to have my child?' His eyes twinkled, and he seemed unduly happy at the prospect.

'I'm not saying anything of the sort...' I replied as sternly as I could.

'Of course not. I'm far too limited to understand the subtleties of your superior mind.'

'I'm clearly much cleverer than you.'

'Much.'

'I can read and write. What do you say to that?'

'I say 'well done'. What else?'

He got to his feet and lifted me up by my belt. He draped his cloak over my shoulders, and it dragged on the floor at my feet.

'Maybe you can write yourself a cloak,' he said with a boyish smile.

He started towards the path and reached out to take my hand. I grabbed his forearm instead and held on tight as he wrapped his long fingers around my elbow.

He looked at me with a mix of emotions, happiness but also pain. I wondered whether I had hurt his feelings after all with my jibes about his illiteracy.

It wasn't his fault Clanspeople were so woefully unedu-cated. Even amongst my people, soldiers were not supposed to be great thinkers.

I didn't like hurting him. I thought I would, but in fact I didn't. I promised myself never to mention this to him again.

He had done me a lot of good, and it was the least I could do to do him no harm.

The sky was completely dark when we reached the edge of the forest, and I followed his footsteps as he led me safely home.

The end

∾

Learn more about the origins of the Clan in Book 3 of the Skyriders Trilogy, 'Fate of the Skyriders'! On Kindle and Paperback.

In the meantime, for free spin-off stories and book news, please sign up for the Skyriders' mailing list by visiting www.florencephillips.co.uk/join-the-clan-2.

Otherwise, stay in touch on Facebook (www.facebook.com/clanoftheskyriders) or on Instagram (www.instagram.com/florencephillipsauthor)

Finally, please, please leave a review for this book, either on Amazon or on Goodreads. It makes a huge difference to the book's visibility and you can share it with others.

Check out my step-by-step guide to leaving a review on www.florencephillips.co.uk/how-to-leave-a-review

ABOUT THE CLAN

Following a worldwide catastrophe, industrial civilisations crumbled, taking down with them all global communication networks. With no access to oil or electricity, humans have gone back to nature and lead a self-sufficient existence in small groups that eke out a living in an inhospitable landscape. Illiteracy has again become the norm.

Before the events of this story, the Clan was one large extended family, living in self-imposed isolation on a mountainous territory. The Clan consisted at all times of 130 to 140 people, including 52 workers, aged between 18 and 60, and approximately 30 retired workers and 50 children under 18.

Their long history spanned several hundred years during which they strictly implemented a zero population-growth policy thanks to a contraceptive potion inherited from their early days. The Clan's Chiefs allowed only enough births to replace worker numbers. Outsiders could not become part of the Clan, and no Clan member had ever left the Clan.

Purposeful breeding

The founders of the Clan – often referred to as 'The First Twelve' – decided that stable numbers were the key to their survival in their wild environment. They postulated that their territory could only feed and sustain about a hundred people: enough to work and replace each generation, but not so many that resources would become stretched.

They also came to believe that certain mental or physical qualities were necessary to best perform specific tasks. They assumed that these qualities ran in families.

Therefore, the Clan's Chief chooses the parents of each child to be born so that he or she may inherit the qualities required to eventually replace a specific worker. Children are trained from a young age for their intended job by the very worker that they will replace. Every time a worker retires, the child born to take their place enters the workforce as an apprentice.

Men and women are interchangeable and will take up any vocation for which they are conceived, regardless of their gender. Women fight, and men raise children and vice versa.

Unplanned children are very rare, one or two per generation at most. They are called the Surprises and raised for a broader skill set so that they can support different workers on a temporary basis. They also replace workers on a more permanent basis when someone dies before their appointed replacement is old enough to take over.

Vocations

The Clan had 11 vocations, each with three key skills or attributes.

Chief: (Intelligence – Memory – Compassion) One Chief and an Apprentice. The Clan Chief makes the decisions for the Clan. He or she enforces Clan laws, chooses a mother and a father for each child depending on their intended vocation. The Chief also records and safeguards bloodlines, and has ultimate responsibility for the welfare and work appraisal of each member of the Clan. A cross between general, judge and human resources director.

Singers: (Memory – Intelligence – Creativity) The three Singers are the guardians of the Clan's oral traditions. They memorise and perform all of the Clan songs that record the history of the Clan. They advise the Chief on the interpretation of Clan's rules. A cross between lawyer, journalist, historian and musician.

Teachers: (Compassion – Patience – Intelligence) Four Teachers care for and educate the children under 18. A cross between teachers and foster parents.

Makers: (Creativity – Practicalness – Intelligence) The four Makers are designers and craftspeople. They invent and make everything from tools and weapons to clothing, houses and everyday items. A cross between inventors, designers and artisans.

Keepers: (Compassion – Practicalness – Patience) The five Keepers breed, train and look after the Clan's birds.

Healers: (Memory – Compassion – Creativity) The three Healers are the doctors, nurses, pharmacists, therapists and dentists to the Clan.

Gatherers: (Practicalness – Memory – Diligence) The five Gatherers pick fruit, nuts and plants, collect eggs, forage for wild foods, and gather natural materials like firewood, wicker, and grasses for cordage.

Farmers: (Practicalness – Strength – Diligence) The seven Farmers farm the fields for oats, rye or corn. They grow vegetables, breed and shear the sheep and keep chickens, ducks, and silkworms.

Cooks: (Practicalness – Creativity – Diligence) The four Cooks butcher the meat, preserve and stock food, and prepare meals for the Clan.

Hunters: (Practicalness – Intelligence – Strength) The four Hunters hunt for rabbits, birds, deer or bears to provide food and fur, and they protect the Clan from dangerous or nuisance animals. They're also in charge of aerial surveillance and defence of the Clan's territory.

Guardians: (Strength – Practicalness – Diligence) The nine Guardians guard and defend the Clan's territory, as well as manufacturing and maintaining the Clan's weapons. They accompany and serve as bodyguards to those who work outside the Territory.

Clanspeople come of age at 18 in a special naming ceremony during which they choose their patronymic or matronymic name, a compound of their mother's or father's name with the suffix 'born'. At the end of the ceremony, they are officially introduced into the workforce and become Apprentices in their particular vocation. At age 21, they become fully fledged workers.

Exceptionally gifted workers may be given the honorific title of 'Master'. Masters take on a supervisory role for the other workers of the same vocation. They are entitled to a separate house.

Workers retire between 55 and 60, depending on their health and the availability of their replacement. Retired workers continue to serve the Clan as Helpers, either in their original vocations or in any other capacity they choose.

Health

Infant mortality is high. One-third of children do not live past the age of five. Life expectancy at five is 55 years. Some Clanspeople die of accidents or diseases but most die of old age. Death in childbirth has been virtually eradicated by strict rules regulating which women can bear children. Women will normally have their children between 20 and 25. Only women with wide enough pelvises are allowed to breed. Clanswomen are fit and slim, and although many will take up to a month to recover from childbirth, very few die. When faced with the choice of saving a mother or a baby, it is Clan rule that the Healer will always save the mother. Women who become depressed after childbirth are not called upon to breed again.

Stringent precautions are taken to promote good health. Water is systematically boiled whether for washing food or cooking. The Healers impose frequent bathing and hand washing, adequate clothing for any weather and regular health checkups. These, combined with natural sleep patterns, a varied and nutritious diet, all-day physical activity and a strong sense of belonging and usefulness, keep Clan members healthy and strong.

Clanspeople believe in good hygiene, hair and oral care, regular clothes washing and thorough cleaning of dwellings and particularly kitchens and kitchenware. Healers are allowed to quarantine sick people, no matter what their illness is, to avoid contamination of workers. The sick are then looked after by the Helpers until they either die or get better.

Food

Clanspeople have a varied and wholesome diet of grains, game meat, fish, eggs, mutton or lamb, potatoes, carrots and various greens either foraged or grown, as well as mushrooms, apples, berries and nuts. They make cheese and butter from ewe's milk and cook oats, acorn or rye flour into porridge, gruel or pancake-like cakes. They favour soups, stews, roasted meat, boiled or sautéed vegetables and sandwiches made with flatbread cooked on hot stones or twisted bread dough roasted on sticks. They have re-invented the art of preserving food by drying, curing or smoking and thus eat three solid meals a day all year round. They drink milk, or infused leaves such as sage, nettle, thyme or mint and a tea made from chopped greasewood. They eat little sweet food apart from fruit, beetroot and wild honey. They think it strange that Outsiders should drink alcoholic beverages, but they distil a type of vodka for cleaning wounds.

Clothing

Clanspeople wear woven or knitted wool fabric, leather or furs over silk underclothing. They favour layers with leggings and vests worn underneath leather trousers and knitted or woven tunics.

Woollen knee socks are held in place by leg wrappings and leather shin pads. Hunters, Guardians and Farmers strap leather arm braces over their shirt sleeves, and wear thick belts or waistcoats to gather their shirts round their middle to free their movements. In winter, Clanspeople keep warm with knitted scarves, mufflers or cowls, fur hoods or shoulder capes. As Hunters and Guardians may be away from the Village for days at a time, they each own a travelling cloak made of oiled animal skin and lined with rabbit fur at the neck and hood. The cloaks are large enough to double up as sleeping bags or tent material if need be and have retractable sleeves to protect the arms while birdriding.

Boots, gloves and hats are made of tanned animal skins and lined with wool or fur.

Clothes are the property of the Clan and are designed to be worn by men or women interchangeably. Belts and arm and leg wrappings are worn to adjust garments to the size of the wearer. Women may at times wear dresses or longer tunics, especially during the warm summer months.

Housing

Clanspeople live in the 11 Lodges that circle the Fire Pit and the Village Square. Each vocation has its own lodge where workers sleep and keep their tools and possessions. Children live in dormitories inside Teachers Lodge until they are 18, then move into the Lodge that correspond to their vocation. The children of the Master workers may live in their parent's house although this is a rare occurrence, which may for instance follow a bereavement. The retired workers and the Surprises live in the Great Lodge with the Chief.

In addition to the Lodges, the Village consists of a large bath house with several separate bathrooms, two sets of latrines, a wood store, a grain store, a food store and five bird sheds. The Village is nestled against the tallest mountain of the Clan's territory. It is surrounded by fields dedicated to farming or grazing as well as by allotment-type vegetable plots maintained by the Farmers.

The buildings are mostly made out of wood although some are reinforced by stone walls and abutments. Roofs are made of shingles.

Sanitation is provided by a mountain stream that runs through the Village and brings fresh water and flushes sewage into an underground drain system. Recycling and up-cycling is one of the Clan's strictest rules and waste is kept to a minimum and fully biodegradable.

Birds

The Clan breeds giant birds descended from condors and eagles that they ride for travelling long distances. The Clan's territory is not accessible on foot. This has been key to preserving the Clan's isolation.

There are about 20 birds. The Chief, the Master Healer and each Hunter or Guardian has his or her own bird. The rest of the birds are available to anyone who needs to travel to carry out their work.

Birds are trained from chick-hood to carry people on their backs and are taught simple commands. They wear a leather saddle and harness with bridle and reins around their head and beak.

These exceptionally large birds are omnivores and eat a range of small animals, but also grains and vegetables.

Clanspeople do not eat either the eggs or the flesh of their birds. Dead birds are cremated and their ashes scattered in the wind at a special ceremony attended by all the Clan's members. Clanspeople believe that the birds' souls return to the air and continue flying beyond the clouds.

Geography

The Clan's territory consists of three mountains surrounded by thorny hedges ten to twenty feet tall, collectively called 'the Hedge'. It includes several woodlands of oaks, pines and cedars as well as orchards and grasslands. The river that forms from the different streams cascading down the mountains provides fishing for the Clan; it river ends near the Hedge in a spectacular 500ft waterfall. The Clan's territory is teeming with wildlife from deers to rabbits and wild birds.

The climate is temperate with four distinct seasons, and the temperature varies from 15°F (-10°C) to 90°F (30°C).

It is surrounded by a plain area, called the Lowlands, and further out by a semidesert called the Wastelands that stretches for hundreds of miles in every direction. The landscape is dotted with patches of grass and small woodlands due to fresh-water springs rising from the ground. Strong winds sweep the plains, and the vegetation is sparse with mostly bushes and grasses.

~

For more information about the Skyriders' world, please visit:
www.florencephillips.co.uk/The-World
www.facebook.com/clanoftheskyriders
www.instagram.com/florencephillipsauthor
https://uk.pinterest.com/florencephillip/skyriders/

ACKNOWLEDGMENTS

I would like to thank my husband for his constant words of encouragement and my children for their interest and patience.

A huge thank you to the two best-read women I know, my dear friends Linda Sansum and Rachel James who, by their example, challenge me to get off Pinterest and read more books.

As always, special love to my sister, who believed in me when no one else did. She thinks she knows – but she really doesn't – how important she is.

The song referred to in Chapter 16 is an Icelandic lullaby called 'Soðu unga ástin mín' or 'Sleep young love of mine', written by Jóhann Sigurjónsson (1880-1919) for a play about 18th century Icelandic outlaws, Fjalla-Eyvindur and his wife Halla. In the story, Halla sings the song to her baby before throwing it into a waterfall so she can escape with her husband. There are so many beautiful covers of it on YouTube, but the English version that stands out for me is that of Alice Dillon.

I also borrowed a traditional Scottish song called 'Kelvin

Grove' which I truncated and slightly rewrote to suit my story. Lovely renditions can be found on YouTube!

Finally, thumbs up for the French education system, for where else could you learn all about Rousseau, Thoreau and Maslow without paying a penny for the privilege?

Once again, last but still not least, a round of applause for my lovely editor, Catherine Rubinstein. Her patience and expertise know no bounds!

Florence
July 2017

ABOUT THE AUTHOR

Florence Phillips was born in 1972 in the South of France.

She is a graduate of an Institute for Political Studies, holds a Master's Degree in Law and worked as a corporate lawyer both in France and in the UK.

She is the author of the Dystopian epic series 'The Skyriders Trilogy'.

She lives with her husband and two children near Henley-on-Thames, England.

ALSO BY FLORENCE PHILLIPS

The Skyriders Trilogy

'Clan of the Skyriders' – Skyriders Book 1

'Guardians of the Skyriders' – Skyriders Book 2

'Fate of the Skyriders' – Skyriders Book 3

The First Twelve Trilogy

'The First Twelve' – Skyriders Book 4

(*Coming soon on Kindle and Paperback*)

Printed in Poland
by Amazon Fulfillment
Poland Sp. z o.o., Wrocław